WOMAN FROM ANOTHER PLANET

By
FRANK BELKNAP LONG

I0616788

ARMCHAIR FICTION
PO Box 4369, Medford, Oregon   97501-0168

*For more information about Armchair Books and products, visit our
website at...*

www.armchairfiction.com

Or email us at...

armchairfiction@yahoo.com

COULD HE CONQUER HIS DESIRE...

This is the unusual story of David Loring, an artist, and his beautiful fiancée, Janice Reece. David loved Janice but the Martian Empire had a plan to entice David away from his beloved. With their plan for world domination at stake the Martians selected these two lovers' for their first attack. Together, David and Janice became involved in a highly emotional and physical conflict that broke through the barriers of outer space itself.

Join renowned horror and sci-fi author Frank Belknap Long for a 1960 sci-fi tale he wrote for Chariot Books, a book company famous for their sexually provocative paperback novels. Although this tale is fairly tame by today's standards, it's interesting to see how Long weaves the elements of sex and science fiction together.

FOR A COMPLETE SECOND NOVEL, TURN TO PAGE 123

CAST OF CHARACTERS

DAVID LORING
This man's behavior was being monitored for an alien experiment he didn't even know about…

JANICE REECE
Her self-controlled manner was widely-known and respected, so what could have caused her sudden panic?

TRAGOR
He thought his masculine wiles could win any woman over, but the feisty redhead he set his heart on was one tough cookie.

SULL
Eager to see the Martians' "Great Plan" to fruition, he was not happy with his Superior's sudden lovey-dovey distractions.

COORDINATOR KRAII
He was in charge of the whole Martian enterprise and he had the authority to terminate the plan—or the man—at any time.

PETER SUMMERS
An extraordinary specimen of human fineness, this man was hand-picked as the ultimate male for android cloning.

COLONEL RICHARD CLEGMAN
Sharp-witted and discerning this airman had earned his silver eagles—and saved the world!

CHAPTER ONE

The alarm clock was ringing. There was another sound in the room as well—the more distant peal of door chimes. Oddly enough, it was the chime music that penetrated most sharply into David Loring's awakening mind. Each fragment was a tinkling and the tinklings ran the gamut of the musical scale. An ice-crystal music in caverns measureless to man. Rising, falling, almost dirge-like at times.

The alarm clock, having exhausted itself, stopped ringing. But the chimes continued. The ice crystals broke, shattered and reformed again.

Another day, Loring thought, stirring drowsily and blinking sleep from his eyes. He let his gaze roam over the room. The floor was thick with dust, and the record player on its handsome walnut stand, the ornamental decoy duck on the mantel and the uneven bricks on the built-in fireplace all needed dusting badly. In fact, the whole damned apartment needed the attention of a cleaning woman.

Well, it wouldn't be long now. The mere fact that he could afford a cleaning woman and no longer had to worry about the expense was reason enough for putting it off. The place could be made spic-and-span at a moment's notice and he profoundly disliked having his precious knick-knacks roughly handled by a stranger. It would be all right for Janice to take over. Wonderful, in fact.

Just bide your time, boy, and before you know it your bachelor days will be over. In two or three weeks you'll have a wife. And you can support her now. Two hundred dollars for just one ten-by-twelve picture, and the next one you paint will be better than any of the earlier ones, and you can go on from there with a wife to keep you out of the doldrums.

No reason to move either. Janice likes Greenwich Village and the apartment is spacious enough for two, and cheap, since you high-pressured the landlord and got the rent whittled down to a song. He was mixing his metaphors, but it didn't seem important to him at the moment. Only the future seemed important. It was brighter with promise than he could have imagined when he'd sat holding hands with her on a bench in Washington Square on the evening before he'd sold the painting.

He was a little startled when the chimes stopped abruptly, as if a hand had reached out and ripped the press-button mechanism from the door. The sudden, loud knocking startled him even more. It came from the short entrance hall just outside the room—three sharp knocks followed by a pause and a knock so loud that it hinted at more than just impatience. He knew that it had to be Janice, for her knocking—when she did knock—followed a pre-arranged pattern. A fourth knock was part of the pattern. But not a thump that rattled the door chain.

He sprang out of bed and seized the first garment that came to hand. It was a terry-cloth bathrobe, which Janice had urged him to have laundered. But he just hadn't gotten around to it, and now it contributed nothing to his male aplomb and early morning dash. He hoped she wouldn't mind too much when he took her in his arms and brought his lips down hard on hers. And smoothed her red-gold hair and ran his rough artist's hands up and down her back until she began to shiver a little and purr like a kitten.

He hoped she wouldn't think about the robe and how untidy he looked in it. Making women forget little disharmonies like that could be tougher than painting a picture that would put Utrillo in the shade. Well...what the heck? He was an artist, wasn't he? Not all women went for artists, but when they did they usually liked them a bit on the unkempt, disorganized side.

You just had to keep the disorganization from getting out of control. If you allowed it to spread to the romance department you were sunk. But that couldn't happen with Janice—not when he took her in his arms and told her how beautiful she was.

As he strode toward the door a tiny muscle in his jaw started twitching. Something was seriously wrong. He was sure of it. Self-containment was Janice's specialty. Her self-control was phenomenal and no matter how eager she might be to see him it just wasn't in character for her to try to break the door down.

Something extraordinary must have come up to make her act that way. It was hard to imagine what it could be, to bring about such a change in the way she ordinarily behaved. Fright? Hysteria? But Janice didn't have a baker's pinch of hysteria in her makeup. His alarm increased as he reached the door, and started fumbling with the chain. His fingers were all thumbs and the knocking was so loud and continuous now that it further unnerved him, so that it took him nearly a minute to get the door open.

She came in with a sobbing gasp, her hair disheveled, her eyes so wide with fright it gave her a staring, almost China-doll aspect. She was startlingly pale and hadn't bothered to cover up her pallor with lipstick and rouge.

For an instant the machinery of Loring's mind was barely able to function. It moved slowly, as if ice-clogged, with one dread thought uppermost. Village streets were likely to be deserted in the early hours of the morning and a scream could be quickly smothered. Had she been fleeing from someone who wouldn't have let her failure to use lipstick discourage him? A brutish someone who cared only that she was a woman?

She was trembling violently and her voice was so agitated that he had to strain to catch the words which tumbled from her lips as she clung to him, her eyes still China-doll wide, her fingers tightening on his wrists.

"Darling, darling, hold me tight. Just keep your arms around me for a moment, and I'll be able to tell you what happened. Right now I can't seem to think straight."

Loring stood for a moment without moving, holding her close, his temples throbbing. "What is it?" he urged, trying to keep his voice calm but not succeeding very well. "Tell me. I've got to know."

"There was a man in my room when I woke up this morning. A complete stranger. I'd never seen him before."

Loring's heart skipped a beat and for an instant he couldn't seem to breathe. "A man—"

"Yes. The door was locked and I don't see how he could have gotten in. I never forget to lock the door when I go to bed. I'm very careful about it. The windows were locked too. I'm sure of it. I—I was terribly frightened. He just stood there looking at me. I don't think he was a burglar or anything like that. He was tall, dark and very good looking. Young, about twenty-seven. Just about your age. I don't think I've ever seen a more attractive looking man. If I'd met him at a party before I met you—I don't know. I just don't know."

"You don't *know*. You mean you'd have gone overboard for him at first glance, without knowing a thing about him?"

"I might have. I'm being completely honest, because the experience was so terrifying that I have to get it straightened out in my mind. And I want you to understand too, darling. I thought of you, and something deep inside me protected me, so that I didn't really feel that way about him at all. But I almost did. I had to struggle against it, before I overcame it. If he'd moved forward and taken me into his arms I'm quite sure I would have screamed. But before I thought of you I might have—"

"Janice! For God's sake."

"I know, darling. The thought torments you. In a way, that makes me happy, because I love you so very much. So very, very much. And the torment you're experiencing proves that you love me. But it's cruel of me to feel that way—but all women do. There's something very primitive in us that makes us want to be fought over. If the man you love will fight for you, to the death, if necessary, it brings him closer to you."

"If he's dead that won't give him any pleasure at all."

"I know, darling, I know. I hardly know what I'm saying. Forgive me, be patient with me."

"I'm trying to. But don't you see what you're doing to me? You've told me nothing so far. Or very little. I mean, did he try to make love to you? Did he—touch you?"

"No, darling. He didn't. He just stood there by the fireplace staring at me. He had a strange way of looking at me. As if he could see deep inside my mind and knew exactly what I was thinking. And there was a kind of—tenderness in his eyes, as if he would have cut off his right arm before he'd take advantage of the fact that we were completely alone and I was wearing only—"

"Never mind what you were wearing. Do you have to tell me? All right, I want to know. I must know."

"That lace-fringed nightgown you gave me, darling. You know, the one with the black lace at the neck and sleeves. It really isn't so very revealing. Only—"

"Only what?"

"It may have slipped down a little at the shoulders. Of course I was embarrassed as well as frightened, but I don't think he gloated over it or took advantage of it in his mind in any way. Try to understand what I'm trying to say."

"I'm trying."

"He apologized. He was very nice about it."

"He apologized for what? For breaking into your room like a thief in the night? You can't clear yourself of a criminal charge by making a simple apology. The courts would take a very dim view of that."

"But he didn't do anything criminal. It was all a mistake. His exact words were: 'I'm terribly sorry. I hope I haven't embarrassed you. I live on the next block, and I've been to a party and—well, you know how it is sometimes when you've had a little too much to drink. All these buildings look alike…'

"He didn't finish. He just smiled, hoping I'd understand, and there was something boyish and even a little pathetic about the way he smiled. As if he was pleading with me to forgive him for forgetting himself and drinking a little too heavily. And of course I did understand. It wasn't a crime. After all, darling, I do live in the Village."

"Why don't you say what you mean? He was probably reeling drunk."

"No, he wasn't. I could see he wasn't. He might have reached the reeling stage for just a moment, when he made a mistake about the apartment. But it must have passed very quickly, because when he spoke to me his speech wasn't slurred and he held himself very straight."

"What happened then?"

"Nothing you need to be alarmed about." Most of the agitation had gone out of Janice's voice, but there was still a look of fright and sharp apprehension in her eyes, as if she were trying hard not to think about something she hadn't yet told him.

"He—he just crossed to the bed, bent and kissed me lightly on the forehead."

"Good God! I thought you said he didn't even touch you. What right had he to take such a liberty? He must be a clownish Village character of some sort. I wish I could get my hands on him."

"Aren't you being a little absurd, darling? The man was emotionally upset. It was a crazy thing to do, but I wasn't offended. Everybody who lives in the Village does things like that occasionally. It was just a spur-of-the-moment, completely impulsive substitution for old-fashioned gallantry."

"You think so? I don't. What did he do then?"

"He just turned without saying another word and walked straight out of the door. He opened the door and walked out, and I could hear his footsteps dying away on the stairs. He didn't come back."

Loring let out his breath in a long sigh of relief. Then he seemed to regret having allowed himself to feel relieved. He tightened his lips and his voice became that of an angrily bewildered man who has a great many questions to ask and is not at all sure that the answers will satisfy him.

"And the instant he left you dressed and came rushing over here to tell me all about it, in a condition bordering on shock. Why were you so terrified? Why do you still look so frightened? You've done nothing but make apologies for him. You keep telling me that you weren't offended in the least. Then why—"

"David, darling, there's something I haven't told you."

"What was it? For God's sake, don't keep me in suspense."

"I—I felt myself being embraced."

"You *what?*"

"Felt his arms about me, felt him lifting me up. Of course it had to be just something I imagined. He was gone. I'd seen him walk out of the room, and close the door. But for an instant I could see him again. The outlines of his head and shoulders were very hazy, and—well, ghostly isn't just the right word. Not ghostly. Shifting, smoke-like—like an image in a mirror wrapped in mist. But I could feel the strength of his arms, his hands moving across my back, even fumbling with the shoulder strap of my nightgown, crushing the lace—"

"Stop it, Janice! Keep quiet! You don't know what you're saying. If I thought for a moment…"

Loring's face was very white, and his fingers clamped tightly on Janice's arm, causing her to cry out in pain. He released her instantly, stroking the arm with his hand.

"I'm sorry, Janice," he said contritely. "I got a little carried away. Let's get out of here and get some breakfast. Maybe we can talk more sensibly about this. What you are saying is too confusing to take on an empty stomach."

"All right, darling. That sounds like a fine idea." She followed him to the dressing room and leaned against the doorjamb as he stripped off the bathrobe without any self-consciousness, revealing the compact, finely muscled body she knew and loved. He appeared so agitated that Janice's own hysteria left her, and she felt a sudden, overwhelming tenderness sweeping over her, making her forget her own need for reassurance.

She walked over to him, and reaching up, drew his head down and opened her lips, murmuring endearments and running her fingers through his hair to enhance the ardor of her embrace. His arms tightened about her and for an instant he was not only holding her close, but saw her as if she were standing a little apart from him in warm sunlight, with whispering tropical palms at her back, and the trade winds ruffling her red-gold hair above the exquisite beauty of her face. To him it was the loveliest of all faces, and he had painted it a dozen times, from the stubborn, loyal chin to the slightly tilted nose and the precious, adorable brow with its sprinkling of enchanting freckles.

When he released her, her eyes were shining. Then, slowly, the look of near rapture faded and her face clouded over. She shuddered and took a slow step backwards. He had the feeling that she had more to tell him, that she was more deeply disturbed than he had imagined. Suddenly, he didn't want to hear it.

He lost his head then completely. It was a strange time for lovemaking, but he couldn't help himself. He gathered her in his arms and carried her across the living room to the couch that could be folded back into the wall when he had no occasion to stop painting and turn his attention to a different kind of artistry.

He put her gently down and unfastened her dress, easing the zipper over the places where the cloth fit tightly. He drew the dress down over her shoulders, freeing her brassiere-ensheathed breasts and allowing the light to caress the soft, white skin of her truly lovely back, and the shadowed recess in the small of her back from which it was so easy for a hand to glide downward over the smooth roundness of equally lovely hips.

He could not quite persuade himself to do more than run his fingers lightly along the curve of her neck for an instant, to nibble at her ear, and then plant a single firm kiss in the middle of her back. It was not, he reminded himself, with an effort, quite the right time for reckless abandon. She was still too nervous and upset and was trembling violently.

It was only when it slowly dawned on him that she was not trembling because her nerves had been strained to the breaking point but for a quite different reason that he ceased to be constrained and scrupulous, and embraced her with so fierce an ardor that it put a complete end to all restraint, and led them both along pathways of rapture in a continuously unfolding intimacy…

Later, eating Danish pastry and tasting steaming coffee in the coffee shop a block away from Loring's apartment, the world seemed normal again. Their eyes met across the table, and they smiled, a little sheepishly, at one another.

"Feel better, sweetheart?" Loring asked.

"You know I do," she said softly. Then her smile abruptly disappeared and she frowned slightly. "But David, I have to tell you the rest of it, even though I want to forget it, and I know you would. After I had this feeling of being embraced—"

"You had an erotic fantasy, Janice." David interrupted firmly. "It's nothing to be ashamed of. It's an honest, sound objective appraisal of a scientific reality that every man has experienced a good many times in his life, and every woman too."

Janice shook her head.

"It would be all right if my erotic fantasy involved a man with no particular cast of features, just a man in the abstract. But it involved a living man, a man whom I'd just met and described to you. He's alive and a rival and you have to think of him in that way. You can't help yourself—no matter how scientifically enlightened you may try to be."

"I know," Loring said. "I was lying to myself and to you. I'd be jealous if it was just a man in the abstract. I'd be jealous if that man wasn't me."

She tried to laugh, tried to force gaiety into her voice. "You don't have to carry it quite as far as that," she said. "The man would be you, without all of the very dear, very special details filled in. You create a mental image first, in the abstract, a kind of unconscious clay model. Then you meet the only man in the world for you, and fill the details in.

"It was a terrifying experience. I knew he couldn't be real but his strength was so great I couldn't free myself. Even if I'd struggled violently and clawed at his face he'd have caught me again before I could reach the door."

Loring's face had gone very white. "But he was so attractive to you that you didn't struggle. Is that it?" Even before he words left his lips he hated himself, but he had to say them.

She shook her head, her eyes firmly denying it. "He was attractive, yes. The handsomest man I've ever seen. But his attractiveness had nothing to do with it. Oh, if he'd been an ugly-faced brute I suppose it might have seemed worse. But not much worse. I couldn't struggle because I'd gone numb all over. I couldn't even raise my arms."

"A man doesn't have to have an ugly face to be a brute!"

"There's nothing more, so you can stop torturing yourself. Quite suddenly he was gone, almost as if he'd never been there. It was all like some hideous nightmare, one of those dangerous, utterly terrifying dreams from which you awaken just in time. They're dangerous because people have died in their sleep just from shock. But I did awaken in time. You'll never know how relieved I felt, how inwardly glad."

"Then why are you still so frightened? Nothing happened to you. It's over and done with. Even his actual presence in your room, when you heard him speak, may have been an hallucination. Perfectly normal people can have hallucinations. What else is bothering you, Janice?"

She toyed with her coffee cup for a moment before answering, then spoke in a low voice. "An even stranger, more terrifying, thing happened. Harder to explain and ghastly in a completely non-human way. I don't think I was in quite as much danger, because it just stood there in the hall watching me without moving at all. But I had the feeling that if it did move I'd be in even greater danger."

"It? Janice, what are you talking about?"

"Just give me a moment, darling. I'll tell you, but please don't rush me. Let me tell it in my own way. It was so frightening, so unbelievable that the mere thought of it makes me almost physically ill. In a way, it could be an hallucination, because I did have the shock of the other experience before I saw it. No shock preceded the first experience, as I told you, but this one—"

"All right now, try to stay calm. You're in no danger now. You're safe here with me. Remember that."

"I'll try."

"I love you very much."

"I know you do, darling. Well, I calmed myself down so successfully that I believe I could have gone back to sleep again. But I decided instead to get dressed and go out. I thought the fresh air might help to clear the cobwebs out of my brain.

"My nerves had stopped screaming, but I couldn't shake off the feeling that there were still cobwebs deep in my mind crisscrossing, forming a hideous pattern. Down one of the gleaming strands a black widow spider was crawling slowly toward me."

"Black widow spiders devour their own mates," Loring said. "But the female is about fifty times as large as the male. Only the males have to worry."

It was the wrong way to ease her tension, and he instantly regretted that he hadn't kept silent.

She went on quickly, her voice tightening. "It took me only a moment to get some clothes on and I didn't waste any time with makeup. But I was trembling so I kept dropping things, and I thought I'd never get the door open. I didn't realize just how badly shaken I was, though, until I got out into the hall. There was a dim light bulb at the end of the hall and there were shadows everywhere, large dark shadows that seemed to change shape as I stared at them. Then I saw it."

Her voice shook and she looked quickly around the nearly deserted restaurant, as though expecting someone to be eavesdropping.

"Just remembering it is terrifying. The creature looked almost human. It had a face with nose, eyes, ears and the body of a man. Darling, I—I can't describe it. Not really, not perfectly, because I only saw it for an instant and it was standing in shadows. But I saw enough to know that it wasn't human—couldn't have been human. It wasn't a man or a woman. It was a *thing*."

CHAPTER TWO

Ten minutes later they were back in Loring's apartment again. David had thought it best to hear the rest of Janice's revelation there. As they entered the large studio living room an oppressive pall seemed to burden the atmosphere; as though they had stepped from the cheerful bustle of the Village street into a place where fear and uncertainty dwelled. David shook off the feeling resolutely; this was his own apartment, and no one dwelled here except himself, and he was a realistic, if somewhat romantic fellow.

They sat down together on the couch that had held them rapturously entwined in one another's arms such a short time ago.

"Now Janice," he said, trying to keep his voice calm and patient, as though he were a doctor dealing with a difficult patient. "You probably had an hallucination. But tell me about this Thing you saw. And remember I am right here beside you."

She spoke with an effort. "I saw it distinctly enough to be sure it was alive and watching me. I saw its face. It was flat, coldly impassive, hideous. No animation in the features at all. The nose was bulbous. Like the nose of an alcoholic. Oh, I know that sounds almost ludicrous, but it's the right description. I can't think of a more accurate one. Its eyes—"

"Go on."

"They were small, dark and smoldering, buried in folds of pinkish flesh. I said no animation, but the eyes were alive, riveted on me as if it were—yes, a ghoul. As if it wanted to pounce on me, sink its teeth in my flesh and suck all the marrow from my bones. There were two little knobby outgrowths protruding from its forehead, one from each temple. They were pinkish too, and if they had been a little longer they would have looked like horns."

"Let me get this straight, Janice. Its face was flat and yet the nose was bulbous. And when the eyes are animated they have a great deal of expression. It makes the other features seem animated too. Aren't there contradictions there?"

"No, I don't think so. Its face did look flat, mask-like, despite the bulbous nose and the smoldering eyes. I had the feeling that its features just weren't human—that it was incapable of feeling as we do, thinking as we do. I told you how I felt. It was some kind of monster, despite its almost human body."

"Did you see its hands?"

"That's what terrified me the most, David. I don't think it had hands. Its arms were in shadow, so I couldn't be sure. But I think it had claws. Talons. I didn't wait to make sure. I ran on past it and down the stairs. It made no attempt to follow me."

For an instant Loring sat motionless, shaken in spite of himself, not quite knowing what to believe. Then, quite suddenly, a look of relief came into his eyes. In another moment his expression had changed again. The relief was gone and his eyes were blazing with anger.

"A prank!" he said. "That's what it must have been. All of it, from the moment you saw that lacquered, good-looking joker in your room to the caricature in the hall. Some Village character is having a time for himself, at our expense. Damn him to hell!"

"But David, I told you—"

"Never mind what you think you saw. I know exactly what happened now. It happens often enough, not only in the Village but wherever artists and writers throw parties and allow envious people to drift in. There's always some joker with no talent who wants to get back at people who have talent. Sex can get mixed up in it, too. Someone is making a play for another man's girl, or—"

"You mean you think the whole thing may have been directed at you."

"Quite possibly. At me through you. I wouldn't put it past Iack Durbin." He rose and paced the room, excited by the possibility of a rational answer to the strange tale.

"But it wasn't Durbin I saw in my room. Or anyone we know."

"Naturally! Durbin's looks would eliminate him right off. But he could have talked a friend into helping out with the prank. There are a dozen other people I could nominate for the role. You don't always remember the faces of people you meet casually at parties. You may have been staring into a cocktail glass when the good looking guy was introduced to you. You may have met him and forgotten all about it."

"I wouldn't forget."

"All right, you wouldn't forget him. So he's new, someone you've never seen before. That doesn't rule out the possibility that he was talked into helping out with the prank by Durbin or someone else. We've attended thirty or forty parties in the last eighteen months. All kinds of people. Beatniks, Madison Avenue gray flannel suiters, painters who have crashed the midtown galleries, piano players, wrestlers, trapeze artists, lads who have been writing the Great American Novel for forty years. You can take your pick. I'll cast my vote for one of the far-out, real gone Beatniks."

"Darling, if I could really believe—"

"Let me finish, Janice. All kinds of people can get erotically compulsive ideas, dangerous and malicious ideas. They become lost to all honor. That's an old-fashioned word, but I've always rather liked it."

"I've no quarrel with it, David. But I can't believe it was all a malicious prank. I just can't reconcile what I saw with any such convenient, easy-to-accept explanation. You've convinced yourself that the figure in the hall was wearing a mask. It was the first thing I thought of, but I couldn't go on believing it."

"Why not? It makes sense."

"Not to me. That creature was real, David. Real and alive and a monster. Not a man disguised by a mask. Its face had a fleshly look."

"But you said yourself that its face was mask-like. And modern mechanical masks can be almost unbelievably lifelike. Mask making has become a fine art. It always was, in a sense, but it's genius-inspired today. I've seen a few of the extraordinary ones—both the Frankenstein monster type and the kind that wouldn't scare a woman if she woke up and saw it beside her on a pillow in the morning. She might even—"

"Don't say it, David, or I'll get angry. I've been holding myself in, but I *can* get angry. You've been pressing the jealousy pedal too hard, damaging the sound track, jamming the keys."

"I'm sorry, Janice. It just slipped."

"What are you going to do, David? If you really believe it was just a malicious prank."

"Find him, of course. Find him and take off the mask and flatten his face out so he won't really need a mask to look like a ghoulish monster. That way we'll be helping each other."

"You may end up in jail."

"It will be worth it. Finding him may not be easy, but there's a good chance I'll get my hands on him if I work at it hard enough. I'm going over to your apartment right now, alone. I want you to stay here until I get back. I'll question the neighbors. Someone may have seen him coming or going. I'll describe him and try to locate someone who knows him well, or has seen him often enough to recognize the description. Then I'll go through the halls and your apartment with a fine tooth comb. He may have left a clue to his identity somewhere about the apartment."

"That seems unlikely, David."

"You never know. Even professional criminals get careless and he isn't a professional. It's surprising how often intruders leave traces somewhere. They get careless and drop something, even a slip of paper with a name or address on it. I know a detective lieutenant who's firmly convinced you have at least a forty percent chance of tracing a criminal intruder if you're thorough enough and explore all of the possibilities."

"All right, David, go ahead. I won't try to stop you. Find out all you can. I think you're wrong. I don't believe it was a prank. I'm sure it was something stranger and more terrifying, something we can't even begin to understand. But I don't want you to blame me later. Although I really can't see what good catching him would do."

"You don't? I should think you'd be the first to understand how I feel."

"I can understand how you feel, David. But what good would knocking him down do? If you're right about its being a prank he's a very sick man. Actually, you ought to have compassion and want to help him."

"I'm afraid I can't be that objective about it. It's a matter of male pride."

"Well, go ahead, indulge your pride, David. I'm not stopping you…"

The parting shot rankled a little as David stood outside the apartment building staring down the long length of MacDougal Street, his eyes alert for a cruising taxi. Simply being angry with her made no sense at all, he told himself. A woman couldn't understand how a man felt when he was caught up in an ugly situation that could only be straightened out in one way if he wanted to go on living with himself.

Being angry made no sense, but he should have explained to her exactly what would happen to his integrity if he shrugged the whole matter off and forgot about it. Emotionally she would never understand, but he should have made a serious effort to at least straighten her out intellectually and correct the impression he'd left with her that he was scientifically moronic and still living in the Middle Ages as far as mental illness was concerned.

The prankster was quite possibly psychotic, or, at the very least, a psychopathic personality. But even so, his integrity demanded that he give the scoundrel at least one sturdy biff in the jaw. After that, he could afford to feel generous and enlightened and drag the man by the scruff of his neck to the nearest mental institution.

A taxi swung to the curb at last and Loring got in and gave the driver Janice's Horatio Street address. He relaxed a little and watched Village stores, restaurants and dry cleaning establishments sweep past the windows of the cab. The almost completely deserted aspect of the Village before ten in the morning never ceased to fascinate him. He didn't quite know why.

Three minutes later, the taxi drew in to the curb in front of a four-story brownstone. Loring paid the driver, climbed the stoop and walked up two flights of stairs to the door of Janice's apartment. He inserted the key she had given him into the lock.

Janice's apartment seemed completely peaceful—quiet and appealing in the early morning light which streamed in from a high window directly opposite the daybed. The covers were in disarray and there was a slipper in the middle of the floor and a small oaken stand had been overturned in her hurry to get away. But otherwise the room was in order and her presence seemed to hover over everything that Loring touched.

He was staring at the slipper when a chill thought crept into his mind, and made his heart stand still. What if she were not alive and safe and waiting for him in the apartment they'd soon be sharing? What if he were a lover returning alone to a house that would never echo to her footsteps again? What if she occupied a narrow home beneath a row of cypresses and he was alone now with only memories to comfort him, or tear cruelly at his heart?

If he were returning alone to such a dwelling, could he bear even to look at the slipper, the unmade bed, all of the dear, precious things her hands had touched?

He remembered suddenly that in the past when he had allowed his mind to dwell even for a moment on some great and inconsolable loss which had never actually taken place he was the better for it—a man more capable of taking full advantage of every moment of joy and happiness in the narrowing orbit of his days. You had to live every moment to the full, with as much heightening of consciousness as you were capable of experiencing, because the orbit started narrowing when you were twenty and never grew any wider even when it stopped narrowing for a time and stayed the way it had been.

In the past such thoughts had not shaken him too profoundly or left a cold chill in their wake. But now they did, somehow. The room felt perceptibly more somber and the chill seemed to spread out from his mind in widening circles to envelop the chairs and bedside table, the bricks of the fireplace and even the pictures on the wall.

He did not hear the door open, though it made a faint click which would have been audible to anyone less preoccupied.

He did not even hear the woman's footsteps approaching him across the room. Her tread was very light and the rug was deep-napped and very soft. But her quick, excited breathing and the heady perfume which was distilling its essence through the room—an odor of jasmine—and the rustle of her dress as she moved quickly made him aware that he was no longer alone.

He turned abruptly and stood staring at her, unable to move or speak, a look of dazed disbelief in his eyes.

He had never seen the woman before. Once seen, her face would have stayed forever in his memory and he could not possibly have forgotten how tormentingly beautiful it was or failed to remember every first-encounter impression, the time, the place, the exact moment when she had ceased to be a stranger.

Her beauty was so overwhelming that it stirred the heart in ways that were dangerous. Instantly, tumultuously, like a drug injected directly into the aorta, tightening the muscle fibers, drawing them together, increasing each pulse beat, turning each beat into a hammer blow in a bursting stillness.

CHAPTER THREE

David Loring had no way of knowing that he was under observation and that his every movement was being watched. He could not see the lighted tele-communication screen or the cold, alien eyes trained on his image as he inserted the key which Janice had given him into the door of her apartment and stood for an instant motionless, with an angry set to his jaw.

He did not know that an alien electronic pickup device was transmitting his image from an apartment house hallway in Greenwich Village to a hovering flying disk high in the sky. Within the disk the screen glowed brightly and Loring's image was life size. It stood out with a startling, three-dimensional clarity. Not only was the image studied carefully, it was relayed to a dozen other flying disks within a radius of six hundred miles. The eyes that watched were dark and inscrutable, buried in folds of pinkish flesh. They did not blink, but stared steadily and without noticeable animation. Each eye was like a smoky lens, concealing more than it revealed, keeping its many secrets hidden. Each eye was a Sphinx-eye, brooding and unfathomable.

And each was the eye of a Martian.

The truth would have staggered Loring and broken down all of his defenses. He would have stood motionless, his hand on the doorknob, struggling to remain calm but feeling his sanity imperiled. Fortunately he did not know, did not even suspect that everything he said or did was being constantly scrutinized.

His ignorance was shared by every man, woman and child on Earth. Not even the sharp, wise eyes of the astronomers had detected the rocket flares on Mars when the Martian ships had taken off from the red planet on their three-stage journey across space.

There were other things that Loring did not know or suspect. The Martian invaders of Earth had been woman hunting. They had been woman hunting so relentlessly for five days that even as Loring's image flickered on their tele-communication screens their great, silvery mother ship was moving slowly above the autumn-resplendent countryside one hundred and forty miles from New York City, at an altitude of ninety feet above ground level.

It was a deserted region of sapling spruce and birches and dwarfed evergreens, growing so symmetrically on the sloping hillsides that each isolated group of trees had a deceptive appearance of greenhouse cultivation.

The Martian invaders were taking a calculated risk. They were almost sure that the sparsely settled region would contain no eyewitness whom they could not quickly capture and silence. But they could not be completely sure. The screams of the captured women or the barking of savage dogs on the scattered farms or in the streets of the small village communities might be just loud and frantic enough to alert the hard-eyed, stony-faced men whose duty it was to carry arms and be always on guard.

The inhabitants of Earth had already seen far too many Martian ships. Fortunately their Martian origin had not been stressed even by the credulous, and the majority of eyewitnesses preferred to believe they came from Venus, or the dark side of the moon, or some unknown region of outer space. No scientist of worldwide prestige had even seen a flying saucer, and scientists in general refused to take Unidentified Flying Objects seriously, and were quick to dismiss the many rumored sightings as superstitious nonsense—a product of mass hysteria.

Nevertheless it was a dangerous undertaking. If a Martian ship should meet with an accident and be forced to land, tangible proof would exist in abundance. There would be a fiery crater in the quiet countryside, which would flame more brightly than a cluster of burning buildings. The walls of the crater would be eroded and smoke-blackened, its circumference sprinkled with radioactive dust from the descending ship's exploding rocket jets. A search party would be likely to find, scattered about in the immediate vicinity, fragments of a radioactive metal unknown on Earth.

A wave of terror would sweep from city to city, from continent to continent, until it engulfed the entire planet. Emergency warning signals would be broadcast everywhere, from New York and London, from Paris and Moscow, to the remote Asian villages: *It has come. The ultimate horror, the unbelievable. Earth has been invaded by the intelligent inhabitants of another planet.*

And if a Martian should be captured alive... The thought could be accepted by the human mind perhaps and even embraced with a momentary, wholly unjustified feeling of triumph. But to a Martian it would be a death thought, too hideous to contemplate.

A Martian in a cage or in a laboratory, stared at, jeered at perhaps, completely at the mercy of his human captors. A Martian stretched out on an operating table, with sharp instruments of human science glittering in a cone of radiance above his strapped-down body. Pain, torment beyond endurance. Martian pride humbled, and dragged through the dust.

A dissecting laboratory. Would Earth display pity or stay its hand if it needed knowledge to forge weapons to combat an intelligent race bent on space conquest—a race so different from Man in some respects that it would be easy to think of its captive members as caged beasts or hideous and dangerous monsters?

No mercy would be shown. No mercy could be expected. It would be a battle to the death, and in some respects Earth's technological knowledge was formidable. No Martian ship could hope to survive a full-scale atomic attack. The hydrogen bomb was far more destructive than any Martian weapon, deadly as some of those weapons were. A single nuclear bomb could destroy ten or twelve Martian ships moving in close formation.

It was not a thought that Tragor cared to dwell upon. He stood in the observation compartment of the mother ship, staring out at the bright autumn foliage directly beneath him. The ship was hovering so low above the sloping countryside that its hull almost brushed the branches of occasional tall trees, looming like sentinel posts above the dwarfed pines and the slender trunks of young birch trees, spruces and cedars. Some of the hillsides were rocky and overgrown with lichen, their leaf-choked recesses and bramble patches casting purple shadows. Others were bright with a riot of autumn colors, reds and browns and golden yellows.

Tragor could see his own reflection in the viewglass, tall and grave and commanding. It seemed incredible to him that even on an alien world his appearance could cause a female to recoil from him in terror and revulsion. That he should seem handsome and desirable, an outstandingly virile male, to all humanoid women—no matter what their lineage—was something he had taken for granted.

Was he, after all, so different from the males whom women mated with on Earth? Did he not have a strong, robust body, well shaped eyes that could burn with an unquenchable ardor, hands that could clasp and caress? Why, if the women of Earth seemed so maddeningly attractive and desirable to him, did he not seem equally desirable to them? Why should they recoil from him in horror? Why should they regard him as a monster?

There were physical differences, of course, but they were biologically superficial. He was in every vital aspect of his being completely human. Human enough to make love, to embrace a human female and convince her in a hundred ways that in him she had a lover indeed. And every other Martian felt the same way. They had made a tragic blunder, but it was a blunder that could be wiped out, forgotten, and compensated for. It was not too late.

Had it not been, after all, a natural blunder, a credit to a male with pride? To conquer and colonize another planet was a hazardous undertaking. To expose females to so great a danger, to such unimaginable hardships, would have been unthinkable. But still, a mistake had been made. A male cannot live alone. The woman-need must be appeased, or unendurable frustration and wretchedness will result.

And on Earth there were women who, by a miracle that could not be easily explained, were even more desirable to a Martian than the females of his own race. If only—

Forget the "only" Tragor told himself with vigor. Their fear can be overcome, their resistance broken down. Ardor will do it, flaming ardor, all the delights of the dark, the words of love, the whispered reassurances. Limbs crushing limbs, with a passion irresistible, gentleness with fierceness intermingled...

Yes, yes. He only needed to be bold, virile, fearless. And he had a great boldness within him. He was stronger than any male on Earth and wiser and more understanding. In the long run no human woman could resist him.

Had they not already captured and studied dozens of human women? They had needed to do that for a quite different reason, a reason not associated with lovemaking at all. They had held themselves in restraint, because they had not been so long cut off from the women of their own race that the torment and frustration had become unendurable. Studying the women of Earth had been part of the master plan, the Great Plan for Earth conquest.

Nothing must be allowed to interfere with that plan even now. But now there was another need—compulsive, overwhelming. For every Martian a mate must be found—a woman tender and yielding.

For every Martian.

Tragor straightened in sudden alertness, his eyes on a stretch of open countryside a few hundred feet in front of the steadily advancing ship. Between a winding brook and a small, tree-shadowed grove eight or ten tiny human figures were moving slowly about or sitting in pairs on the grass.

He had seen such groups before and the sight did not surprise him. They were hikers, relaxing after a strenuous tramp over the green-yellow hills, and enjoying one another's company by a cool stream in the shadow of whispering boughs. They had unwrapped packages of food and spread a white tablecloth on the grass and at the edge of the stream a girl with gold-red hair was filling a pail with water.

He could see the girl clearly now, her slender supple form bent seductively above the pale, sky-mirroring water. There were other girls in the group but even at a distance they seemed far less attractive. Two were very stout and one was a gaunt, big-boned woman with almost mannish features and no roundness where Tragor looked for roundness with anticipatory delight.

He saw now that the group consisted of eight people, and that four of them were men. The men could be destroyed without difficulty and presented no problem. But he studied them carefully never-theless. He studied their physiques for muscular sturdiness and their faces, as the ship drew rapidly nearer, for qualities that might prove troublesome in a struggle, however heavily the odds were weighted against them: resolution, defiance, firmness of mind and will.

He knew that a few men would fight to the death, counting their own lives of no importance, if a monster threatened a woman dear to them. Tragor recoiled a little at the thought, cursing himself for allowing such an image to torment him at a moment when his triumph seemed assured. He was not a monster, and he intended to make sure that the woman by the brook did not think of him as one for long. She would very soon find out he was the most perfect lover she had ever known.

How many human lovers had she known? he wondered. A woman that beautiful could hardly have escaped lovers, but it did not matter to him at all. It disturbed human males, sometimes even drove them to acts of violence, but he was not that kind of a fool. He could make any woman forget any lover in her past. He was sure of it. He could blot the memory from her mind, make it seem less than the shadow of a dream. She would exist for him alone and believe that she had come into his arms completely virginal.

A little violence at first perhaps might be needed. He must be firm and unbending, but it would not be for long. She would quickly enough dissolve in his arms when the monster image was destroyed by an embrace more passionate and unyielding than she could have dared to hope for, even during those moments of wild surrender when a woman is asleep and dreaming and restrained by nothing sternly forbidding and unfair to her nature in the waking world.

The four men and four women had seen the ship now and were on their feet, pointing, shouting, their faces contorted with terror. The girl by the brook had dropped her pail and was running toward the others, her red-gold hair whipped by the wind, her white limbs gleaming in the sunlight.

Tragor swayed a little, so aroused and stimulated by her great beauty that he was unable to take command. He stood very still, his heart beating wildly, knowing that it was not really necessary for him to act. Others would act for him, as they had often done in the past. In the absence of direct orders the ship would veer slightly, and then remain stationary, hovering above the women who were to be taken captive and the men who were to be destroyed. A wide section of the hull would swing open, and five heavily armed Martians would descend to the ground over a collapsible metal stairway. The stairway would be instantly withdrawn and not lowered again until the men had been killed, the women taken captive.

It was happening now. Tragor could hear the thrumming of the opening hull section, the metallic clatter of weapons and equipment as the marauding party waited with no attempt to conceal their impatience for the stairway to be lowered.

Then, through the view-glass, he saw the stairway go down and the first of the five Martians start to descend, his massive shoulders and hairless skull giving him the formidable aspect of a trained warrior who would give and expect no quarter. The brutishness of the warrior caste never failed to repel Tragor a little, but he realized that warriors were necessary.

A human woman might almost be justified in looking upon a Martian warrior as a monster. A straggle-legged brute, hairy and uncouth and utterly lacking in refinement. To be seized by a warrior, roughly slapped, and carried screaming and kicking to a space ship could hardly fail to be abhorrent to a sensitive and delicate woman. But a desirable woman could not be allowed to escape and the women of Earth were often incredibly fleet of foot.

Two warriors were descending the stairway now and a third was just emerging. The structure grazed the ground, but did not rest solidly upon it. It was necessary to keep the ship in motion, and a grounded stairway could cause unimaginable havoc.

Below there was havoc of a different sort. Two of the men were standing their ground and one had picked up a rifle. But the fourth man was in headlong flight, his shoulders jerking as he ran, his coat flapping open. He stumbled and fell and picked himself up again, stopping for an instant to look back in horror. He did not seem to care that he had stamped himself a craven and cut a woefully pitiful figure, for he added to his shame by crying out hoarsely. He changed his course slightly and headed directly for the grove, moving slowly and awkwardly now, as if fear had begun to paralyze him.

The gaunt, mannish woman was standing very still, shading her eyes with her hands and watching the Martians descend with no pronounced change of expression. But her face was drained of all color. The two stout women were clinging to each other and screaming.

But the girl whom Tragor had seen first by the brook and now saw in a different light, with the sunlight aureoling her hair and a man to defend her, did not appear to be the kind of woman who could be easily demoralized. She stood straight and still by the man with the rifle, her head tilted back in defiance, her lips slightly parted.

All five of the Martians were on the stairway now, and the first to emerge from the ship had been passed by the second, an equally muscular warrior with an even more brutish countenance. With a quick leap he was on the ground, his puckered, heavy-lidded eyes darting toward the four women with lascivious eagerness, the pupils strangely luminous.

The Martian directly above him paused for an instant on the stairway, raised to his shoulder a small, compact weapon that bore a slight resemblance to a sawed-off shotgun despite its technical complexity and took careful aim at the running man, who had almost reached the grove.

The weapon leapt in the Martian's clasp and a sharp crack echoed like a pistol shot across the open countryside, from the hollow, metallic sounding board of the ship's hull to the distant cluster of trees.

The running man screamed, threw out his arms and crumpled at the edge of the grove. The spurt of blood from a severed artery was visible from the ship, a thin, crimson jet that spattered the grass and the foliage and gleamed brightly on the boles of the trees until the crumpled body began to smoke. The smoke spiraling up from the slain man obscured the gleaming, and was blown by the wind between the trees, filling the entire grove with a thin, drifting haze.

One of the stout women swayed, released her hold on her companion's arm and sank to the ground in a dead faint. The other went on screaming, so shrilly and hysterically that for a moment no other sound could be heard—not even the heavy tread of the Martians moving toward the four women and three men with their weapons raised.

The slender girl, who Tragor coveted, gripped the arm of the man beside her in desperate appeal. "Don't shoot, Kenneth," she whispered, her face pale with fear. "They'll kill you too!"

"They'll kill me anyway," the man said, closing his hand tightly over her trembling fingers and gently freeing his arm. "This is one nightmare that seems to be real. They're certain to kill us all. But I'm going to get one of them first."

The rifle was at his shoulder before she could cry out in protest.

There was another sharp crack, not unlike the report that the Martian's complicated weapon had made. The nearest Martian came to an abrupt halt. For an instant his green-fleshed, mask-like face remained totally devoid of expression. Then the lineaments seemed to shrivel and darken. The cruel, slitted mouth lost its firmness and the flesh around the eyelids began to sag. Slowly, horribly the entire face changed color, the green fading to an ashen gray, the pinkish hue of the eyelids darkening to a deep crimson, which did not fade.

From a ragged cavern in the Martian's chest there came a brighter flood of crimson. It stained the fabric of his dark-textured, tight fitting garments, dripped from his garments to the ground and formed a widening pool at his feet.

He swayed a little, but he did not totter and fall. He died standing up, with the animation fading slowly from his eyes. The eyes clouded over, became opaque. But still the Martian remained upright, a standing corpse that maintained its equilibrium by the sturdiness of its firmly planted legs and the sheer massiveness of its barrel-shaped torso and dangling arms.

The mannish woman sank to her knees, covered her eyes with her hands, and began to moan. The man with the rifle stood motionless, his lips white, smoke pouring from the barrel of the half-lowered weapon. The stout woman had ceased to scream. Her face looked gray and frozen and her fingers had gone to her throat. She was plucking at the flesh of her throat, as if the sudden tightening of her vocal cords was causing her unendurable torment.

The slain Martian's costly delay in killing the man with the rifle appeared to enrage his companions. With brutal callousness two of them moved forward, and hurled the lifeless body to the ground. Then, they took care not to repeat his mistake. They killed all three men, with such rapid bursts of weapon fire that they were lifted into the air, hurled backwards and were dead before their bodies struck the ground.

The slender woman whom Tragor coveted cried out in anguish and ran toward the crumpled form of the man with the rifle, her eyes shining with a near madness that went far beyond shock and made her waver as she ran. He was still clasping the rifle, his fingers snagged in the trigger frame. There were no visible wounds on his body, but blood stained his left temple and his eyebrows and hair had been singed. His face was ashen, the eyes blankly staring. She knew at once that he was dead and flung herself upon him, weeping, moaning, her body racked by uncontrollable sobs.

She did not hear the slow, heavy tread of a Martian drawing near and if she had heard she would not have cared. She had no desire to go on living, and had ceased to know the meaning of fear. Her life was over. At that moment she realized, as never before, that no one dies alone.

He had taken her with him and she had died too. Only the hollow shell of a living woman remained. She did not care what happened to that shell. There is no fate worse than death to a woman who has ceased to live.

At first, when she felt herself being seized and lifted up, she struggled only to remain where she was—close to the man whose life she had shared and would go on sharing forever, despite death and change and Time's relentless tyranny in a universe which spared no one.

She was not even aware of the Martian's fleshly strength, the savage cruelty of his embrace, the way he was drawing her to him mercilessly, encircling her shoulders and refusing to relax his grip on her arms until his flat, hard chest bruised her numbed breasts.

At first the Martian was no more than a hindrance, an obstacle, a disembodied force that was keeping her from her dead lover. It was as if a magnetic web had enmeshed her limbs and was lifting her from the slain man's side, forcing her to abandon him.

It wasn't until the Martian had swung about and started back toward the ship, his arms tight about her, that she started to struggle. Even then her struggles were blindly instinctive, her flesh rebelling while her mind remained remote and grief-shattered.

She was not the only captive. Both of the stout women were struggling furiously in the arms of warrior-caste Martians, their faces flushed and despairing, their bodies arched backwards, as if to remain pressed cruelly to the board-like chests of captors so brutish and alien, their screams silenced by force, was a horror and a degradation which no woman could sanely endure.

The gaunt, large-boned, mannish-looking woman was not being carried to the ship. She was being propelled forward by nudgings from the weapon of a Martian who wore upon his mask-like face an unmistakable look of distaste.

There was a cold anger in her eyes and she walked with dignity despite the proddings, her composure completely restored now, her lips set in tight lines.

Tragor, staring through the view-glass, had missed nothing of the deadly, ten-minute struggle. He was pleased and almost beside himself with eagerness to take the captive whose beauty had so maddeningly aroused him from the arms of the warrior-caste brute and carry her to his own sleeping compartment.

The warriors had done well, but he had no intention of congratulating them. Discipline forbade it. A wave of revulsion swept over him again when he thought of how crude the warriors were in their lovemaking. They had no delicacy of perception, no true understanding of how to make love to a woman. They went about it in the most brutal imaginable way. Firmness, yes—that was necessary. You had to be very strong and sure of yourself. The slightest doubt or hesitation could be fatal.

In fact, you could develop what human psychologists called a complex in regard to one particular woman if you failed at the wrong moment, no matter how accomplished you were with other women. He had been on Earth long enough to understand these things, to realize that Martians were no different from human males in that respect. One failure and a woman could be lost to you forever. And she might be the most desirable woman you'd ever known, and couldn't do without.

It was important to understand all this, because when a Martian made love to a woman who regarded him as a monster, failure might very easily occur the first time. And that failure might be impossible to overcome later on.

No, no, he told himself angrily. It wouldn't happen this time. The captive who had stirred him beyond reason was now being carried up the stairway into the ship. She was still struggling and her red-gold hair had come unbound and fallen over her shoulders and he could see the entrancing curvature of her half-revealed breasts. She was slender and yet her beauty seemed full-blown in a pulse-stirring way, as the beauty of a young girl often seems in the magic mirror which draws no sharp distinction between a girl of twenty and a woman of thirty. If she is lovely enough, she becomes not one woman, but two, her youthful charms blending with the ripeness which will soon be hers and making that ripeness another aspect of her present self.

It couldn't happen this time, he told himself again. He desired her too overwhelmingly and her beauty was too irresistible. She would stir him instantly to an amorous frenzy. He was sure of it. He would experience no misgivings, no apprehension. Already he could feel her lips moving against his. Her lips were full, red and enticingly curved. He would drain the sweetness of her mouth like a thirsty man, a parched desert wayfarer...

He straightened, anger creasing his brow. The warrior-caste brutes were taking unwarranted liberties with two of the captive women when they were under strict orders to do no more than clasp them firmly and carry them into the ship. It did not anger him too much, because the women the brutes had captured would probably soon become their mates. But what if it gave the warrior who was carrying the slender woman ideas?

The brute did not know that she was the woman of Tragor's choice. He had not assumed command and he had issued no orders. What if the warrior assumed that Tragor was hard to please and would not be likely to have made a choice when so many opportunities were open to him? Hadn't he surrendered even more beautiful women to warriors with a shrug, simply because they hadn't seemed quite so desirable as the slender woman who might, unless he acted quickly, find herself in the deadliest kind of danger?

A sudden trembling seized him. His worst fears seemed about to be realized. The warrior-caste Martian had paused a short distance from the top of the stairway, and had taken firm hold of his captive's unbound hair. He was drawing her head backwards, with the unmistakable intention of implanting a kiss on her lips—a kiss that would be savage and prolonged. Just to be kissed in that way by such a brute was a desecration in itself. And Tragor knew that the brute would not be satisfied with a kiss. It would not stop there. His hands...

Tragor left the observation compartment in three long strides, dark anger surging up in him, a fury that he was powerless to control. He knew that the warrior was not too much to blame, for he had issued no orders. But if it went beyond a kiss, he swore that the brute would die.

He had gone beyond a kiss but not too much beyond. Standing at the head of the stairway, with the opened section of hull looming at his back, Tragor took careful note of what the warrior-caste Martian was doing. The brute had placed one of his taloned hands squarely on his captive's back, and was running the other over her body, over the smooth curvature of her hips and back and forth across her knees. Her knees were drawn up and she was kicking her legs in protest, but her efforts to free herself did not seem to be discouraging the Martian.

Tragor did not move at all for a moment. Then he stepped forward into the light that was flooding up from below and spoke to the warrior-caste Martian.

"Come into the ship. Put her down and walk away from her. Do you understand? I expect instant obedience."

The warrior obeyed in complete silence. He cast one doubtful glance at Tragor and then did as he was told. The slender girl slumped to the deck the instant she was released, rolled over on her side and moaned.

The warrior spoke then, for the first time. "I did not harm her. You saw—"

"I saw," Tragor said.

"If I did her no harm, why are you angry?"

"Your orders were to bring her into the ship without making love to her."

"But you gave no orders—"

"They are permanent orders. All captive women are to be brought to me first. I will decide who is to claim them."

The warrior nodded. "I am sorry," he said.

"You had better be. Turn now and walk away from me."

The warrior-caste Martian took a slow step backwards. He began to tremble. "You will not—"

"You heard what I said. Walk away from me." The Martian turned without a word and walked away from Tragor along the deck.

Tragor removed a small metallic box from his three-pocketed waist jacket, opened it, and withdrew the dart projector from its sterile container. He raised the projector to eye level and took careful aim.

The dart struck the warrior-caste Martian at the base of the neck and went completely through his skull, passing upward through his brain to emerge at the top of his head.

He did not die standing up. The needlelike sliver of metal severed a cerebral nerve that controlled the functioning of his muscles and his entire body went flaccid, so that he slumped to the deck without uttering a sound, but with a conclusive shudder that would have been pitiful to watch if Tragor had been capable of compassion or remorse.

But Tragor felt only dark, terrible, anger, ebbing away a little now that he had found a target for his ire and had laid that target low.

He turned and walked to where the slender woman was lying. He was more shaken than he would have cared to admit even to himself. He had never experienced a rage quite so uncontrollable and he knew that it did him no credit. Jealousy? No, that was insane. How could he be jealous of a brutish, warrior-caste Martian?

The brute had held her tightly in his arms, kissed her savagely, dared to embrace her in a more intimate way. But he had not possessed her. And she had not responded in any way to his brutal lovemaking. She had struggled instead, had shown unmistakably that she would have preferred death to a night in the dark with so primitive a lover.

But that was all over now. He had avenged and protected her and with him it would be different.

It would be very different. He would destroy the beast image very quickly by his tenderness and solicitude, and his virile, forthright love-making. There was no brutishness in him but she would find him very firm, accomplished, determined to make her realize that Martians were completely human in every way that mattered—with minds and hearts that worshipped at the shrine of love, and with bodies which were lithe-limbed and well formed. Anatomically there was no actual structural difference between Earthmen and Martians that went beyond skin coloration and the more superficial aspects of posture, muscular coordination in the higher cerebral centers, and the distribution of body fat. Martians walked with a slightly stooped posture, but they could stand straight enough when the need arose. In addition to the difference in skin coloration their facial contours were at variance with the human form, and their hands terminated in nails so sharp and long that Earthmen thought of them as claws.

They were claw-like, but only because the nails contained a network of tiny blood vessels and could not be cut without causing a Martian to writhe in pain. Why did it so seldom occur to Earthmen that their own bodies were primitive to an equal degree and that the heritage of the jungle had left its mark on them? Why were they so slow to realize that only the great beauty of their women could overcome such flaws?

Martians were human—as that term was used on Earth. To think of them as merely *humanoid* did Earthmen and Earthwomen no credit, for it was a reflection on their intelligence. And in one respect at least both races possessed a splendor that no primitiveness could dim. In both Martians and Earthmen the great organ of love was the same.

Tragor remained for an instant deep in thought, his eyes on the slender woman for whom he had killed—and he would kill again, if necessary, to make her completely his own. Then he bent and slipped one arm about her slim waist, and gently raised her to a sitting position on the deck. For an instant she seemed scarcely aware that she was no longer alone with her grief. Her failure to struggle or offer any resistance at all surprised him. She had surrendered limply to his guiding strength, allowing him to lift her up and change the position of her body without crying out or pleading with him not to touch her.

It was a good omen, even though it seemed strange and unnatural under the circumstances. Then, quite suddenly, he realized that she wasn't looking at him at all. She was staring dazedly beyond him, at the blank expanse of metal surrounding the slowly closing hull section. Her eyes were very wide, the pupils slightly dilated, and her lips were parted, as if she lacked the will or desire to bring her thoughts to a focus, and exercise control over the muscles of her face.

She appeared to be in a state of shock. Well that was understandable, he told himself. He should have anticipated such a frustrating development and made allowances for it. He could wait. She would find him an impetuous lover but not an inconsiderate one. He would know how to be gentle with her.

He would wait patiently and—it suddenly seemed to him that he could no longer breathe. Her closeness, the pulsating of the veins in her soft, white throat, the swelling firmness of her breasts, bursting like honey mounds from the constraining tightness of her dress made it impossible for him to wait.

It was all like a terrible dream that is both rapturously intoxicating—sweet beyond anything the waking mind can experience—and laden with the blackest kind of guilt. He had not wanted to be cruelly importunate with this woman whom he desired so ardently—this woman he had already begun to worship.

But now he had no choice. Restraint had become impossible.

His arms went out and around her. She was not the first human woman he had ever made love to, but in that instant of fierce passion no other woman existed for him. There were no memories to distract him and provide comparisons, for all past amorous conquests dwindled to a pinpoint glimmering in his mind, and then vanished completely.

He was only aware of *her*. Aware of her hair, which his taloned hands caressed lightly, and the soft flesh of her shoulders that he also caressed, and the tender swell of her bosom, which drew his eyes, and her mouth, which he wanted to smother with kisses. He wanted to envelop her completely, and in every pore of her being, to make of his body a palpitating web of love which would bind and imprison her and make her his captive and a slave of love through long months and years of amorous dalliance.

He wanted to hold her tightly and never let her go. There were lovers who remained entwined the whole night through and he wanted to be such a lover now, but a single night would never suffice and he wanted it to be a hundred nights, a thousand.

Earthmen were too quick in their lovemaking, headstrong and foolish. They thought of love as a kind of explosion, which quickly burned itself out and left only ashes. He knew better. He was far wiser and now that wisdom and knowledge was a living flame consuming him. Not a flame that could be extinguished in one soaring burst of ecstasy or a hundred such bursts but a flame that would burn forever.

First her mouth. Claim and possess it, parted lips over parted lips with the dartings of love between. Yes, her moist and yielding lips. She would bend to him and he would kiss her with such ardor…

But it was not as he had expected. As his arms moved to envelop her more completely and his lips approached her mouth she shuddered convulsively and strained backwards, crying out in wild terror.

It was not the cry alone that unnerved him. He could see her eyes now. They were very close and he could look directly into them. They were no longer glazed and uncomprehending. They were trained on his face with a blazing intensity of hatred and loathing.

It was horrible. It shamed him. He himself began to tremble and turn pale. Not only had his ardor failed to arouse her, it had stirred her to the kind of response that he most dreaded—anger, contempt, revulsion. She was no longer even frightened. He could see that she despised him too much to be afraid of him. He revolted her, sickened her. But strongest of all was the hatred—a blazing hatred such as he had never before seen in the eyes of a woman.

It was not even a womanly hate. It was the kind of hate that could crush and destroy. She was clubbing him with it, using it as a gladiator would use a mace—a mace encircled with cruel, blood-drawing spikes.

He had no defense against such contempt, such hatred. It unmanned him, so that he cowered back from her as if she had turned suddenly into a savage beast with bared fangs, slowly pacing about in front of him, and waiting for his knees to give way before closing in for the kill.

The words she flung at him were the worst of all. He had hoped never to hear such words spoken by any woman. But from her lips they seared all that remained of his pride, so that his image of himself as a lover, accomplished and irresistible, shriveled and blackened and fell apart, like a leaf on a burning tree.

Her words were destructive to more than his pride. They even made him doubt the genuineness of his past triumphs, his success with Martian women. Had his fierce lovemaking not been what Martian women wanted? Had he been less than an artist in love? Had they submitted to him only because of his high station, while secretly holding him in contempt? If they had spoken such words as were coming now from the lips of the woman before him would their voices have rung out with the same biting contempt?

He could imagine a Martian woman saying such things to him. He could picture it now. But the words of the slender woman before him were infinitely more cruel and vindictive and even as he listened to them he could feel his virility ebbing away. They were terrible and crushing words and they burned into his brain like a firing rod glowing white-hot.

"If you touch me again I will kill myself! I will find a way! If only you knew how loathsome you are—what a beast thing you are! I would rather be embraced by a toad! I do not know where you came from or what you are. But you are inhuman beasts, cruel and cold and merciless. We will fight you until every man and woman on Earth is dead. If necessary, we will all die. But we will fight you. You can be sure of that. Oh, you can be very sure! You killed my husband! He had every right to defend himself. He saw what you did to the man who fled."

Tragor heard himself speaking in reply. How he managed to find the right words he did not quite know, and perhaps they weren't the right words at all. But he had to say them. He had to speak.

"Listen to me," he said, with a pleading urgency in his voice that he could not repress and did not perhaps really want to repress. "I can speak your language. We have been on Earth for almost two years but we have taken care to keep our presence well concealed. We are from Mars. We call our home planet Jagroon, but to you it is Mars. A few of our spaceships have been sighted in the past, for almost twenty years now. But we sent only a few ships to Earth to explore the planet at first and did not come in force until two years ago.

"Do you understand? I want it all to be very clear to you."

The woman's lips had gone very white. "It is clear enough. It is what I feared. Beasts like you, and men like my husband cannot live on the same planet in peace. You will either destroy us or we will destroy you. My husband took the flying saucer sightings seriously. I did not. I only wish that my blindness had not been shared by so many."

"If that blindness had not been widespread you still could not have struck a single destructive blow against us," Tragor heard himself saying, knowing that he lied but determined to prevent the woman from knowing. "You have atomic weapons, but so have we. And our weapons are more destructive than yours. We could destroy all of your cities overnight. We could destroy them instantly."

"Then why have you not done so? Isn't that what beasts would normally be expected to do?"

"We have a better plan. It is not our purpose to destroy but to build. That is why we are here. To build a better world for both men and Martians."

"With the beasts in the saddle, is that it? Peace on your terms. Peace with slavery for every man and woman on Earth."

"I did not say that."

"No, but you are thinking it. I can see it in your eyes."

"And what if it were true? Should a higher race bow to a race that could not hope to build a ship like this? If you could see the Martian cities you would understand."

"I have never seen a city built by beasts, filled with beasts. I doubt if I would care to visit such a city. The constant stench would be intolerable—the stench of cruelty and death."

"We are not beasts," Tragor said, still looking at her almost pleadingly. "If I were stretched out on a table in the operating room of a New York hospitals, the surgeons busy with their scalpels, there would be no horrified faces, I can assure you. There is nothing about my body or brain that is in the least beast-like."

"You forget. I have seen a demonstration of just how beast-like Martians can be."

"Is there nothing I can say to convince you then?"

"Nothing. You killed a man I loved more than my own life. You've killed me too. I died with him. You are looking upon a woman who no longer places any value upon the mockery life that remains. That is why I do not fear you."

It seemed to Tragor that he, too, had died. At least a part of himself had perished. For a moment life had flamed so brightly in him that he had feared it might consume him. But now that vision of beauty, of desire's complete fulfillment, had been snatched away. There could be no rapture in the night with a woman who looked upon him with loathing and contempt.

He could take her by force, easily enough. But how could love have any meaning when it was completely one-sided? Just to make love was not enough. You had to be loved in return, loved for yourself. He had never been able to endure a completely unresponsive woman, a cold shape of ice in his arms. The warrior-caste brutes felt quite differently about it. They preferred either complete passivity in a woman, or protests, tears, and wild strugglings. He had no great liking for either. He preferred a woman who was as passionate as himself and who could return his caresses with unrestrained ardor.

Perhaps it was a limitation in his nature. He had never felt completely happy about it and now it returned to torment him. Why couldn't he be primitively ruthless? Had not an Earth philosopher said that all women were alike in the dark? Perhaps in the dark even a completely unresponsive woman...no, no, it was unthinkable. He was not a warrior-caste brute and never could be. The small, fleshy protuberances growing from his head were a mark of his high station. The ruling caste alone possessed them, and no man who wore them could ever descend to that kind of barbaric lovemaking.

It seemed suddenly horrible, unendurable to him that he should have to surrender all hope of fulfillment. He had never before been quite so stirred by a woman. Her great beauty had enraptured him beyond reason. Not only her physical charms in the light of day when she was standing close to him, but the promise of delight which those charms hinted at when the daylight was gone and they would be alone together in the night.

No, it could never be now and he had lost her forever. He felt like a man adrift in an open boat, far from land, his throat parched, the sun beating down. Water everywhere, but not a drop to quench his thirst.

If only he were a man in a completely human sense, a man like her husband. Then, no matter how much she hated him, he might be able to overcome her resistance by continuous, passionate pleading.

But now there was no hope. No hope at all.

He turned and gestured to a waiting, warrior-caste brute, whose stationary bulk cast a long shadow on the smooth metal wall opposite the drawn up, now completely telescoped stairway. The warrior stepped forward and stood waiting expectantly.

Tragor spoke tonelessly, as if the tumult within him had risen to such unprecedented heights that its ebbing had left him exhausted.

"Take her to my sleeping compartment. I am quite sure that she will go willingly." He looked at the woman as he spoke, and was not too surprised when she nodded. She at least had the good sense to realize that further struggle would be useless.

"If you harm her in any way I will kill you," Tragor said, surprised and shocked by the explosive violence which gave his words so much added weight that the warrior-caste brute paled and stared with alarm in his eyes at the slumped form at the end of the passageway. From the slain warrior's dart-pierced skull a thin ribbon of blood was descending to the deck and spreading out in a widening pool, which gleamed in the overhead lamps.

"I warn you," the slender woman said. "If you touch me again I will find a way to kill myself."

She turned then and followed the waiting warrior down the passageway to where it turned sharply to the right.

CHAPTER FOUR

The landscape beneath the Martian mother ship was changing rapidly now, but no Martian eyes watched a lake sweep into view and the dwarfed evergreens surrender their sovereignty to a forest of tall, straight pines, their boles dark against the pale, blue-gray sky. A speedboat came suddenly into view from behind a mile-wide island densely overgrown with scrub oak and hemlocks, and headed northward, throwing up a curtain of silvery spray that slowly blended with the haze that hung over the southern part of the lake.

The observation compartment was deserted and only the telecommunication screen opposite the view-glass glimmered with light and movement.

The light was very bright, the movements of absorbing interest to Martian eyes on every ship that had tuned in on that particular broadcast. Twenty-two Martian ships had tuned in. On the screen a man was fitting a key into a lock in the hallway of a building in New York City.

The man was an artist and every Martian watcher knew that the man's name was David Loring. They knew that he was about to walk into the apartment and change the entire pattern of his life. And that change would be a small but vital part of a larger change—the Martian pattern for world conquest.

It was all a part of the Great Plan. And every Martian knew exactly what that plan would do to the man even if he failed to behave as he was expected to behave. Even if he failed. He was in deadly danger, but he did not know that and it was not important that he should know. Nothing but the Great Plan itself was important.

It was a plan tremendous in scope, unbelievable in its daring.

It was a plan that had to succeed or Martian hopes would go down into everlasting night and darkness. It was a plan for the conquest of Earth by infiltration. But it was not the infiltration of spies and fifth columnists. Not even the infiltration of skillfully trained saboteurs. It was a quite different kind of infiltration.

To perfect the Great Plan five hundred women had been captured and studied. And five hundred men. Their desires, hopes, dreams, intelligence native and acquired, manner of thinking, loving, dressing, walking, eating, sleeping; their habits and methods of choice in every aspect of living, taste in women—or, in the case of the women, men. Sex proclivities, sex drives, physical appeal, were all approached scientifically, and the effects of enhancement of the sex urge and what happens when it is enormously diminished by accident or design.

The Earth people were kept in captivity for eight months and then released, with all knowledge of what had happened to them blotted from their minds.

Five hundred men. Five hundred women. Living models. Living models for—what?

Only the Martians knew.

The Great Plan was protected, guarded, veiled in secrecy. But now one man was about to know, to be tested, to enter into the inner workings of the Plan. His name was David Loring and he was an artist and he was a man of very great talent, perhaps even a man of creative genius.

One man alone first and then ten thousand men, the wielders of political and social power, statesmen, generals industrialists of the first rank, influential molders of public opinion, atomic physicists, the key men in a hundred laboratories. Ten thousand men who could strategically determine, by the power invested in them whether human civilization should resist or surrender when the Martian mask was lowered and Martian intentions were made unmistakably plain.

Ten thousand men who must be made to say: "We must surrender. We shall. The Martians will not destroy us. They wish only to live with us in peace, in a world so strangely beautiful that we cannot understand why we were content to live in the world as it was, with its poverty and wars and widespread human misery. We have received from the Martians a living gift that has transformed our lives and made us men indeed. Let us surrender freely and joyfully, with everlasting gratefulness to the gift-bearers."

Ten thousand women too, in high places, in the front ranks of industry and politics, women of enormous wealth, of great and commanding talents who had found no man to please them, or had foolishly allowed themselves to believe that they did not need men to enrich their lives and continuously adore them. Ten thousand women who must also be made to say: "Let us surrender with gratitude, for in the world as it was there was no true happiness for career women. Now all that is changed and we are deliriously happy."

In the thrumming observation compartment of the mother ship, as it moved southward toward New York City, the landscape beneath a riot of autumn colors, the sky clearing now and the haze dissolving, the telecommunication screen continued to glow brightly.

And on the screen the man named David Loring was moving into a room fragrant with woman-scent, with the lingering perfume of his beloved and another perfume that mingled strangely with it, barely noticed but impinging on his senses in a subtle, and beguiling way—the odor of jasmine.

A low, droning sound arose suddenly in the observation compartment and a wall panel swung open.

Two Martians stood framed in the lighted aperture, remaining for a moment motionless, neither advancing nor retreating, but staring steadily at the telecommunication screen, as if it were commanding all of their attention and had for them an almost hypnotic fascination.

One of the Martians was Tragor. The other was a shorter, less heavily muscled ruling-caste individual, stern of eye and lean to the point of emaciation. His name was Sull.

Tragor seemed to have aged and almost to have shrunken in stature. There was a smoldering bitterness in his eyes, a look of savage frustration.

If only her rejection of him could have wavered slightly, he might have been able to endure her scorn. He had tried in a thousand ways to please her, had humbled himself, had knelt in desperate appeal at her feet.

He had beaten on the panel of his sleeping compartment when she had locked it—and he had given her permission to lock it—until the bruising of his flesh had become too painful to endure and blood had dripped from his taloned hands. The back of his right hand was scraped raw.

Never had a woman been wooed so ardently, with such utter abandonment, with such a thrusting aside of all pride. Even a woman of ice should have been stirred to compassion, should have relented a little. Was there not something in all women that responded to the lovemaking of the stricken, the hopeless, the lost? Should not her maternal instincts have been aroused?

They had advanced into the observation compartment now and he was suddenly aware that Sull was talking to him.

"You must be quite mad to forget in so dangerous a way why we are on Earth, Tragor. The Plan is about to be tested, an actual experiment is at the crucial stage, and you let a woman make a complete fool of you."

"I am sorry," Tragor heard himself replying. "I did not intend—"

"You did not intend. You are sorry. What a pitifully weak excuse that is! We should not have gone searching for women at all at so crucial an hour. The success of this experiment is vital to us. We may be needed to silence the man if the experiment is not a success. If you were not my superior I might be tempted—"

"Do not allow yourself to be tempted, Sull," Tragor heard himself saying, his bitterness and frustration giving way to rage. "I warn you. I am in no mood to countenance insubordination. I would be quite capable of silencing you, in a way that would cause you exquisite torment."

"I am not afraid of you, Tragor. My lineage is almost as high as your own. I have a right to speak my mind."

"Speak it then, and let us be done with it. I know where my duty lies. I have not neglected it in any way."

"You are trembling so I am concerned for your sanity. You are thinking of that woman and you are thinking of her compulsively and that is bad. I would never allow a woman to hold the whip hand. They must be made to obey."

"You have never been in love, Sull. You cannot force a woman to love you."

"You can force her to respond."

"Sull, there is something about you that I do not like. I refuse to listen to you. We have come to watch the experiment. Let us watch."

The two Martians approached the telecommunications screen and stood before it. The man named David Loring was in the room of his beloved staring about him now, his eyes on the unmade bed and a slipper that she had dropped in her haste to leave the apartment. He was standing very still, his image very sharp on the lighted screen.

Tragor turned and glanced for an instant at the view-glass, which mirrored the shining waters of the lake far below and the launch that was heading northward.

He stiffened in instant alarm, gripping Sull's arm. "That speed boat," he whispered. "Sull, look! Quickly! Can you see it? They've observed the ship and are turning about. We can't allow that many eyewitnesses to remain alive when everything is so crucial. It would be dangerous—the height of folly. We must silence them immediately."

Sull turned and stared in the view-glass, his lean body and the emaciated lines of his face making him look almost mummy-like in the cold overhead light.

"Three men and three women," he said. "One of the men has a camera."

"It would not be the first time that photographs have been taken of our ships in daylight," Tragor said quickly. "But we cannot risk it now. Events are moving too rapidly."

"Yes, it would be a very clear photograph, with identifiable scenery in the background. The kind of photograph it would be difficult to fake. It would carry conviction, if backed up with the observations of six eyewitnesses. I do not like it at all."

"Neither do I. And it is too late to get out of range. They have started taking pictures and they can see us clearly. I'm afraid we shall have to destroy the boat."

Tragor turned, strode quickly across the compartment and picked up a communication tube. He spoke into it, issuing detailed instructions, pleased by the steady way his voice rose above the faint buzzing and clicking of the instrument, feeling within him the sureness and firmness which he always experienced when he knew himself to be in command...

On the bright waters of the lake the occupants of the launch were no longer in a merrymaking mood. It had been quite wonderful to be in such a mood and it had lasted for five hours before the huge, shining disk had come into view. Both the men and the women had been drinking heavily and had felt gloriously relaxed and at ease, the way they had known they would feel on a speedboat excursion with no holds barred. Even now on the foredeck there was still a sprawl of arms and nylon-encased legs and a sleepy voice whispering: "I'm not going to get up, lover. Not even going to get up and look. You hear me, lover? It's too dee-licious right here. What do I care about an old flying saucer? You are sending me, lover. Sweetkins, come closer. Closer...that's it. Never mind that silly old flying saucer. We can do our own flying right here."

All of the others had gotten up, however and were staring up at the sky. One of the women was very tall, but otherwise no fault could have been found with her from a man's point of view. She was wearing only a halter and a transparent, black gauze brassiere, which was having no success at all in concealing her rose-tipped, sharply pointed breasts. Her legs were long and so beautifully shaped that they could very easily have persuaded a man at the wheel of a speedboat to ignore the safety of his companions in a dangerous gale. The whiteness of her body where it wasn't suntanned was a specialty of the house, and her face went with the menu like the rarest of Parisian wines.

The man who stood at her side had tossed the menu aside for a moment, apparently. He was almost as tall as she was, with curly blond hair and a rugged, outdoorsman aspect. He was wearing a gray tweed sports jacket and a stubby pipe was clamped between his teeth, the smoke drifting out over the water.

The woman sprawled on the foredeck, who still did not seem in the least interested in the saucer, was a redhead, and she also wore a halter. But her companion, who had a Latin profile and hair so black that it could have been mistaken for the wings of a crow, was doing his best to conceal most of her charms. The third woman was a short, almost dumpy brunette, but there was something attractive about her.

The man with the camera was heavy set and ruddy-faced and attired in a bathing suit. He seemed the most excited member of the party.

"And I thought people who took UFOs seriously were whacks!" he shouted. "Good Lord! Look at it. Just look at it. It's an Unidentified Flying Object, all right, but when I get it on film the lads in Washington will drop the 'Unidentified'. It's from, somewhere in space. Mars, Venus! Who knows? Big—oh, my God!"

"You've got a good camera there," the man in the tweed sports jacket said, removing the pipe from his mouth and speaking very calmly. "A Leica, isn't it?"

"Sure it's a good camera. The best. But why in hell does that interest you now? A kid's box camera would do the job just as well. You're a funny guy, Jim. Does nothing excite you?"

For reply the tweedy man glanced significantly at his tall companion, his eyes lingering for an instant on the black gauze brassiere, and then passing downward to her shapely legs.

"Blondes, brunettes and redheads," he said, rather tritely.

"Oh, come off it. No guy could see a flying saucer—actually see one at close range—and not bust his seams with awe. Yeah, that's what I said. *Awe.* A fancy word, but I'm not ashamed to use it. Boy! Brother! It's so big it fills half the sky."

"I see what you mean," the tweedy man said. "But I never allow myself to get too excited. It doesn't pay."

"Do you have to take photographs?" the tall girl said. "It makes me terribly nervous. Suppose they don't want to be photographed?"

"I thought of that. But it's the chance of a lifetime. I'm not passing it up."

"Oh, lover!" came from the foredeck. "Oh, darling, sweet, I never imagined—don't stop now."

"Oh, Gawd!" the tall girl said. "Do we have to put up with that?"

"It's a crazy world," the tweedy man said. "That's why I'm such a skeptic. A flying saucer? Maybe. But I'm not convinced by any means. It could be a Naval Observatory plane, some new fancy kind that's disk-shaped and very large. Or maybe the Russians have come up with a low flying satellite. Anything is possible. I'll admit that if I was convinced I would get excited."

"I'm frightened," the short brunette said. "I'm so scared I can't think straight."

"I guess we all are," the tweedy man admitted. "I take back what I said. I guess we all are. But if we just sit tight it will be gone in two or three minutes."

"I've got thirty-two exposures on this roll," the man with the camera said. "I'll get it from every angle. There won't be any argument about it this time. They'll be banner headlines and every paper in the country will give the pictures a front-page spread. I'll be in *Life*. Both the pictures and the guy who took them. The best kind of publicity for a writer. He made it on the flying-saucer circuit."

"I agree with Ellen," the tweedy man said. "I don't think you should be taking pictures. And it's not really a joking matter."

"I'm not joking. Believe me, I'm not. I'm just being a little light-headed. Can you blame me for that? You get keyed up and you think of the craziest things. Like in the poem. Two lines. His life was scarlet but his books were read. To a writer that's important. Just to be read. Starting tomorrow, I'll have fifty million readers."

"You're over stimulated," the tall girl said. "Calm down. The right place for over stimulation is where it can be appreciated. There's a time and place for everything, Freddy boy, as you should know. If that flying saucer was a woman, I bet you wouldn't be half as excited."

"That's where you're wrong. But if flying saucers really exist, do you realize what that means? The whole universe could cave in on us. Anything is possible, as Jim said. Only he was thinking of Russian satellites. I'm thinking visitors from space who may bear us no love, who may want to see the whole planet go *pouf.*"

On the gleaming waters of the lake four frightened people and two who were too preoccupied to be frightened, lived out the last five minutes of their lives with the unique individuality that sets every man born into the world apart from all other men, every woman apart from all other women.

They were no different from a million other people as people go: thoughtful, whimsical, lighthearted, unselfish and self-seeking, generous and tight-fisted, courageous and cowardly, aggressive and self-effacing as changing circumstances dictated. Each was a world in himself or herself—each a universe, a spiral nebula.

And in a blazing split second of time six universes were blotted out.

It happened so quickly there was no pain, no shock even. From the hull of the Martian mother ship a shaft of blinding incandescence lanced down, white, flaring, terrible. A dull concussion shook the bed of the lake, ran in earthquake-like waves to both shorelines, toppled a few trees, and traveled on with an electrically generated surcharge to the brushwood-covered summits of adjacent hills and set the brush aflame.

Where the shaft struck the water geysered. Elsewhere it was churned into whitecaps and miniature whirlpools. A dozen gigantic catfish were killed instantly and rose slowly to the surface to float, white-bellied, near the shore.

When the incandescence vanished, both the boat and its occupants were gone.

"Let us hope we encounter no more men with cameras before we have made certain that the Plan will succeed." Tragor said.

He had returned to the telecommunication screen and was standing at Sull's side, watching the image of the man who, more than any other member of his race, had become the trigger mechanism that would make or break the Plan...

David Loring had not turned, but now the door was slowly opening behind him and someone was coming into the room. On the bright and flickering screen Loring's image seemed a little larger than life size, the planes of his face a little sharper than when he had first stepped into the room. Even his shadow on the floor seemed to lengthen as Tragor stared, and Tragor found himself wondering—the thought, of course, was absurd—if that shadow might not continue to lengthen, slowly and relentlessly, until it filled the world and brought the Martian Plan crashing down in ruin.

Had they taken too great a risk? Was it not highly dangerous to use a man as a guinea pig? No, no—not a guinea pig. Only Earthmen used guinea pigs in laboratory experiments. Had he lived too long on Earth, two years that seemed like a lifetime? It was outrageous the way Earth terms sprang naturally to his lips, both outrageous and disturbing. He must try not to think in such terms. Loring was a guinea pig only in the sense that he could be destroyed if he failed. But Martians did not really use men as guinea pigs. They used them as pawns.

CHAPTER FIVE

The woman who had come into the room stood silently staring at him for a moment, her lips slightly parted, her young breasts taut and pressing tightly against the silken constriction of a dress that did full justice to their voluptuous roundness. The dress was pale blue, with a plunging neckline, and its semi-transparency seemed to accentuate her beauty beyond the scope of Nature's design. Absolute nudity could hardly have enhanced her loveliness at that moment, for she seemed more than unclothed to the inner eye, wrapped in a splendor so revealing that for an instant Loring could scarcely breathe.

Her femininity was so extreme as to seem unbelievable. She was all woman, her very stillness a male-stirring miracle. It excited him instantly and overwhelmingly, so that all of his thoughts became centered on her, and he forgot that he was in love with another woman. He forgot even that there were strict physical limits to any one man's capacity to experience desire.

He felt himself to be not one man but ten thousand, each from a different age, each bursting with an uncontrollable urge to clasp and hold, and satisfy to satiety the most primal and compulsive of human needs.

The wonder of her, and the strangeness, the voluptuous softness and sweetness enticed him away from reality and then drew him back to the throbbing, pulsating core of Nature's supreme reality, and held him captive there, caught up in a web of time-obliterating instinct, which reason and all of Man's higher faculties had made the opposite of blind.

She seemed both a wanton and a wanton's opposite—a virginal and tender creature, shy and withdrawn. Her very breathing seemed to whisper: "I could be to you mistress and wife, dear companion and seductive enchantress, mature woman and girl-child, first love of the boy you once were and still are in dreams of youth, which will never fade. I could be your lady in ermine, a goddess of fertility rites, a Paleolithic woman with great breasts swelling, and a Grecian Venus rising slender-limbed from the foam."

Even as he heard the whisper deep in his mind, the whisper of a voice that was hers, surely, though it seemed to float through his consciousness like a feather blown about at random by the slow rise and fall of her breathing—even as he heard the voice her physical attributes seemed to change.

She became a woman of woodland enchantment, a slender nymph darting in and out between the trees of an autumn-colored forest, her skin berry-stained. She became a woman pirouetting on a stage, clad like a Russian ballet dancer. She became a dancer in flowing robes, moving in slow, sensual rhythm under the spell of a weaving baton. The baton rose and fell, gleamed and swayed and the music became tumultuous, and then, abruptly, the baton ceased to move and there was only silence and darkness on the stage.

Then, all at once, he saw her again as she really was, standing with slightly parted lips within reach of his arms, so unbelievably near that he could have clasped her and drawn her to him by taking a single step forward. The fantasies conjured up by the voice—were they hallucinatory or merely mind beguiling?—became shadowy and unreal, and her actual physical presence was all that concerned him.

In daring dreams Loring had, like most men, imagined what it would be like to make instant and completely uninhibited love to a woman without preamble and with no need to rely on past acquaintanceship, however brief, or to summon to his aid any of the social devices by which ardor without limit can be excused or palliated in the eyes of the world.

It was primitive, perhaps, but he had often imagined himself walking between the huts of a South Sea Island village, seeing in a doorway a brown native girl who set his pulses to pounding and wasting not a second's time in gathering her into his arms and carrying her inside the hut. The girl would have to be willing, of course, even eager. Even in his most audacious dreams Loring was not a brute.

Making love that impetuously was certainly frowned upon by society, even if a man wasn't a brute, and very difficult to achieve in reality, because almost all women preferred the slower, more graceful and romantic approach. The whispering of at least a few sweet nothings into a woman's ear could work wonders and it helped to have known her for at least ten or fifteen minutes.

In sober fact, Loring had never quite been able to reconcile himself to an amatory pattern that was taken for granted in the Village. You went to a party and met a girl you liked and slept with her the same night. He liked to tell himself he couldn't be shocked and yet, almost invariably, he was shocked. Some vestigial Puritan remnant deep in his nature, perhaps. He was glad that it hadn't happened that way between Janice and himself.

And yet, strangely enough, he experienced no such inhibiting emotional reaction when he looked deep into the eyes of the woman standing before him. He felt completely freed from all conventional restraints, untouched by scruples of any kind. Her eyes both mocked and challenged him, with an almost animal sensuality, as if even his few seconds of hesitation were wholly inexcusable and were becoming intolerable in her sight.

She was unsurpassably young and vibrant, a temptress with sultry eyes and heaving bosom. Her lips were full, red and curving, her hair silvery blonde, her skin fair and smooth, unmarred by the tiniest blemish.

She gave a little cry when he seized her. At the touch of his hands on her back and thighs a spasmed aliveness took possession of her and she writhed in his clasp with an ardor that drove the blood in torrents from his heart. Her lips were fire, her kisses a burning that dissolved the barrier of flesh where their tongues met in molten sweetness.

Her body molded itself to his, pressing against the hard muscles of his chest and thighs. His own passion equaled hers for an instant and then surpassed it, and in the fierce, unrelenting masculinity of his embrace she became suddenly passive, content to surrender completely to his guidance. But in that very surrender there was a continuing wild responsiveness, a fervor that matched his own, as if she had been caught up in a wilderness of desire where bright bursts of lightning forked down and the trees were sheathed in flame.

He had lifted her up and was carrying her toward the bed, the passion seething within him making him oblivious of his surrounding and blotting from his mind all thought of Janice, when his hand on the throbbing warm flesh of her thigh, just above the knee, encountered a startling coldness. An obstruction and a coldness—something solid and very hard, which sent a shock through his arm when he touched it.

For an instant his fingers tingled and he felt a sudden, very acute stab of pain, as if he had touched an open electric circuit. It was followed by a burning sensation, and a distinct mental shock, a feeling of blank bewilderment verging on horror. Suddenly the room became very real again, and he remembered that it was Janice's room, Janice's bed. A sickening sense of guilt and self-reproach swept over him. But only for the space of a dropped heartbeat. The obstruction beneath his hand was too mysteriously strange for even guilt to obliterate as an immediate, impossible-to-ignore threat to his sanity.

The object was metallic and unmistakably disk-like. Beneath his exploring fingers its configuration dispelled all uncertainty as to its shape and it had the smoothness, the coldness, and the general feel of a metal object. It was about three inches in diameter and seemed to be embedded in the flesh of her thigh. There were no wires or prongs projecting from it. The shock had come from the disk itself, but there was no further shock as his fingers rested upon it.

He found himself tugging at it, without quite knowing why he felt such a compulsive need to find out all that he could about it except that it filled him with alarm and foreboding.

The woman in his arms was still clinging to him, her arms tight about his shoulders, her body, moving with the slow, voluptuous amorousness that kisses could distract but for an instant. She seemed unaware that he had found the metal disk, so entranced was she by the soaring breathlessness of a moment from which the mechanical was by necessity barred and kept at bay by love's physical rapture in a temple of love's own choosing. She was breathing heavily now, her eyes glazed, a deep flush suffusing her face and throat.

But Loring's pulses were no longer pounding. Her kisses were feverish and had to be returned, but he returned them now without enthusiasm, a cold fear constricting the muscles of his heart. A dozen frightening question clamored in his mind for answers that did not satisfy him, and did nothing to lessen his dread.

Was the disk a surgical device of some sort? If it was, what was its purpose and function? A metal plate inserted in a man's skull could protect his brain from damage, if natural suturing failed. But why should a metal device be embedded in the flesh of a woman's thigh, just above her right knee? What possible purpose could it serve?

Had some unusual and tragic accident left her partially paralyzed? Was the metal disk a surgical device designed to restore the circulation or correct the impaired muscular flexibility of an injured limb? An electrical device? It seemed probable, since touching it had given him a shock. But the rest of it was hard to accept. The shock had been more than physical. Momentarily it had done something to his mind, chilling him to the core, and making him remember something that he had once read—that a man in the grip of stark fear can lose all sexual drive.

But why had his discovery of the disk so profoundly alarmed him? Why had he experienced such sharply mounting apprehension? It was merely an electrically charged metal appliance, small, flat and circular and—yes, not unlike a hearing aid. Could it be a hearing aid? He would have liked to believe so, but it seemed unlikely. No woman, however vain, would wear a hearing aid on her right thigh.

Her hands were moving back and forth across his back, and she was moaning a little and pressing her lips against his throat. He knew that he could not maintain the pretense of desire much longer, that she would begin to suspect he was responding like an automaton, with the desperate clumsiness of a man whom heated kisses and the most fervent of body movements could no longer arouse.

He felt detached, remote in some vital part of himself, with a cold objectivity growing in his mind that he could neither explain nor understand. There was a pain in his heart also, an agony of indecision. He was backed up against the bed now, his arms still tight about her, but love's culmination would now be a mockery and something deep in his nature rebelled at carrying pretense that far.

It was incredible; it stunned him, because he was susceptible beyond the average—so overwhelmingly so that there were times when the mere touch of a beautiful woman's hand on his arm could set him to trembling.

And now he was clasping a woman who was almost savage in her direct approach to passion, a woman utterly without inhibitions, primitive as few women would have dared to be. But a woman of flesh and blood notwithstanding, with an eagerness to love and be loved that was as human as his own demanding need of her had been.

That was as human... The thought was insidious at first, a small, gnawing doubt in an obscure recess of his mind, emerging fearfully crawling out into the light like some tiny rodent with razor-sharp teeth.

Hadn't her great beauty seemed from the first almost unendurably tormenting, as if no woman had a right to be quite so beautiful and to drive a man to such a wild, uncontrollable frenzy of desire? Hadn't he felt for an instant that she could have very easily destroyed him, simply by withholding her favors and refusing to let him touch her? And the fierceness of his desire, his feeling that all of his ancestors lived in him and desired her with a deep, racial urgency, a Dawn Man's primitiveness—hadn't that been a little different from the strong virile desire which a perfectly normal, civilized man of ardent temperament would feel even in the presence of an extraordinarily beautiful woman?

He was completely human, all too human, and it was useless to pretend that he hadn't found the going a little rugged at times since he'd set himself the difficult task of staying loyal to just one woman. It had been tough, but he had proved to himself that he could do it. Not once, but a dozen times. And yet, when he had taken this strange woman into his arms something dark and terrible had stirred in his blood, and blotted out every loyalty.

Why? What did it mean? The metal disk on her thigh, her great beauty, the strangeness of her. The strangeness... There was something in the Song of Songs about that. "The magic and wonder of a strange Woman."

According to Biblical legend there were two women in Eden. There was Eve, who was Adam's lawful wife. And there was Lilith, the enchantress, the dark sorceress, a creature of fire and dust who was not human and who gave birth to demons. But Lilith was beautiful beyond imagination—more maddeningly desirable than a human woman could ever be.

She was clothed in garments of flesh, but she was not flesh. She was the eternally seductive male that Man cannot do without, lest his manhood wither on the vine. He must pursue and clasp her, in wild dreams of madness and desire, or his Earthbound lovemaking will be futile and absurd and living women will turn from him to seek a more accomplished lover elsewhere.

The sorceress came bearing gifts—the greatest of all gifts, a wealthy fruitage that was hers alone to share. "Love me at your peril," she whispered, "but love me well, or you will be less than a man and you will live to regret it. Why should you fear the kind of love I bring you? All life is uncertain; all men dwell in the shadow of the grave. But there is one supreme fulfillment, one joy that, once experienced, can never be taken from you. I am Lilith, all woman, all soft yielding flesh, and I have come to you alone, in a secret place, and in the joining of our bodies there is rapture unspeakable."

They were not the words of the woman in his arms. That Loring knew. But still they found an echo in his thoughts, as though the woman he was clasping could see deep into his mind and knew that from myths and dreams and legends Man had built an imperishable inner world that no reality, however harsh, could wholly shatter and destroy.

And what if modern science could illuminate and transform that world without altering its strangeness and its dangerous beauty, making it in every respect real? What if modern science, with the technical knowledge of intellectual giants and the lightning at its fingertips could create a Lilith? A woman of more than human beauty but still in every way a woman. A woman not fashioned of fire and dust but of living, breathing flesh, laboratory-created, perfect, flawless, in every aspect of her being.

Only a fool would think it impossible. Had not modern science achieved as great a miracle when it had released the wild stallions at the Atom's core? Why not...why not? Modern science or—a technology alien to Earth?

Both were possible. There could be intelligent life on Mars, on Venus. What was it H. G. Wells had said? Great cool minds watching us, plotting our destruction...

The woman in Loring's arms spoke then, for the first time. She was no longer clinging to him, no longer moving her limbs in amorous abandonment and tugging at his hands in an effort to draw them to the warm cavern between her taut young breasts.

"Yes," she said.

Loring's temples began to pound. He stared at her wordlessly, looking deep into her eyes, unable to believe what he saw there. A calmness, a quiet depth of understanding—even a measure of pity.

"Those were not all your thoughts," she said. "Some of them were mine."

"Who are you?" Loring breathed.

"Lilith," she said. "As you have thought of what such a woman could be to you if you believed in her as a scientific reality. Lilith, in that sense. Your dark enchantress—if my hair were not silvery blonde and my eyes were not blue. Laboratory created. Yes, that's true. And the disk gives me life and warmth and fire. I am a telepath. I can read your thoughts. But you were not supposed to know that. And you were not supposed to discover the disk. You stirred me beyond reason and I became careless. Your too eager hands."

She sighed and the pity in her eyes seemed to deepen, widening her pupils in an unfathomable way.

"The harm is done now. There is nothing I can do. If I hadn't told you, you would have tugged at the disk and I would have gone limp in your arms. Then your curiosity would have become insatiable. Fear alone would have made it insatiable. I know exactly what you would have done."

"What—would I have done?"

"You would have ceased to be a lover. You would have become ruthlessly scientific and clinical. You would have stretched me out on the bed and removed all of my clothes. You would have examined me from head to foot, not sparing even the pores of my skin. Without a magnifying glass you would be handicapped, not quite as well equipped as one of those thorough little men whose task it is to peer at beetles under glass or butterflies pinned to a board, or a human body stretched out naked and helpless on a mortuary slab. But you would have seen enough to disillusion you. No woman can be peered at quite that relentlessly. Even a body like mine is not perfect. There are a few flaws."

Loring drew in his breath sharply. She had drawn away from him and was sitting on the edge of the bed, a faint, enigmatic smile on her lips. Then the smile vanished and her eyes clouded over.

"I am sorry. It is all very serious—and I am deeply troubled. I did not intend to speak with bitterness or levity. But sometimes levity helps when you are inwardly greatly disturbed.

"Good heavens, if I really believed—" Loring's mouth had gone dry and he had difficulty in getting the words out. "You don't actually expect me to believe—"

"How much proof do you need? If I hadn't the ability to anticipate some of your thoughts would you know as much as you do about me? Telepathy at that level of complexity would only be possible between a human and a not entirely human mind. Surely you must realize that. The faculty is more highly developed in me than it is in you, but it is strong enough in you to be stimulated artificially when our minds are in contact."

"Then you must have wanted me to know."

"Up to a point. Your erotic ardor might have been less intense if you had thought me completely human. There would have been less mystery to stir you and make you my slave."

"Your *slave!* You must be quite mad."

"Oh, no, I'm not. You may think the shoe was on the other foot, but it wasn't, not for a moment. You have a term for it. Love slave. Don't misunderstand me. That is not a reflection on your masculinity, on the relationship that exists between a man and a woman in biological sense. No truly feminine woman wants to dominate a man in a love relationship, and no really masculine man would stand for it. But I am not talking about the purely physical relationship. In an ultimate sense it is the woman who enslaves the man, by her beauty. If that beauty is great enough he becomes her slave night and day. He thinks of nothing else, desires nothing else."

It was a subject that Loring had always felt so strongly about that for an instant he forgot his fear, his growing bewilderment and even the threat implicit in her reference to him as a slave.

"Slave is too harsh a term for that kind of entanglement," he said. "The world calls such a man a romantic fool or a fool for love. But I've never had any objection to being that kind of a fool. What else in life is one-tenth as important? There's nothing else that you can be completely sure of; that no one can take away from you once you've experienced it. Even the memory is better than a Long Island estate or seven Cadillacs and almost anything else I can think of that I wouldn't pass up if it were offered me. A poet once put it better than I could: 'Who gets more than the lovers, in the dust, in the cool tombs?'"

"I wasn't thinking about tombs," she said. "But it could be very serious for you."

"Why? Because I wouldn't object too strenuously to being what you foolishly call a love slave?"

"Yes. Because, you see, that's why you were chosen. Because you feel that way. And that's why Janice Reece was chosen."

Loring started, his lips tightening, his face becoming pale beneath his summer tan. "Chosen? What do you mean? Are you talking about what happened here this morning, when Janice woke up? The man in her room?"

"You shouldn't have to ask that. Why do you suppose you found me here? I'm surprised you didn't have more curiosity right at the start. You couldn't think of anything, see anything, but the cut of my dress and the way it clung to me, and I'll be very blunt—the bed on the other side of the room."

She looked at him steadily, almost angrily, but he had the feeling she wasn't angry because of what he had done. She was angry in a more impersonal way, as if she was cursing fate for bringing about a tragedy that should never have taken place.

"They wanted you to make violent love to me and you did," she said. "At least, you started to. And your lovemaking was very wonderful. It would have stirred a woman of ice. If my response was all that they could have desired, it wasn't a pretense. I want you to know that. When you took me into your arms I could have—well, never mind. It's over now, and you're in very great danger. I wish there was something I could do."

"There is," Loring said, trying to keep his voice steady, but not quite succeeding. "You can stop talking in insane riddles. You say you're not entirely human. But I can't accept that. I've the kind of mind that just can't adjust to a thing like that. Speculating about it and telling yourself that it's not impossible, not beyond the scope of what modern science could accomplish, isn't quite the same thing as out-and-out acceptance. You look too human, act too human, you're warm and alive. You're right here with me, and I took you in my arms and kissed your eyes and lips and hair. I can't believe—"

"You must believe," she said, "because it is true. I am completely human in a physical way, with warm human blood in my veins, and a heart that beats steadily, and I can be stirred to passion like any young girl by the caresses of a lover. Even my mind is human, although there may be certain differences. If you could see my brain it would not startle you. No medical student would be puzzled or disturbed by it. It is no larger or in any way different from the brain of a quite ordinary woman."

She paused and moistened her lips, still looking at him steadily. "I have warm blood in my veins and I can be as yielding and generous as any man could desire. But I'm unlike any other woman. I was never born."

He started to speak, but she silenced him with a gesture. "Don't look so startled. Have I not prepared your mind for such a revelation? Does it not follow the pattern of your thoughts a moment ago, when our thoughts merged? I was never born. I was laboratory-created. But I was not created by *human* science. Human science has soared miraculously and a tiny, furry creature with bulging eyes has descended from the trees and become a big-brained biped who has exploded the energies at the core of matter, explored the universe through a great, stationary eye for millions of light years and may yet succeed in disrupting a sun, and hurling a blinding incandescence through space as a symbol of what Man alone can accomplish."

She nodded, her eyes beginning to shine. "Yes, human science can accomplish miracles, but it has not yet succeeded in reproducing the human form in all of its complexity—brain, heart, arteries, bone structure, the pulse of life itself—within a transparent incubator bright with nutrient fluids, weaving filaments of flame, stabbing needles of nuclear energy…"

She stopped, her breath quickening, and lowered her eyes. "I have told you too much," she went on with a slight tremor in her voice, as if she were forcing herself to remain calm, but knew that she was treading on dangerous ground. "There are some things I can't tell you. They would destroy me instantly if I told you more than a small part of what I know. I am in danger because you discovered the disk that controls my breathing, my pulse rate, and my ability to move about at will. But you are in much greater danger. You are in danger because you were able to resist me. They may feel that their plans are in jeopardy."

"Their plans—"

"Let me talk. Let me say what has to be said now, before I think about it too much and fear make a coward of me. If you who are a fool for love—I am only repeating what you told me and what they believe about you—if *even you* could resist me, more hard-headed, practical men who think of love only as a diversion, and often hate themselves when they succumb to it, men who sit in high places and rule the Earth with a humorless kind of harshness, may not succumb at all."

She had raised her eyes and was looking at him steadily again, with an unexpected warmth and sympathy in her gaze. "It is not a mistake to think of love as the most important thing in life. I agree with you. It is. There is a greatness in living that only love can make complete and glorious. Even though I am not completely human I know that without desire, without the need to give and receive love, my brain and heart would shrivel. But not all women feel that way. And not all men. There are some men who so despise love that they think of it as shameful, the physical act of love as a degradation."

"I know," Loring said. "And they are tragically crippled men."

"You are not crippled," she said. "That is why you were chosen. They had to make a test first, a carefully controlled exploratory—" She hesitated, an evanescent smile hovering for the barest instant on her lips and then vanishing, leaving her eyes even more deeply troubled. "The technical term for it, in human laboratory experiments is, I believe, 'test run.' They had to make a test run with just one man and one woman before my great beauty could be transformed into a weapon for the conquest of Earth."

Loring stared at her wordlessly, stunned, unbelieving. He would have liked to trust his reason completely, to dismiss what she had said as the meaningless ranting of a madwoman. But somehow he couldn't quite ignore the look of desperate appeal in her eyes, her aspect of absolute sanity. He had turned deathly pale.

"You must believe me," she went on quickly. "I am risking destruction by telling you this. They have a plan for world conquest that is audacious beyond anything the human mind could have conceived, audacious and terrible, with every detail coldly thought out, weighed, decided upon. I will become not one woman, but many. I am the first, but there will be others. A thousand women with my lips and hair and eyes, and my white and beautiful limbs that almost brought you to your knees in adoration. A thousand women like me will be laboratory-created.

"A thousand women and a thousand men. Your Janice saw the man when she awoke this morning. There are men who only have to look once at a woman and she begins to tremble. Her breathing quickens and she knows only the insensate joy of immediate and complete surrender."

Her lips were trembling slightly and she cast an apprehensive glance toward the door, then went on quickly. "Your Janice is a very strong willed young woman. When she saw the stranger in her room she was startled and frightened at first. That was only to be expected. She had just awakened and it was only natural for her to experience nothing but fear for a moment. Then she lost her fear but she not instantly and overwhelmingly drawn to him. She should have been, but she wasn't. She was very strongly attracted to him, but she did not lose control."

Loring moistened his lips. "She told me," he said. "She told me exactly how she felt. But what happened when he left the apartment made me jealous beyond reason."

"That was a hypnotic illusion, deliberately introduced into her mind. I will tell you a strange thing. When her breath did not quicken with passion, anger overcame him. He did not step forward and embrace her simply because he could not. *We must not make the first advance.* Deep in our minds they have implanted a command: If you do not succeed instantly, do nothing. Your presence alone must stir the chosen ones to an ardor they are powerless to resist. We cannot judge the strength of that ardor otherwise.

"Do you understand? She did not respond with instant, overwhelming ardor and he could do nothing. He stood there as if paralyzed, staring at her. He is as human as I am in that respect. In that moment of repudiation—and it was a repudiation even though his physical nearness stirred her—he experienced great bitterness and anger. But he had to pretend that he was not angered. So he advanced to the bed, kissed her lightly on the forehead and left the apartment.

"Then I think *they* lost their heads for a moment. It is what I have been told. They introduced into her mind an erotic fantasy, so powerful, so compelling, that she was powerless to resist. They know that to the human mind an erotic trance, dreamlike and unreal, can be more compulsively irresistible than any waking moment of rapture and abandonment, enforced by fervent kisses and caressing hands. In dreams of desire, the human mind is completely set free. All inhibitions are dissolved. But such dreams cannot last. They do not permanently enslave, because the dreamer is bound by no physical chains."

"But—"

"Listen carefully. You must listen. That erotic fantasy accomplished nothing, proved nothing. They realized that almost at once. They were defeated and discouraged. Your Janice had disappointed them and she had been one of the chosen two—a fool for love. Now you have disappointed them. Your ardor cooled too quickly. You remembered how completely, how desperately you loved her and you ceased to desire me. Do not tell me otherwise. I know better. Your discovery of the disk may have helped to cool your ardor, but she was the real reason. She is all beauty and all grace in your sight. She is the mistress of your heart and will always remain so."

A sardonic smile appeared for an instant on her lips. "I should be angry, as he was angry. But I am not. I do not know why, but there is something about you."

She sighed and looked away quickly. "Perhaps some impulse, some pattern of behavior they implanted in me went wrong. Perhaps I myself distorted it. I feel for you a strange liking—"

Suddenly she laughed, a little wildly and was instantly sober again. "We must not talk about such things. The danger is too great. Even now they may be—"

"Tell me," Loring said, and his voice sounded strange to his own ears. "Who are *they*? I must know."

She started to speak and then, all at once, her body stiffened and a look of horror came into her eyes. She clutched at her right thigh and half rose from the bed, her lips livid, and her mouth twisting strangely, as if she had been gripped by a spasm of sudden, almost unendurable pain.

She staggered and almost fell and then in that instant she seemed to age. Her face took on a waxy pallor and hollows appeared in her cheeks, so that the bones of her face became faintly visible. Her skin sagged a little, losing much of its firmness and even the fresh look of youth. Her great beauty remained. Nothing could efface it, for the very structure of her face was beautiful, its every lineament a miracle of loveliness. That beauty was marred now, but only by stark fear and the deceptive aging that great shock imparts, at times to even the very young.

That she had had a very great shock, Loring knew the moment she began to scream.

She staggered and almost fell and then she was swaying back against the wooden bedstead, clutching it with both hands in an effort to steady and support herself. The next instant she was on the bed, doubled over, her body straining forward, her breath coming in choking gasps.

One leg was crumpled under her, the other thrust out straight, and on the smooth, unblemished flesh of her thigh Loring saw a circle of flame take shape and grow to the size of a half-dollar. As the circle grew its brightness increased, until it blazed with light and fire, enveloping both limbs in a blinding radiance.

Loring had to look away quickly, and when he looked back the woman was no longer moving. She was sprawled out on the black satin bedspread, her head thrown back, her hair a tumbled mass that lay in shining strands across her white breasts and unmoving shoulders.

She had torn open the front of her dress and there was a bleeding gash on the smooth flesh of her throat in an effort to relieve her torment.

Loring went to the bed and stood over her, feeling a tightness in his chest. His breathing was ragged, and his heart had begun a furious pounding.

He thought for an instant that she was dead. The he saw that a faint flush suffused her cheeks and that her eyes were not expressionless. Her eyes were wide open and she was staring up at him. There was awareness in them, but it was not the awareness of recognition. It was as if she knew that a man was standing by the bed looking down at her, but did not know who that man was or why he had drawn near to her.

He reached out and put his hand on her bare shoulder. Her skin was warm, almost hot to his touch. She stirred slightly and a questioning look came into her eyes. Shaken as he was, that almost imperceptible moving of her body in response to his touch made him feel almost as he would have felt if he had deliberately caressed her and she had shivered with pleasure and shown him unmistakably that she was not displeased.

Nothing had been further from his mind, but now he found himself wondering what would happen if he touched her again, and this time more boldly.

He reached down and gently cupped one of her breasts, taking care to let his fingers encircle its smooth roundness without suggesting that he was engaged in anything more than a medical examination. He told himself that he felt that way about it—a purely clinical test.

Something terrible had happened to her. He had to find out just how terrible as quickly as possible. Any kind of response would tell him whether her reason had been shattered completely and could not be restored, or whether she was merely in a state of shock and could be aroused by guiding her firmly along pathways of passion, taking care to think of himself only as a concerned and solicitous physician.

That and nothing more. But he was not prepared for the violence of her response and the sudden, almost convulsive tightening of her arms about him. He had not expected her to come so instantly alive again, with lips so demanding that he found himself struggling to breathe, smothered by the insatiable frenzy of her kisses. Her mouth melted into his, her tongue became a darting shape of fire, fluttering, pulsating within the cavern of his mouth. She was a moth with fiery wings fluttering, a wild temptress.

Her hands moved up and down and across his back, and her mouth unlocked itself and fastened on his ear, nibbling first at the lobe and then whispering softly into the chambered recess words of love sweet beyond endurance, dripping with the honey of forbidden ecstasies, unimagined delights.

"No," he whispered, but found himself surrendering to her guidance and then, suddenly, he was guiding her, anticipating her every desire, responding to every writhing of her body, every straining of her lips with a passion now as great as her own and now surpassing it, for he was not a man who needed to be instructed in the refinements and subtleties of love.

What sobered him he never knew. But something did. One moment he was in a golden paradise with no memory of how he had come to be there and no desire to depart and the next he saw a woman with glazed eyes arising from his side, and movements so blind and purposeless that they chilled him and made his blood run cold. He saw her arise from the bed and step swayingly to the floor and move away from him across the room, her shoulders held rigid, her arms pressed stiffly to her side.

He called out to her and she turned and stared at him for a moment, the veins in her white throat pulsing, her moist red lips slightly parted. Her cheeks were still flushed and her bosom rose and fell with her breathing, rose and fell with a slow trembling and she seemed aroused still and if he had pleaded with her he was sure she would have come running back to him. But he did not plead, because there was no recognition in her eyes.

Her eyes were cold, empty, drained now of all expression. But it was not only her eyes that chilled him. It was the jerkiness of her movements, the stiffness, the rigidity. He had never seen a woman move in that way before.

The woman who stood facing him was not dead and yet she was moving, not as a living man or woman would move, but as an automaton would move if it were clothed in garments of flesh, and knew more about life than an automaton should know and had perhaps even held converse with the dead.

She did not wait for him to call out to her again, but turned and continued on until she stood before the door. She remained for an instant motionless, staring at the white panels on both sides of the door and then raised her head and stared up at the ceiling, as if the room was totally unfamiliar to her and she was puzzled and disturbed to find herself imprisoned within it.

Then slowly, jerkily, her hand went out and fastened on the knob of the door and it turned in her clasp. She opened the door and went out into the hall and closed it very firmly behind her.

The instant the door closed Loring started to get up from the bed. He quickly discovered that he could scarcely move at all. His limbs seemed weighted and when he tried to raise his arms agonizing stabs of pain darted through them.

He sank back against the pillows, feeling alarmingly lightheaded, his vision beginning to swim. The room seemed to waver and recede, the floor to tilt, the furniture take on grotesque and unfamiliar contours. The chairs elongated, the mirror above the mantel misted and seemed to melt, the pictures on the wall changed color. Blues became yellows, yellows blues, the purples deepened, the reds and greens faded out. Landscapes changed their pattern, hills dissolved, rivers widened or broke up into dozens of small streams that snaked in all directions over a gray and desolate plain.

The walls seemed to converge and increase in height and then to sweep away from him like the sides of a towering wave receding from a crippled ship, caught in a storm-wind and whirled helplessly about.

He saw the door opening as in a glass darkly, the knob a glowing ember amidst a weaving wilderness where nothing else glowed except the faint outlines of dissolving shadow shapes.

There was someone in the room with him now, but he could not see the intruder clearly, only the looming massiveness of his shoulders and his flickering shadow on the walls.

He could hear the slow, heavy shuffling of the shadow-caster's feet, however, and his labored breathing, and a more distant sound as of glass shattering as the intruder drew near to him.

He struggled to rise but could not and fell back with a groan, his shoulders jerking as he tried desperately to move his arms and propel himself backwards against the wall at the head of the bed.

The intruder's bulk seemed to grow larger, to hover so ominously above him that if he had been some monster of hideous legend with drooling fangs and fire-ensheathed limbs he could hardly have inspired more terror or seemed more on the verge of leaping toward him, sinking cruel talons in his flesh and tearing him limb from limb.

Then, quite suddenly, his vision cleared and he saw that the intruder was just such a monster!

With a convulsive contraction of his entire body Loring managed somehow to retreat further, to hurl himself backwards against the wall. But he might as well have remained where he was. The intruder's arm went out and up, and something white and glowing flowed from the shadowy end of his arm and hovered above Loring like an air-suspended shroud.

He had no way of knowing that it was not a shroud but a net, quivering as it unfolded—a floating web that remained hovering above him for an instant and then slowly descended, enmeshing and imprisoning his limbs.

"You must come with us," a cold voice said. "We must study you further. We are not content with what has happened here."

CHAPTER SIX

"Tragor, Coordinator Kraii wishes to see you at once."

Tragor awoke with a start from a dream transcending in splendor anything his waking mind could have imagined. In his dream Tragor had been surrounded by the wisest and boldest of his people. He was standing on the heights looking down on a planet ripe for plunder.

The green hills and valleys of the planet Earth stretched out beneath him, with its golden harvests, winding waterways and populous cities stretching away for miles.

"It must be a bitter blow to you, Tragor," the voice that had awakened him went on relentlessly. "Frankly, I couldn't live with myself if I had to tear up a Plan I had worked on for a third of a lifetime. But no matter. Coordinator Kraii insists on seeing you immediately. It's a command."

Even before he opened his eyes Tragor knew it was Sull's voice he heard. Sull was standing there quietly looking at him. Sull the fox, bland of voice and gesture, but with cruel, shrewd eyes that saw too much.

Sull was looking at him derisively, his lidded eyes gleaming with triumph. Yes, the crafty wretch did look remarkably like a fox—that cunning little animal of Earth that scurried in and out of burrows on the new planet, waiting for just the right moment to bite and draw blood.

But with an effort Tragor controlled himself. "Thank you, Sull," he said. His voice was satirically polite, edged with contempt. But Sull managed to look guileless, as if anger verging on violence between two similarly dedicated Martians would have been unthinkable.

Tragor knew that the interview with the Chief Coordinator was going to be unpleasant. Mortally dangerous and unpleasant. He was sure of that. He might not even return from it alive.

He went to his dressing compartment first, and put on his most resplendent uniform, carefully assembling on his chest the many decorations he had earned by risking his life in a hundred Martian conflicts. He arranged the medals painstakingly, with just the right indifference to precise spacing, so that the most important ones were half obscured by the overall glitter of the rest. It was just the kind of negligence which a truly modest Martian might be expected to display. Then he inspected himself in a mirror and was satisfied with what he saw.

Kraii was waiting for him in the central coordinating compartment, his huge taloned hands, blue-veined, in ominous repose on his knees. Kraii was at his dangerous worst when he appeared to be completely relaxed. He sat before a black metal document stand that shone with an ebon luster in the cold light, which streamed down from above.

"Sit down, Tragor," he said.

Tragor sat down and waited for the Coordinator to question him. The chair he was sitting in was narrow and straight. His own face was in light, but the Coordinator's face was partially shadowed. He could see enough to know that the Coordinator's jaw was very firmly set. Coordinator Kraii had the rose-tinted complexion of a quite young Martian, but his eyes were bleak with half a century of hard living. An irreverent, almost outrageous thought flashed across Tragor's mind as he returned Kraii's noncommittal stare. How many Martian women had Kraii known, and what had they done to the iron assurance he was supposed to possess?

If he had been very successful with women a little of the edge might have been taken off his rumored ruthlessness. But if he had not fared too well in his amorous conquests frustration might have made him potentially malignant. It was not a possibility that could be lightly dismissed.

Kraii was speaking now and his voice had a harsh edge to it.

"As you know, Tragor, a leader in an undertaking as momentous as this must do his duty as he sees it. He must not spare the guilty if he is to be faithful to his trust. I like you, Tragor. I have always liked you. But that is not the point at issue. You were the chief architect of our Great Plan for the conquest of Earth and you have failed."

"But surely—"

"No, wait. Do not interrupt me, Tragor. You have failed tragically. Now I am going to ask you to be very frank. I want you to tell me in your own words just why you were so sure the Plan would succeed, and why I had to discover for myself, indirectly, that you had made a serious, perhaps fatal, blunder."

Tragor's mouth had gone very dry. He tried to swallow, but there was a tight constriction in his throat.

"I may have made a few mistakes," he heard himself saying. "But everyone makes mistakes. There is still hope…"

"I could enter into a long discussion with you, Tragor," Kraii said. "I could take the tragedy of your failure from the beginning and carry it forward step by step. But nothing would be gained by that. I want you to summarize, very briefly, the whole intent and purpose of the plan. I want to hear you explain it. I am familiar with it, of course, or I would not be where I am. But I want to hear about it again from its chief architect."

The full, ghastly truth dawned on Tragor then the awful certainty that he was on trial for his life. He might never leave the compartment with the blood warm in his veins. He might never see another sunrise, on Mars or on Earth, never experience again all the joys of the flesh; never feast and dine and dance and hold a beautiful woman in a fierce and ardent embrace. He saw himself crying out in agony, his flesh blackened by the fiery blast of a handgun, blood streaming from a horrible, gaping wound in his chest. He knew that he must talk fast and talk convincingly, if he hoped to go on living. And he knew that he had to keep it brief.

"The success of the Plan—" he began, and stopped, frightened by the look on the Chief Coordinator's face.

"Yes, Tragor. Go on."

"It was not a complicated plan. But it was a brilliant one, carefully thought out, and I was sure it would succeed. We would take captive five hundred men and five hundred women and study them with every laboratory technique available to us. We would use them as models— to discover as much as we could about the human race. Then we would free them, with all knowledge of what had happened to them blotted from their minds."

"Yes, I know. Go on, Tragor."

"We would use our new knowledge to fashion men and women miraculously perfect in body. Mind-living, breathing androids who could be controlled by us with a disk-like mechanism embedded in their flesh. They could be controlled by us at will, robbed of all volition and made almost mindless if we decided to send a charge of energy pulsing through the disks. Their very thoughts and desires could be controlled, regulated."

"Perfect men and women, yes," Kraii said thoughtfully. "But more than that, of course."

"Far more than that. Android women so beautiful it would be impossible for Earthmen to resist them, so beautiful they would enslave all men instantly with their white and clinging arms, their rose-tinted breasts, the swelling voluptuousness of—"

"You forget yourself, Tragor. No description is necessary. There is no need for you to become erotically stirred by an android, an artificial robot-woman created in our own laboratories. You know what they are."

"Yes, of course. I do know. But Earthmen do not. Our plan was to make Earthmen slaves of love and obedient to our bidding, to forge about them chains of love they would be powerless to break. Only Earthmen in high places, naturally, for we were not concerned with the rest. Only the rulers, the powerful who are in a position to control the destinies of nations and surrender Earth without a struggle. Our androids would command them to obey us, and they would have no choice. Men so enslaved would be completely at our mercy.

"And women too."

"And women too. The male androids have everything an Earthwoman could desire in a man. They are physically handsome beyond belief, irresistible in their wooing."

"But the Great Plan went wrong. Why, Tragor?"

"We—we selected as experimental test subjects one man and one woman. The man is an artist, a painter. Sensitive and imaginative; so much so that if a beautiful woman so much as lays her hand on his arm he begins to tremble. He has to struggle with himself to exercise control. If ever a subject seemed ideal for our purpose—"

"But you did not succeed with him. Why, Tragor?"

"I do not know. I really do not know. He resisted twice. The first time he was almost at the point of capitulation but he resisted in time. The second time we controlled the android woman by means of the disk embedded in her thigh. We made her almost mindless, a creature given over entirely to sensual delights. We made her a body solely—a body that could twist and writhe—and drive a man to madness."

"And still he resisted."

"Not—not exactly. But his ardor cooled instantly when deep in his unconscious mind something warned him that he was holding an android in his arms. We could not hope to succeed with the Plan if such a warning signal were to be flashed to the men and women in high places we intend to enslave."

"And the woman? I have been told she also resisted when she saw the android man in her bedroom."

"That is true. They both resisted. So far we are at a dead end. So far we have created more than a hundred android women and half that number of android men. But we cannot release them on Earth until we are sure that the Plan will succeed. It would expose us to the deadliest kind of danger. It is bad enough that Earth has the hydrogen bomb and could destroy our ships if we resorted to open warfare. Even the Great Plan itself could fail."

Tragor could have bitten his tongue out when the words had left his lips, for it brought a sudden dangerous tightening to the Coordinator's face.

"And so you think the Plan will fail."

"No, no, I did not say that. I would like—"

"What would you like, Tragor?"

"One more chance. One more chance with both the man and the woman. I want to take them to Mars."

Kraii stared at Tragor for an instant as if unable to believe what he had heard. But he controlled himself with an effort and spoke in a calm tone.

"Why?" he asked.

"We have taken both the man and the woman captive. The woman remained in his room when he went to her apartment, expecting him to return. We captured him first and then we captured her. She is very beautiful, almost as beautiful as the android woman. Perhaps that is why he was able to resist the android woman the first time."

A totally irrelevant thought crept into Tragor's mind. *She is very beautiful, with red-gold hair. The woman I took captive this morning has hair of almost the same color. But she loves the man and I am not loved. Would it matter so much if Kraii killed me? Why should I be afraid to die? Why should I care?*

"Well, Tragor," the Coordinator said, impatiently. "I am waiting to hear why you want to take them to Mars."

"I have a plan."

"Another plan? It would seem that your brain is cobwebbery with plans, Tragor."

"It is all part of the same Great Plan. We must make the Earthman and the Earthwoman slaves of love, we must break down all of their resistance. I believe I can accomplish that on Mars."

"How, Tragor? This is most interesting."

"When men and women have been subjected to a great and almost unendurable strain, when they expect every moment to be their last, when they have to struggle desperately to stay alive—amorous impulses often overwhelm them. Love becomes to them a refuge and a solace, a temptation impossible to resist. They have a saying for it on Earth. 'Let us drink, love and be merry, for tomorrow we die.' "

"I see. But the temptation would have to be very great, the love offering exceptional."

"Have we not Temples of Love on Mars? What if we should fill those temples with android men and android women? Expose both the Earthman and Earthwoman first to danger, see that they walk in the shadow of death. Frighten and terrify them, make them struggle desperately to survive. Drive them to the brink of despair by confronting them with unknown dangers on a planet alien to them. Then imprison them in a Temple of Love. It would not be a prison to them. It would be a garden of delight after such terrible experiences. They would be sure to succumb. They would yield themselves to all pleasure with no thought for each other."

As Tragor contemplated the images his own mind was conjuring up his eyes began to shine. "Imagine what it would be like. A man and a woman surrounded by a thousand temptations, every bursting fruit that voluptuousness can give birth to! On Earth there is no such paradise. But on Mars…"

For the first time the look of cold condemnation went out of the Chief Coordinator's eyes. He arose slowly, nodding, looking at Tragor with an unmistakable glint of admiration in his gaze. He raised his arm, and Tragor felt a great wave of relief and warm gratefulness flooding over him, for he knew that it was a gesture of benign dismissal and not a sentence of death.

"Very well, Tragor," the Chief Coordinator said. "You have my permission to take them both to Mars."

It was only when Tragor had left the Central Coordinating Compartment and was proceeding down the cold-lighted passageway which branched off from it that everything that he had been saying to Kraii rebounded on himself. He too had just been in great and terrible danger, fighting desperately to stay alive. And now he felt himself in need of love's solace. He had never needed a woman more, never needed the touch of a woman's hand and a woman's warm and eager lips with quite so compulsive an urgency.

If only she would…

Five minutes later he was standing before the locked door of his sleeping compartment, raising his voice in passionate pleading, calling out to the woman within to give him—at least, pity.

"Let me in," he begged. "I promise that I will not touch you if you do not wish to be touched. Just let me stand near you, and look at you. That is all I ask."

There was silence for a moment beyond the locked door. Then he heard her say: "You killed my husband. Even if you were not so repulsive to me I would hate you. Do you hear? I would hate you with my dying breath and if necessary, I shall die. I will find a way. Go away, or I will beat my head against the wall until I can no longer hear your loathsome voice. Go away. I will never let you in and if you try to force your love upon me—"

"No," he pleaded. "I want you to love me willingly."

"That is strange talk for a Martian. I will tell you something. One of the women who was taken captive may soon find herself with child. Did you know that? Didn't those brutish lovers tell you? Lovers! What a mockery, what an insult to the very name of love! If I found myself with child by a Martian I would strangle—oh, no, no. I did not mean to say that. I could never be that cruel, no matter how great my loathing. But if that happened to me, I would make doubly sure to kill myself before such a cruel choice was forced upon me."

It seemed to Tragor that he could endure no more. His triumph of a moment before had the taste of ashes. He had argued persuasively with the most formidable Martian on Earth, and—for that matter—on Mars. He had argued and won. His life had been spared. But now it seemed unimportant to him, of no consequence whatever. Only the woman beyond the locked door was important to him. She was more than important. She had become his whole life. Without her he felt, drained and empty—a hollow shell of a male.

He sank to his knees and covered his face with his taloned hands. If only she would pity him and open the door a crack and let him see her!

Just the sight of her would enable him to endure the loneliness and emptiness of space when he took the two captive lovers to Mars on the mother ship. Just the sight of her beautiful white body and her face so torn with grief and torment that he could scarcely bear to meet the accusing fury in her eyes.

CHAPTER SEVEN

On Earth a man named Peter Summers and his wife Ruth—two people out of Earth's teeming millions, but chosen with care because of their exceptional courage and comeliness of form—went about their daily affairs with no memory of what had happened to them on board a Martian ship a short month previously.

Summers was a writer of mystery novels and his wife an artist whose paintings had been widely acclaimed by critics. They were quite ordinary people in some respects, brilliantly exceptional in others. They had both been used as models by Tragor in constructing experimental android men and android women, but those particular androids had been discarded as not quite what the Plan called for. The android who resembled Summers and the lithe-limbed, sultry-eyed robot woman who was almost an exact duplicate of Summers' wife had not been destroyed, however. They had been kept immobilized in a laboratory on Mars, the disks on their thighs turned off.

Summers and his wife had not been harmed. They had been released at the completion of what had been one of the earliest of the android-constructing experiments, with all knowledge of what had happened to them on board the Martian ship blotted from their minds.

They were no longer of any interest to Tragor. However, the two androids who resembled them had now become of vital interest to Tragor, for the writer, Peter Summers, was a strong-willed, imaginative and sensitive man and greatly resembled the crucial figure in the entire Plan. David Loring. Not physically, but in the subtle and complex configuration of his mind, and that configuration had been duplicated in the robot-man fashioned in Summers' image. And Ruth Summers bore a quite striking resemblance, even physically, to the woman whom Loring loved.

The man and the woman awoke and stared about them. The man was not Peter Summers. The woman was not Ruth, his wife. But the man resembled Peter Summers in all respects. He had the same physical build, the same eyes, ears, nose and mouth. Not only were his facial contours the same, his body was a twin-duplicate of Peter Summers' body. He moved in the same way, with the same gestures and mannerisms, and his voice would not have seemed in any way strange to his wife or to any of the people who knew him well.

The woman looked exactly like his wife. Her face and body would have deceived anyone who knew his wife, knew precisely how she gestured and talked. Even the tiny mole on her right shoulder was the same, and the way her eyes crinkled slightly at the corners when she smiled.

In fact, the resemblance was almost too perfect, for there is something obscurely and indefinably artificial about a duplication that is flawlessly exact, unassailable in all of its parts. The living organism changes constantly, is never quite the same from moment to moment. In a duplication such elusive changes are hard to capture and preserve. Even when the effort has been made and can be looked upon as successful a faint aura of artificiality remains.

The man's first words were simple and direct. He asked: "Where are we?"

"I do not know," the woman replied.

"How did we get here?"

"I do not know."

The man looked down over himself. He was attired as Peter Summers had been aboard the space ship. There was no recognition or surprise in his eyes. Simply acceptance, as if he'd known he would be attired in precisely that way and would only have been surprised if he had found himself naked or clothed in garments strange to him.

He looked at the woman and saw that she was also attired in garments familiar to him. There was no need for him to recognize the garments in a strict sense, for a knowledge of what they would be like had been deeply grooved into his mind. His garments were as much a part of him as his slightly heightened breathing and the calluses on his palms. And so were the garments of the woman facing him with slightly widened eyes.

"I can remember so little," the man who resembled Summers said. "Everything here is strange. I am quite sure that we have never been in this place before. Do you also feel as if you have never been here before?"

The woman nodded. "Yes, I do. It is very strange."

"It is a very large room."

74

"Very large. There is something frightening about it. All of those instruments…"

"They are not navigational instruments. I am quite sure of that. We are no longer on board the ship."

"Were we ever?"

"Yes, I am sure we were once. On board a large ship traveling through space."

"I seem to remember now, too. Some of it is coming back. Slowly, almost painfully. I'm afraid to think about it, to even try to remember. We were far more frightened than we are now. Something terrible happened to us."

"We'd better just relax, take it easy and let it come back in a natural way."

The woman shuddered. "Sometimes not knowing is worse than remembering, worse than any positive knowledge can be. When a memory is crouching like some great beast in the darkness of your mind it is safer to remember. Safer to see the hideous shape clearly, to at least try to force it out into the open."

"Not always, Ruth."

"Ruth. Yes, I am Ruth. You are Peter. You are my husband. The instant you spoke my name it came back to me. Oh, darling, I love you so much. I have always loved you."

"I know, Ruth. And I have always loved you. But beyond that everything is obscure, and in some strange way incomplete. It's as though there are many things which I should recall and understand but which have been—left out."

"Left out? What do you mean?"

"It's hard to explain. But there's a kind of gulf, an emptiness, a falling away when I try to remember what happened to us. The memory doesn't seem to be there at all. I can remember the ship, and how frightened we were. We were traveling through space toward a distant star. There were others. How many I do not know or even what they looked like. It may come back. We must wait and see."

"Wait? What good will waiting do, Peter? We can't just stand here trying to remember or refusing to remember. We don't know where we are. We have no idea where we are, or why we were brought here. Were we brought here against our will? Or did we come voluntarily? Shall we wait for something to happen, or try to make it happen? What shall we do, Peter? Beat on the walls with our bare hands?

Shout and create a disturbance? Some of these instruments look fragile. Perhaps if we smashed one—"

The man who resembled Summers shook his head. "No, Ruth. That would be too dangerous a way of bringing down the thunder."

The man turned as he spoke, and looked more steadily and carefully at his surroundings. The woman stared with him, standing very still, a growing wonder in her eyes.

The instruments that towered on all sides of them differed greatly in size and configuration. Some were metallic and complex, as intricate in construction as the time-regulating mechanism of a great watch, set on a pedestal and reflecting the down-streaming radiance in all of its parts. Others resembled more translucent globes, resting level with the floor, fragile in design and filled with a swirling blue mist. But that globe-like aspect was only partial, for they were pierced by metal rods which projected sharply from their surfaces in hedgehog fashion and obscured or distorted their roundness in various ways.

There were also several flat, box-like structures with a fine mesh covering and one huge box which was heavily screened in front and bore a chilling resemblance to a cage. The screening was enveloped in radiance, so that the mesh was only evanescently visible through the glow and it was impossible to see beyond it. Yet for an instant there was a deepening of the glow and the man who resembled Summers thought he could detect a faint stir of movement behind the mesh, as if some monstrous shape had been imprisoned within; a shape which was self-luminous and very restless in its pacing.

The enormous room was illuminated by globular overhead lamps, which cast stationary shadows on its glass-smooth floor and turned the walls into light-mirroring surfaces that deflected the radiance without diminishing it.

The man who resembled Summers spoke calmly, but there was a slight tremor in his voice. "We will have to wait. We must force ourselves to be patient. It would be easier to let ourselves go, to act impulsively. Inaction is difficult when you feel you're at the mercy of something dangerous that you know nothing about. But we can't afford to take unnecessary risks. We still have one safeguard. Being armed may not protect us, but it's an advantage we can't afford to toss away. We'll be tossing it away if we lose our heads."

It seemed only natural to the man that she should be armed. The weapon he was clasping surprised him no more than his familiar attire had done. Its presence in his hand he took for granted, and its absence would have bewildered him and greatly increased his apprehension. The woman was also clasping a weapon, and taking her possession of it so much for granted that she did not even glance down at it when the man stressed the fact that they were both armed by tapping her lightly on the wrist.

The two small, compact energy weapons glittered in the down-streaming radiance. Outwardly they were exact replicas of nuclear handguns, accurate in range and deadly when fired. Nuclear handguns were capable of disintegrating any object in their path, living or inanimate, within a radius of thirty-five feet. There was no nuclear fallout, no diffusion of destructive radioactivity, no risk to the user at all.

Seventy years of controlled atomic research on the red planet made such weapons available to everyone privileged to carry them: regional law enforcement coordinators, authorized destroyers of dangerous animal pests and explorers in space. But the weapons that the man and the woman were clasping had not been atomically powered. They were infinitely less destructive, with barely enough firepower to kill a man or large animal at close range, or bring down a bird in flight. But the man and the woman did not know that. They had no way of knowing.

The woman was the first to notice the change in the large, cage-like object. The light shifted, and a slow shadow crept across it, elongating as it moved, first parallel with the box and then at right angles to it.

The shadow was sinuous and very dark, and it made a rasping sound on the glass-smooth floor as it advanced in a swift glide. A yard from the cage it ceased to be a shadow.

The woman went rigid. Her hand darted to her throat and all of the color drained out of her face. She stared wordlessly, unable to move or speak, and her stunned helplessness almost led to the man's undoing. He was half turned toward her and did not see the long-fanged, catlike beast until it was within eight feet of him.

He cried out when he saw it and leapt back. It sprang then, straight toward him. Sprang with a terrible, deep-throated roar, its tawny flanks quivering.

The man fired. He had no time to take aim, and there was no need for him to aim with precision. Any blast from any weapon, at almost pointblank range, would have found its mark in so huge a target.

A great gash appeared in the creature's right flank, and turned crimson even before its body swerved and the man fired for the second time, staggering backwards with a sobbing gasp. The wounded beast landed upright directly behind him, and flattened itself. It hugged the floor for an instant as its belly and right flank turned a brighter red, flooding the glasslike surface with a swiftly spreading pool of blood that was startlingly like its own elongated bulk in configuration.

Then it was in motion again, rearing on its hind limbs with a roar and swaying toward him. He swung about and fired three more shots into its body, holding the handgun steady, and taking careful aim now despite the pain-maddened animal's flailing claws and snarling ferocity.

The man did not escape unscathed. The enraged beast raked his shoulders with its claws, tore a deep gash in his flesh from his neck to his waist. The man leapt back and fired again. As the handgun blasted the woman began to scream.

The beast staggered, fell back, and began slowly to crumple, his body arching forward as it sagged, its forelimbs giving way first and the rest of its bulk collapsing like a weighted sack, lopsidedly and with tumultuous heavings. The man stood very still, watching it crumple, seemingly unaware of the grievous wound he had sustained. The long gash did not bleed. It remained a long, livid disfiguration running the length of his spine, as if a scalpel dipped in acid had etched a blemish with ragged edges in the precise middle of his back.

The man waited until the beast ceased to move, his gaze intent, strangely calm. Not a muscle of his face moved. His absolute quietude had followed so quickly upon his first startled outcry and his aggressive action in defending himself that it would have baffled a psychologist whose stock in trade was the reasonably predictable within the limits of what is known about the human mind.

If there was a mental conflict within him it was not mirrored on his features and even his posture was amazingly relaxed. He did not hold himself stiffly, as might have been expected, but simply stood waiting in a completely natural attitude—an attitude free of all strain—for the wounded beast to breathe its last.

The instant the catlike creature's tawny flanks ceased to heave and a rust-colored froth appeared at its mouth he turned quickly, moved to the woman's side and took her into his arms. He held her firmly, stilling her trembling with whispered reassurance and running his left hand gently up and down her back.

"It's all right," he murmured. "I've killed it. It won't move again. Easy now, there's nothing to fear."

The woman was shuddering violently and to quiet her he began more firmly to stroke her bare back, running his hands over the velvety smooth skin between her shoulder blades and even more firmly caressing the twin mounds of her breasts.

Suddenly she was clinging to him, her arms locked about him so tightly he had difficulty in remembering his only desire was to comfort and reassure her. Or perhaps he did not want to remember. Passion awoke in him, fierce, irresistible. He lowered his head and brought his mouth down hard on lips that seemed to melt beneath the demanding ardor of his kisses. She seemed suddenly unbelievably young to him, eager and vibrant, as if he had met her for the first time. Yet she was his wife, surely, and they had known many such moments of rapture in the past. Or had they?

He had the strange feeling that he, too, had been born anew, that he was not quite the same man who had plucked the blooming rose of love many times before. He felt almost like a young boy, clasping his virginal first love in a forest glade and watching her face turn crimson...

"We have seen enough," a cold voice said. "My insight was flawless. They were exposed to danger first—a great and terrible danger. And they were stirred to passion, as I was sure they would be. They are only androids, but the proof is strong and convincing enough. I am quite sure now that we will succeed as well with David Loring and the woman of his choice."

The android man and woman did not hear the voice. It was too remote and Tragor was not addressing himself to an Earthman. He was speaking to Sull, and they both stood at the door of the laboratory.

And then, quite suddenly, the disks on the androids' thighs glowed with a blinding incandescence and they slumped to the floor and lay motionless.

CHAPTER EIGHT

David Loring only knew at first that the room in which he found himself was enormous. He could see the high walls towering up into shadows, and the great distance which separated wall from wall, shadow from shadow.

He saw the room in fitful flashes, between sleeping and waking. He saw it as a prison and a sanctuary, the ward of a hospital, a waiting room at the hub of some of some intricate and planet-engirdling web of communication. He saw it even as a quite simple, peaceful place, soothing to the eye, where a man could sleep and dream with a beautiful woman at his side, their bodies completely at ease in the dawn light, relaxed and languorous.

Finally, after what may have been days, or only hours, he saw the room as it really was. He saw it as a prison on an alien world, and the woman who shared it with him as a captive like himself who had to live with the shattering knowledge that what she saw in his eyes he saw in hers. "Janice," he whispered.

She was nodding at him and trying hard to smile and when he saw the tenderness and warmth in her eyes, tears started to gather beneath his burning eyelids and suddenly he was weeping unashamedly.

She got up quickly and came to him and settled herself at his side, pressing her scantily clad body close to him in womanly solicitude, reaching up and touching his face.

She was wearing the strangest of costumes; a band of golden-textured cloth, which completely encircled her hips and the lower part of her torso, but left her breasts exposed. There were sandals on her feet, and her red-gold hair had been cut short, and was caught up in an entrancing way by a ribbon. She had never seemed more beautiful in his sight or more feminine and desirable.

"I thought you'd never wake up, darling," she whispered, her lips brushing his throat and passing upwards until their moist warmth came to rest against his mouth and stopped his breath for an instant.

"I've been waiting for you to look at me," she said, when he could breathe again. "To really look at me as you did just now. I was afraid to wake you up too abruptly. You seemed so close to exhaustion, so desperately in need of sleep. Oh, David, hold me close. At least we're together again."

"Everything is so strange," Loring said, his hand going out to stroke her hair. "So confused, mixed up. I remember struggling to free myself from a very horrible kind of net—a net with strands that seemed to move and cling to me, strands that seemed almost to have a life of their own. Then I was imprisoned, shut away in the darkness. I saw nothing, heard nothing, for hours. Then I saw a light moving slowly back and forth in front of me. I tried to rise, tried to get to my feet. But something seemed to lift me up and hurl me further back into the darkness.

"There were times when I could hardly breathe, when I seemed to be suffocating. I know that I slept a great deal. The passage of time—that was the most frightening thing of all. Days must have passed and yet I was only obscurely aware of their passing. But I knew that we were no longer on Earth that we were traveling through space to another world. I had no way of knowing through observation, because I was in total darkness and felt nothing, heard nothing. The knowledge must have been implanted in my mind."

"It was," Janice said. "I know, because a strange cold voice spoke to me just once, and told me that when I woke up I would see you again, but that neither of us would remember what happened after you left me alone in your apartment waiting for you to return. Do you remember, David, or was the voice telling the truth? Do you remember what happened after that? If you do—"

Loring shook his head. "No," he said. "It's all a complete blank. I remember going out on MacDougal Street and hailing a cab. I even remember getting into the cab and riding to your apartment. But after that it's as if I had blacked out. I can only remember struggling to free myself from that ghastly web and how the blackness closed in on me, almost smothering me."

"And you remembered nothing more until you woke up here? Think hard, David. Are you sure about that? Completely sure?"

"Just what I've told you—nothing more. The feeling that I was in space, traveling through space. No, it was more than a feeling. It was certain knowledge. But it was nothing that I could have found out for myself."

"It frightens me, David. If you could remember even a part of what happened…"

"I don't think they want us to remember," Loring said. "Whatever their purpose was in bringing us here, they don't want us to know too much about them. That's pretty obvious."

"We've been here a long time, David. I spoke to you once, but you didn't answer, didn't seem to hear me. Your eyes were half closed and your face looked strange, as if everything in the room had gone far away from you. Then everything went far away from me too. I fell into a deep sleep and just woke up a few minutes ago."

Loring was staring about the room, a look of mounting apprehension in his eyes. But he heard her when she said: "I wanted to put my arms around you, and draw you close and bring my lips down hard on yours. But I was afraid, as I said, to wake you up too abruptly. The sudden shock…"

"We'll make up for that right now," Loring said. He clasped her firmly and kissed her until they were both out of breath. "I'm not as exhausted as you might think," he said.

He realized suddenly that he was as scantily clad as she was and was amazed that he had not realized it immediately upon awakening. A Greek athlete in the days of Pericles might have worn less clothing while discus throwing, but he seriously doubted it. He was not a man who liked to strut his maleness and he had no particular liking for exhibitionists. It embarrassed him a little, even in the presence of a woman who had often seen him wearing far less clothing.

"They took away our clothes," she whispered, as if aware of his thoughts. "I don't know how they undressed me and put this ridiculous sash around me but I'll have to make the best of it. I don't really mind too much. Do you?"

"I think it might be a good idea if you removed the sash," he said. "It isn't becoming to you."

"If you wish," she said, and unwound the strange garment.

She stood before him completely unclothed and for an instant his breath caught in his throat. Then she was in his arms again, covering his face with kisses.

After a moment she put the strange garment back on, smiling a little. "If it was just you I wouldn't mind at all," she said. "But we don't know who we'll be meeting."

Her face turned suddenly sober, all of the levity leaving her eyes.

"The window," she whispered. "We'd better see what's outside. Just the thought of looking terrifies me, but we may as well get it over with."

Loring nodded. "If we had any real sense we'd have looked out immediately," he said. "We'd have let nothing stand in the way."

"David! What kind of talk is that? Think of what you would have missed. A completely undraped female, distinctly on the shameless side."

The taunting levity was back in her eyes again, as if she dreaded the thought of walking to the window even now and wished to put it off as long as possible with a whistling-in-the-dark bravado.

"You're right," Loring said. "Forgive me, darling. I spoke without thinking and I didn't mean it in quite that way. I'm glad we waited. It isn't just what I saw. It's what I——"

"David, please don't make me blush now. Shut up, damn you."

"All right, Gorgeous. I won't say another word." They walked to the window together. Janice cried out, and Loring drew in his breath sharply. A tiny vein at his temple bulged and began to pulsate.

The city, which stretched out for miles beyond the pane, transcended in height and depth and grandeur anything Man's creative genius had conceived on Earth, or was perhaps capable of conceiving, even in the realm of imaginative prophecy. Human history supplied no parallels that would have brought such a soaring architectural miracle within the scope of pictorial art as its most prophetic.

William Blake alone might have been capable of portraying it on canvas, if he had been born at a later period in human history and had been familiar with space-age technology and the intricacies of the twentieth century's non-Euclidean mathematics. But even then his vision might have faltered and his palette, lacking the full range of colors, dropped from his hand.

The Martian city was so large it would have completely dwarfed the largest city on Earth. If New York, London and Paris could have been combined in one great wonder city there might have been a few points of superficial resemblance to the metropolis of white buildings beyond the pane. But a few points only, for in a sober and completely realistic sense all comparisons broke down.

It was a city of spider-web traceries against a sunrise sky, of buildings so enormous that their pinnacles seemed to blend with the clouds. It was a city of floating gardens agleam with vermilion--

tongued flowers that seemed to sway and dance in response to some gigantic and invisible baton, so that they resembled myriads of tiny ballet dancers constantly in motion, voluptuously a-twirl, bending first to the left and then to the right and then swooningly backwards.

It was a city of parks and lakes with tree-fringed borders and of column-supported terraces bridged by aerial traffic lanes, where vehicles that resembled gold beetles darted back and forth with a speed so great that the eye could scarcely follow them.

It was a city of clean, strong lines, without elaborate ornamentation to mar a perfection that its builders must have kept constantly before their minds. There was no visible areas of new construction or areas where the buildings seemed to be crumbling. No wrecking instruments at work, or skeleton structures black against the sunrise. Not the slightest sign anywhere of demolition or repair. It was as if the city had been built to endure for centuries, with every stone in place, a monument to the creative genius of a race that had somehow found a means to create a vision of splendor which time or the elements could not mar or efface.

It was a breathtakingly beautiful city and yet, in some strange way, it seemed to be enveloped in an aura of cruelty and wickedness. There was a lewdness about some of its contours—a lewdness that could be physically sensed. It stirred the imagination in a strange way, as a woman utterly abandoned, lost to all shame, may cease to be a capricious wanton, given to light-hearted amours and become so coldly lascivious that she repels the most passionate of men.

And suddenly, as Loring stared, he saw the woman-shape. He saw that the city, its entire circumference, its central mass, was shaped like a recumbent female with great wanton knees and flame-tipped breasts.

Janice saw it too, and retreated from the window with a gasp, her face and throat darkened by a quickly spreading flush.

Loring stared for an instant longer and then turned and drew her to him, holding her tightly for a moment and saying nothing at all.

There were no words that could have eased the shock of what they both had seen, and silence was better, Loring felt. After a moment her breathing steadied and the flush vanished from her cheeks.

"What are we going to do, David?" she asked. "Just stay here and let the builders of that city visit us? Kill us perhaps, or insist that we accompany them on a sight seeing tour? I don't think we'd like what we'd see."

"I don't think so either," Loring said. "And I don't think we're staying if that window isn't locked and opens outward. Or inward, for that matter. I'm going to find out right now. If necessary, we'll conduct our own sight seeing tour. If we can get out fast we may be able to hide somewhere before they realize we've had the quickness of mind to outsmart them."

"Not quickness of mind alone, David. Courage enough to act quickly and descend those stairs."

"You saw the stairs?"

Janice nodded. "Yes, I saw them. A flight of stone steps leading downward, starting just below the window and leading straight down. I was going to push on the window, to see if it would move. You do it, David. Hurry. We've no time to lose."

"All right," Loring said. He returned to the window and pressed firmly on the pane. For a moment the pane held and then, as he increased the pressure, it swung slowly outward.

Janice ran to him with an exultant cry.

They emerged from the room cautiously. The steps began just beneath the window but they were not directly joined to the ledge. They had to take a short leap to reach them. What purpose they had been designed to serve Loring did not know and had difficulty in imagining. The topmost step was very broad and flared slightly, and it occurred to him that a very small flying machine—a midget helicopter or an autogyro—would have encountered no difficulty in making use of it as a landing platform. Perhaps there were hundreds of such structures scattered throughout the city, directly adjacent to the windows of tall buildings. He had no way of knowing and no time to puzzle over it.

The stone stairway was very steep and contained at least three hundred steps. It led to a flaring, disk-shaped expanse of shining metal several hundred feet in diameter. Directly below the disk the tiny moving vehicles which Loring had observed from the window darted to and fro, obscurely visible through its translucent glimmering.

Loring took Janice's arm and supported her firmly, and they started down with a heightened sense of togetherness. "Remember this," he said, with quiet reassurance. "It's some comfort, at least. There are few situations that are absolutely hopeless. They may look that way, but they're not. Escapes take place when every door to freedom seems bolted down tight. Not only in fiction—in real life.

The deadliest diseases often fail to kill. The patient survives and lives for many years. And men condemned to death can always hope for a last-minute reprieve."

"But how often are they reprieved?"

"More often than the average person realizes. There are always possibilities of escape. A failure of intelligence at any point can reverse an advantage. And we've no reason to believe that the minds that planned and built this city, tremendous as it is, are infallible. The slightest flaw in their thinking could give us an advantage which would even the score."

"But this is their world, their home, David. We are aliens here, imprisoned in a web so dark and terrible we can't even begin to understand it. It's like a blind maze with no familiar landmarks, nothing to guide us—"

"It may not be quite as blind a maze as you think," Loring whispered, tightening his hold on her arm. "In another hundred years we'll be building cities on Earth just as tremendous. We use the same basic patterns, and we'll eventually acquire just as much engineering skill."

"It's still a blind maze to me," Janice said. "We may be walking into a trap. Did you think of that, David?"

"I thought of it. But staying in that room would have put us completely at their mercy. Steady now. We'll soon be at the bottom."

"Just looking down makes me dizzy."

"Don't look down then," he cautioned. "Move slowly and stay close to me."

The stairway was enveloped in a faint radiance, which grew swiftly brighter as they descended. They were soon caught up in the brightness, the steps beneath them becoming a descending series of polished stone mirrors which reflected the more diffuse and distant brightness of the sunrise. Their shadows flickered across the brightness, sometimes elongating and becoming immense, sometimes contracting into wavering small replicas of themselves.

They moved arm in arm through a kaleidoscope of shimmering curves and angles, a constantly increasing steepness keeping them constantly on guard, making them feel at times that they were descending an upright ladder teetering precariously in some unimaginable abyss of emptiness.

They were almost at the bottom now and could see the shining surface of the disk that they had seen from above without being able to determine its precise configuration. It spread out from the base of the stairs in a translucent glimmering, a surface of smooth, almost glass-like texture that spiraled slightly downwards for perhaps a hundred feet and then became completely horizontal. Where it rose to a level gradient it widened out, so that its faintly luminous edges graded off into shadows.

There was a pylon-shaped structure at the far extremity of the sloping section. It could have been either a gateway or a small building, but Loring was almost sure that it was a building.

He did not pause when he reached the bottom. He tightened his hold on Janice's waist and then released her, gesturing out across the brightness.

"Walk fast, but don't run," he cautioned. "They may be watching us. That small tower could be anything: a communication control structure, a guardhouse, even a dwelling. We won't know until we get to it."

He nodded and left the stone stairway, moving out across the glasslike surface of the disk without looking back. Janice kept almost abreast of him, quickening her steps but not quite running.

Loring studied the structure appraisingly as he drew near to it. It was smooth-surfaced and completely featureless, a massive block of metal that rose to a height of about eighty feet.

He halted directly in front of it and waited for Janice to join him before he reached out and ran his hand over a square foot of its smooth metal surface. The metal was yellowish with a burnished copper sheen to it.

"What do you suppose it is?" Janice asked breathlessly.

Loring shook his head. "I wish I knew. It could be a guardhouse or a signal tower or something of the sort. There's no entrance on this side, but there may be an entrance in back. It could have been erected here as a kind of sentry barrier to guard this particular part of the city. It could even be a remotely controlled robot structure, equipped with detective devices and destructive weapons."

"You really think—"

"I don't know what to think. I'd like to pound on the metal to see if it gives off a hollow sound. But I'm afraid to risk it. Even raising our voices might be dangerous and activate some delicately balanced instrument of destruction."

A look of decision came into Loring's eyes. "You stay here," he said. "Don't move or touch that wall. If there's an entrance I don't want you to be with me until I've made sure there's nothing dangerous inside."

Janice looked at him, startled. "You're not going inside?"

"I will if there's an entrance."

"But darling, don't you see? If anything happened to you I wouldn't want to go on living. You think of what could happen and all that unrealistic nonsense about shielding a woman, not letting her share a danger with a man she loves more than her own life, breaks down."

"It hasn't broken down with me," Loring said. "I'm sorry, darling, but you're staying here."

"Please, David—"

"No chance. You're staying right here."

Before she could protest again he kissed her and turned quickly, not trusting himself to prolong the embrace. He walked to the edge of the building, rounded it and moved forward cautiously, keeping a short distance from the wall. The side of the structure was as wide as the facade, quite possibly a little wider.

The vague fear, the sense of danger, remained with him, but so far he had encountered nothing alarming. His uneasiness angered him a little, made him impatient with his own perhaps wholly unjustified caution. He came to a sudden decision. If there was an entrance at the rear of the building he would not hesitate but would go immediately inside.

There was an entrance at the rear of the building; an unlighted, oblong-shaped opening without ornamentation, twice the width of a man's body and eight or nine feet in height. Although the structure was metallic, the entrance had a stone-carven look, as if it had been chiseled with precision from a block of solid granite.

Having come to a decision, the swift dwindling of his dread surprised him. It was as if a point of pressure had been removed from his mind, leaving him free to walk without restraint into the structure.

The falling away of tension gave him no satisfaction. He mistrusted it, feared it, for it strengthened his belief that his thoughts were under scrutiny and an effort was being made to influence his emotions. Had he won a momentary victory or was that, too, an illusion?

The tension started mounting again the instant he had passed through the aperture. The darkness was just as bad as he had imagined it might be, totally unrelieved by the faintest glimmer of light. It was a smothering blackness, shroud-like and all engulfing.

He stood very still a few feet within the entrance. The aperture was faintly filmed with light, but the dim glow did not penetrate for more than a foot or two into the darkness. Beyond that slight penumbra of light there was an impenetrable wall of darkness hemming him in on all sides.

The odor that came to his nostrils was equally unnerving. It was sharp, acrid, but with a faint mustiness about it that made him think of tomb rot.

For a moment there was no sound at all, no faintest stir of movement. Then he heard a rustling sound that seemed to come from deep within the darkness. A rustling, a shuffling, the kind of sound that could have been made by a snake unwinding its coils, or someone dragging a heavy sack over a stone floor, or by nothing more unnerving than the slow backward and forward movements of a broom.

Loring did not think it was a broom. The fear which came upon him was primitive, elemental. In some respects it was the kind of fear which a man in a dark wood would experience if he came upon a nest of copperheads while exploring a foliage-choked crevice in search of edible mushrooms. Expecting to find some poisonous varieties perhaps, but hardly death staring up at him out of the opaque eyes of a snake poised to strike.

He moved slowly backwards, keeping the same distance from the entrance but putting as much space as possible between himself and the shuffling. He kept backing away until he came up against a firm metal barrier, which he quickly explored with his hands. It had the solid feel of a wall.

His breathing became a little less strained. With a wall at his back he was at least in no danger of being attacked from two directions. And if the wall made further retreat impossible the danger had not increased, for he was still the same distance from the entrance and could still, if he wished, make a very swift dash for it.

He had no immediate intention of doing so. He stood listening, motionless and alert, his shoulders barely touching the wall. The shuffling sound did not seem to be coming any nearer. It even stopped for an instant. The silence closed in about him and he became aware of the over-loud beating of his heart. When the sound started up again it seemed to come from another direction, closer to the entrance.

Now it was nearer. Unmistakably louder and nearer, very close to him in the darkness. He strained his eyes, but could see nothing. He had to depend on his hearing alone, and hearing, he knew, could be deceptive. It was often very difficult to determine the precise location of a sound, to pinpoint it with any certainty.

Suddenly his heart skipped a beat, and his breathing quickened. His throat turned cold as he swallowed, and tightened as well, the muscles stiffening, cording into knots. Unconsciously he gripped his leg, just above the knee, and dug his fingers into the flesh, as if physical pain alone could keep reality from taking on an aspect so nightmarish that his sanity would be imperiled.

The creature was passing directly across the entrance. It was moving so slowly that he could see it distinctly in the sharply sheared-off glow from outside the building. The glow penetrated the darkness hardly at all, but when the creature paused and half turned about even that abruptly curtailed illumination was strong enough to bring it into stark relief.

He saw the monstrous shape clearly. Saw the long, insect-like legs with their tapering hairs, and the very slender, fly-like body. Saw its gauzy, tightly folded wings, the metallic glitter of its immense, many-faceted eyes and the slow turning of the eyes as they sought him out in the darkness.

The enormous flying insect framed for an instant in the glow was a shape of terror. It was not its size alone that was making his flesh crawl and his chest heave as his eyes remained fastened upon it in the swimming darkness. He was quite sure of that.

There was something rapacious about it, a deadliness that could be instantly sensed. It seemed intent on his destruction, its enormous eyes filmed with a malignancy that made his blood run cold.

Its attitude was just as terrifying, the body poised as if for attack, a rapier sharpness in the writhing mandibles, a wire-tight tension in the rhythmically vibrating thorax, the slender abdomen, and the long, hairy legs which terminated in rust-colored, cup-like disks.

Loring's thoughts went into a mind-chilling whirl. The human mind does not associate ferocity with an ordinary fly. A house fly, a fruit fly, even a blue-bottle fly hovering over carrion and evoking no more than a slight, momentary shiver of disgust. But wasps and hornets are fly-like in aspect and they are equally graceful in flight. Winged insects of great beauty, delicately constructed and the opposite of revolting. Yet wasps and hornets can inflict stings that can paralyze and kill.

A long blue hornet in a drowsy woodland glade can be a flying torpedo, a death-dealing precision instrument, as billions of fat, sluggish caterpillars have discovered over a very long period of geologic time. And if a hornet could become large enough...

A gigantic hornet might well find a man more to its liking on an alien world, a far more delectable feast for its larvae when paralyzed with care and stored in a clay-constructed hive. Or a metal-constructed hive.

The solitary wasps. The mud builders. Every schoolboy was familiar with them, every young naturalist exploring the countryside near his home, the autumn leaves turning red and yellow, the tang of wood smoke in the air. The small, gray, skillfully cemented-over openings to their nests deep underground where unspeakable acts of insect vampirism took place. The paralyzed caterpillar shrinking, turning sere, losing its substance but remaining tormentingly alive while the gnawing, insatiable grubs waxed fat and strong. Dying in the end, its substance liquefying... And a human caterpillar?

Despite his terror Loring knew that he was letting his imagination get out of control. He was taking too much for granted, letting his thoughts lead him into a dark abyss, which probably had no basis in reality. The hideous thought had leapt unbidden into his mind and he had elaborated upon it, filling in the total blankness of the unknown with images so ghastly that they glowed blood red. It was exactly what an expressionistic artist might have been forced to do if his morbidity became a genius-inspired flame and he could no longer restrain an impulse to torture himself to win immortality for what could be, at best, a purely symbolical vision of madness completely remote from reality.

Again he was merely a very frightened man with no particular liking for morbidity who had been trapped in total darkness on an alien planet and had everything to lose by abandoning himself to wild conjecture when only clear, logical, determined thinking could save him.

If he had thought at all of wasps and hornets, if he had instantly seized upon such a comparison—there had to be a reason behind such a forceful, almost irresistible distortion of thought.

He was almost sure that it was a distortion. The mere appearance of a fly-like creature close to him in the darkness, huge and malignant as it appeared to be, would not ordinarily have started such a train of thought in his mind and opened up vistas so specifically ghastly.

In all probability his thoughts had been deliberately guided. The paralyzed caterpillar-feasting grub comparison had been firmly implanted in his mind by a skillful mental manipulation of his imagination.

And if his mind was being manipulated, if the alien city dwellers were—

Loring straightened, cold sweat breaking out on his forehead, his eyes darting to the entrance. The entrance was darkening again. A shadow had fallen across it, partly blotting out the radiance from outside the building.

It was not a massive shadow and he knew that it could not have been cast by the fly-like creature moving about in the darkness. It was an advancing, not a retreating shadow, and it was very slender. It cut off a portion of the light for only a fraction of the time it had taken the insect to pass from the glow into the darkness. It was accompanied by footsteps, quick, uncertain and a brief flurry of movement. Then the slender intruder was inside the building, silhouetted against the glow a few feet from the entrance.

CHAPTER NINE

"Janice!"

Loring spoke her name in a choked whisper, as if an instrument of torture had been applied without warning to his flesh and was slowly crushing every bone in his body. He whispered her name twice, and then his voice broke and he could only stare, gripped by a fear so tormenting that it completely shattered all of his defenses.

He was unable to move or think clearly. If the aliens had chosen that moment of shock to attack nothing could have saved him, for he was incapable of resistance. But they did not attack. It was almost as though they themselves had been caught off guard, checkmated by the very violence of his emotions. Perhaps they had not known that a man in love may lose all concern for his own safety and redouble it in another direction, transfer it to someone whose life is infinitely more precious to him. Perhaps that total forgetfulness of self was so alien to their thinking that they were unable to make instant and effective use of it as a weapon.

Janice's voice broke the stillness, calling out to him in a frightened appeal. "David! David! Where are you? I was too worried about you to wait any longer. When you didn't come back—"

She swayed a little and moved a few steps closer to him, as if groping for something tangible to guide her in the darkness. Then he was at her side, stilling her trembling with the firmness of his embrace, murmuring reassurances.

"What I just said was a lie, David," Janice whispered, holding on to him as if she would never let him go. "Your mind was made up, so I had to pretend I wasn't going to follow you. Now there's nothing you can do about it, is there, darling?"

"No, nothing," Loring said, smoothing her hair, wishing it weren't true but not wanting to alarm her more than he had to.

"You're glad I'm here—glad I did come?"

"Very glad," Loring said, the lie making him tormentingly aware of how difficult it would be to tell her the truth. But she had to know.

The insect might attack at any moment. It was still close to him in the darkness, close to Janice now as well and when he strained his ears he could still hear the faint whirring of its wings. He was aware of its chilling odor too: acrid, and laden with a slight effluvium of mustiness and decay, as if it had just emerged from some airless, long abandoned sepulcher deep underground.

He tried to keep his voice level when he described it to her, holding nothing back, making no attempt to minimize the danger and asking her to listen herself to the faint whirring of the creature's wings.

She began to tremble again, slightly at first and then more violently, so that he had to tighten his grip on her shoulder and draw her firmly back against the wall.

"Something seems to be keeping it from attacking," he whispered. "Perhaps it won't attack at all if we keep very still and think about getting out."

"Think about it?" Her voice was so faint he had to strain to catch the words. "The entrance is right in front of us. Why can't we make a dash for it?"

"We may have to. It may be a risk we'll have to take. But if we can save ourselves in some other way—"

"What do you mean? Why should we even try? If we head straight for the entrance we'll be outside in two or three seconds. Can that—that insect thing move fast enough to intercept us if we know that our lives are at stake?"

"I think it can. If they release it, I think it can. They may expect us to try to get out that way. Remember, an insect can move with lightning swiftness."

"But there's only one entrance. We can't hope to escape in any other way?"

Loring did a strange thing. He leaned back against the wall, pressed himself more firmly against it, and ran his fingers exploringly over its smooth metal surface.

Then he tightened his grip on Janice's arm and moved slowly along the wall, continuing to explore the surface with his free hand as he drew her with him through the darkness.

Before he had progressed more than four yards his fingers encountered a slight roughness. The roughness increased as he advanced, became a series of firmly projecting ridges. He stopped advancing, his breathing slightly quickened, and tugged experimentally at one of the ridges.

Nothing happened for an instant. Then he felt the wall move slightly under his hand. He tugged more vigorously, increasing the tightness of his grip. A section of the wall began to swing open. He wedged one shoulder solidly against it, and exerted a steady, unrelenting pressure, to counterbalance the tugging and keep the movement stabilized.

There was a sudden change in the darkness. It became less impenetrable and by straining his eyes he could make out the shadowy outlines of a flight of steps leading downward. A blast of cold air swept upwards through the aperture, causing Janice to cry out in surprise and press closer to him. She spoke with a stunned breathlessness.

"David, how did you know?"

"I think—they wanted us to know."

"But why, David? I don't understand."

"I had a sudden impulse to look for another way out. It was as if the thought had been implanted in my mind, as if I was being guided. Something started me searching the instant you said there was only one way to escape, through the doorway. They may have feared I'd decide not to make a dash for it. And I think they want us to go on, to at least try to escape. I don't know why. I can't explain it."

He reached out for her hand, clasped it firmly. "We're going down those stairs. Even if it's what they want us to do we're going to take the risk. To stay here would be too dangerous. The slightest display of weakness or indecision could offset any advantage we might gain by staying. With you here, sharing the danger, I couldn't withstand the pressure. I'd be sure to crack."

She was in his arms suddenly, embracing him with a passion so maddeningly feminine in its soft, clinging sweetness that he forgot for an instant that it must have been inspired by terror and desperation, and a mad desire to wed her body to his for the comfort he could bring her.

"David," she whispered. Her hand was exploring him with tender concern. "I want you—now. I must."

"But, darling—"

"That's why, darling," she whispered, "I love you. I want your seed to grow inside me before one of those monsters rapes me. And David, if anything happens to you, I want someone to remember you by. It's our duty David. We must survive."

He was roused. He touched her, and he knew she was ready for him. "It seems crazy, Janice," he protested. "But your reasons are sound. As you say, darling."

Her lips burned on his. Her lovely breasts pressed against his torso. Her small round stomach quivered against his.

"They might see," he warned. "They're watching us."

"I don't care!" Janice cried fiercely. "Let them see how decent human beings behave." She moved against him. "I'll conceive David I know. I'm ovulating. It's one of the unsafe days. Remember how careful we used to be." Her voice was almost gay. "Now we can be utterly careless. With your child in me, David, I won't be scared of anything. Come on, darling."

She took him then. The bliss of their union banished his fears. The warmth of her pulsating body, the rapture of her lips, the quivering of her loins, brought them together in complete harmony. The moment that is eternity for lovers came to both simultaneously.

"Hold me tight just for a little while," Janice pleaded afterwards. "Don't move!" She locked her arms round his waist.

Their bodies still joined, she leaned away from him, hanging her head back exposing the loveliness of her throat. Loring kissed it, because it seemed the natural thing to do. It was an impulsive gesture.

He was startled to feel her tighten against him, as if she were suddenly roused again. Slowly, with a beatific smile on her face, she raised herself, and looked up at him. Love stars were shining in her eyes.

"David," she said seriously. "That was the rightest, purest thing we have ever done. Now we both have something to live for. I am not afraid any more."

He released her wordlessly, tightened his grip on her hand and together they started downward. The stairway was in darkness at first, but it began to glow as they descended.

They moved hand and hand, aware that the stairway was even longer than the one they had previously descended; both longer and set at a more precipitous angle. Vast distances fell away beneath them, and Loring knew that they were descending into the heart of the city.

"Don't look down," Loring warned, slowing his steps. The steepness was one source of danger, but there were others that he feared more: the dazzling brightness of the radiance that now enveloped them or a sudden seizure of dizziness.

"Listen," Janice whispered, halting abruptly and turning to face him with a swift intake of her breath.

"What is it? We can't—"

"Listen, David. Don't you hear it? A whirring sound, right up above us. Not too near, but—David, I'm frightened. That thing must be following us!"

He had to stand very still and strain his ears for an instant before he caught it. It was unmistakable, but so faint that, under calmer circumstances, he would have been amazed by the acuteness of

Janice's hearing. But now there was no room in his mind for amazement. Only horror.

"All right," he said. "It's following us. We might have known that it would. I sensed its rapacity the instant I saw it, and if they kept it from attacking us they must have had a reason."

"What reason, David? Don't try to spare me, if you think you know."

"I don't know for sure. How could I? But I can make a guess that has some ugly implications. It could be an insect-like—"

He hesitated, fighting for control, reproaching himself for his harshness. He was making no attempt to soften the blow and he knew why. He had spoken with a slight edge of angry impatience in his voice because he did not want her to know how profoundly the thought had unnerved him.

It was more than chilling, for there was something diabolically calculated, wholly vicious, about the use of such a horror as a weapon.

A relentlessly pursued man—an escaped prisoner floundering in desperation through a swamp or trapped in a mountain gully—can experience many dreads. But only one that claws at his mind like a sharp-taloned, utterly merciless harpy.

The appeal in Janice's eyes put a quick end to his hesitation. "What could it be, David? Tell me."

"A kind of insect-like bloodhound. A scent-tracking animal can demoralize a fleeing man in a very terrible way, and I'm sure they know it. I think they deliberately kept it from attacking to give us time to escape from the building. Then they let it pick up our scent. They may be planning to prolong the pursuit until we abandon all hope and just wait helplessly for the worst to happen."

He gave her no time to reply. Tightening his grip on her hand he pulled her forward, his voice urgent, rising a little as the distance beneath them dwindled and they could see the shining expanse of metal at the base of the stairway.

"I didn't tell you that to frighten you. But we've got to build up our mental defenses fast. You've got to try not to think of it as a bloodhound. Our instinctive fear of insects isn't as great as our fear of savage, wolf-like animals. Bloodhounds aren't wolf-like, but to a pursued man there are no beasts more sinister. We must keep thinking of it as an insect."

"Are you sure that will help, David? An insect so large—"

"On Earth all insects are small. It's natural for us to think of them as small. Remember, man's fear of insects is real enough. But it can be overcome, thrown off. All small, crawling things make us recoil in revulsion. But the bloodhound image strikes a deadlier chord of fear. We've got to shut our minds to it."

"Then why didn't you keep silent about it? If you hadn't told me, if I hadn't known at all—"

"You had to know. You can't fight the Unknown, can't use the right mental weapons unless you know exactly what it is you've got to overcome. Full knowledge first, and then a choice of weapons. We're choosing a weapon that will clamp a mental block on that knowledge where it has sharp points of deadliness. We'll keep it limited, but we won't forget the danger. The weapon we're choosing is—a controlled self-hypnosis."

Janice flushed and flashed a quick glance at him. She was still trembling, breathless with hurrying, but the strain in her eyes had diminished a little. "Darling, I—I'm sorry. I pleaded with you to tell me. I guess I was being stupidly unthinking and irrational."

"I only told you because I thought it would cut down the danger. You've got to do your best to substitute another, less destructive fear. You're in a garden and a spider is moving slowly toward you across a gleaming web. But even if it's a black widow spider you don't succumb to panic. You know that you have time to leap up and run swiftly out of the garden."

"But I could also reach out and crush the spider between my thumb and forefinger. Or stamp on it. Shake it from the web, and mash it into a pulp. But we're not in a garden on Earth, David. We're trapped on an alien world, with not even a garden wall to protect us. How can we hope to outdistance an insect larger than we are? You said yourself that insects can move with lightning speed."

"Not this particular insect, perhaps. In the building it seemed to move slowly, with a shuffling sound. I was afraid it could move swiftly and that made me hesitate to make a dash for the entrance. But now we can't afford to let such a possibility demoralize us. We've got to seize on the doubt and build it up in our minds. Build it up, do you understand? *Make ourselves believe it.*"

"But the creature is winged! David, I thought—"

"Don't think. Just make yourself believe. Not all winged insects can fly. The wings may be vestigial. You've got to believe that it's slow moving and blot its size from your mind. We instinctively think of insects as small, visualize them as small. Hold fast to that visualization. You can if you try."

"You mean deliberately distort the truth, cling to an illusion which we know, deep in our minds, can't possibly be true?"

"Only in regard to its size. It may well be slow moving. That margin of doubt gives us an advantage we'd be foolish to abandon. If we can control our fear in the right way we won't succumb to panic."

"The right way? Just what is the right way, David? How do you want me to feel?"

"As if you were being pursued by an insect on Earth. A dangerous insect, but small. We've got to stay alert to the danger without succumbing to a paralyzing fear. Just remember that it's not a baying, savage dog."

"All right, David. I'll try."

"Just will yourself to believe that we can save ourselves if we move fast enough. There's a very good chance that we can. We're in no more danger than we'd be if we were well ahead of a swarm of foraging army ants in the African jungle. We could outrun the ants easily enough by keeping our heads and keeping to the trail."

"You think they're trying to break down our resistance by making a deliberate attack on our minds. Is that it?"

"That's about it. We can't afford to lower our defenses for an instant. Our lives may depend on it."

"All right, darling. No doubts. It helps just to know we're together."

"We're close to the bottom now. Just twenty or thirty steps to go. But the glare's getting worse. We've got to be careful. They may be hoping we'll stumble."

"We won't, David. I'm watching every step."

"The steps are tricky. Stay careful and keep close to me. There are buildings straight ahead. Three or four, about two hundred feet from the bottom. I can just barely make them out."

"I can see them," Janice said quickly. "Just the roofs. They look more like shining disks hovering in the air. Are you sure they're buildings?"

"They're buildings, all right. The nearest one stands out when the brightness shifts a little."

"Yes…I can see it now. Quite plainly. Three buildings."

When they reached the bottom of the stairs, Loring paused for an instant to make a quick survey of the shining metal pavement directly ahead of them, and the nearest of the three buildings. The pavement was similar to the slightly mushrooming surface on the level above, widening out as it swept toward the buildings.

The brightness ahead was so dazzling that it was difficult to make out the massive foundations of the nearest glow-enveloped structure, but by straining his eyes he could tell that it was a far larger structure than the one from which they had escaped.

He did not regret having taken the gamble. It was better to be free and pursued than imprisoned with a gigantic insect in total darkness. The memory made his flesh crawl. It had never completely stopped crawling, but even a limited freedom of movement, a freedom that could end at any moment, was better than the feeling that you were hideously trapped and had no chance of keeping terror at arm's length. There was no chance at all if you waited in blind panic with the deadliness drawing closer, relentlessly closing in.

Any action was better than the paralysis of inertia, the helplessness which panic could bring about. Any action. He must keep remembering that. Must force himself to remember, keep all of his thoughts centered on the one aspect of the struggle that was vital when survival became the sole prize to be won, the only issue immediately at stake.

He looked at Janice and nodded, sensing the need for continued haste. They headed straight for the nearest building, with no exchange of words now, for they were both too sharply aware of the danger to experience a need to talk further about it or even to pause for breath.

CHAPTER TEN

It was hard for Loring to realize that they had reached the building so fast, harder still to accept the fact that they were almost inside of it. The high portals arched above them, glimmering in the radiance, and their shadows were flickering on both sides of the entranceway before he remembered that he had at first decided it would be wiser to bypass the structure—to circle around it and keep on fleeing.

Fortunately he had looked back and changed his decision without conscious deliberation, so instinctively that the wisdom of it did not dawn on him until he was less than forty feet from the base of the building. The quick, backward glance had shown him the pursuing insect clearly, etched sharply against the glow, and its terrifying nearness had made him change his mind almost automatically, with a nightmare-like absence of any clear-cut reasoning process.

Only now did he realize that the human mind cannot think or will anything, dreaming or awake, in a completely purposeless way. And he had certainly not been dreaming. The creature was so near, so close on their heels that they could not hope to outdistance it by running.

The building, then, was their only refuge. Into an imprisoning darkness again, but darkness was better than a hopeless attempt to escape pursuit in the open.

Darkness? How could they be sure? This building might be lighted, as bright within as without. And what could be worse, if you were trapped, with all escape cut off, than a blinding burst of illumination?

It could be far worse than any darkness. You staggered and fell, and the light burned through your eyelids into your brain, no matter how tight you tried to shut your eyes.

And through the radiance, through the burning glare that could not be shut out, you saw it coming toward you, its wings thrumming as it closed in with clashing mandibles, while the light turned red around it.

No, no—those were not his thoughts! He straightened and looked at Janice and was glad that she was not being tortured as he was. She was moving ahead of him now, very swiftly, but there was no wavering in her steps, nothing to indicate that a direct attack was being made on her mind.

For some reason they were attacking him only.

And almost unendurable as the torment was he could still recognize it as a mental distortion, a coldly merciless assault on his sanity.

He forced himself to resist panic, to remember that darkness was worse than brightness. It was always worse, because in total darkness unconscious fears, hidden and instinctive fears became monstrous. Darkness was the natural breeding ground for such fears; light, no matter how blinding, an aid in dispelling them. Man's remote ancestors had lived in dread of the coming of night, had huddled together in the darkness of the forest, in the depths of caves, fearing that another dawn would never come for them, knowing how sinister the night could be.

Night fears, hideous and distorted, haunted the dreams of every normal child. It haunted the dreams of savages, and cavemen far back in the Ice Age had crouched around rude fires, fearing an attack from shapes of the night both imagined and real. Cave bears, lions and tigers, invisible demons, the ghosts of the dead. It was darkness they feared, not light. Light, fire, and the dawn were all protections.

The light widened and the pillars on both sides of the building's entranceway dwindled and fell away. A vast interior swept into view. All about them enormous shadow-shapes loomed, beneath a ceiling so high that it had the depth-beyond-depth look of a stretch of open sky.

The ceiling was ablaze with light and the floor threw back the brightness in concentric circles of shimmering radiance, so that they seemed to lie looking at the shadow-shapes through a wavering prism that half blinded them. Then, gradually, their eyes adjusted to the glare and they saw the shapes clearly.

They were no longer shadow-shapes. They were articulated animal skeletons, so large that they would have dwarfed the largest of terrestrial dinosaurs. No Brontosaurus floundering through a Cretaceous swamp in the Age of Reptiles on Earth, no Triceratops or Trachodon had ever loomed so gigantic in Earth's primeval past. But in general aspect the skeletons were unmistakably reptilian, some with shrunken forelimbs, rearing postures and massive skulls armed with sharp teeth, others armor-plated and horned, with bony spikes projecting from their spines, long, angular skulls and short legs of uniform length.

There were three winged skeletons, flying monsters much larger than the horned monsters and a tortoise-like creature eighty or ninety feet in length. At its side stood one of its newly hatched young, with remnants of fossilized flesh still clinging to the splintered egg from which the far from tiny creature had emerged at some remote period in geologic time. The egg was also fossilized and so massive that it would have taken the combined strength of two men to lift it.

For an instant the sheer wonder of it drove all thought of danger from Loring's mind. He forgot where he was and was aware only of that long vista of gigantic skeletons stretching away into brightness. The exhibit dazzled and awed him, made him feel inconsequential, of no importance, a stunned human interloper on a drama of stupendous dimensions. For an instant nothing mattered except the almost hypnotic fascination which Nature imparts to everything colossal in scope and formidable in design.

Janice's voice broke the spell. "David, what are they? They're moving! They must be alive!"

Loring gripped her firmly by the arm and drew her close to him.

"No. It's just the light that makes them waver like that. We're looking at them through a shifting film of radiance. Can't you see? They're only skeletons. No flesh on the bones, no animation, nothing to become alarmed about. They must be gigantic extinct reptiles native to this world. This building is probably a museum."

Janice made no reply. She was staring wordlessly now, standing very still, as if something had started screaming inside of her and she was doing her best to subdue it.

"Size again," Loring said, making no effort to conceal his bewilderment but keeping his voice level. "A gigantic insect and now prehistoric reptiles much larger than you'd expect to find on a planet of this size. But it may have no particular significance. Animal life here may differ in size just as it does on Earth, over a wide range of species. Some of the animals native to this planet may be quite small."

Janice found her voice then. "Some of the living animals may be small. But how do you know these aren't the skeletons of living animals? Reptiles like these may be roaming the planet today. How do you know they're extinct? How can you be sure?"

Loring's voice did not change. He still spoke calmly, staring into the brightness; his eyes narrowed a little. "The bones look fossilized, eroded with age. That gravel pit look could be counterfeited easily enough, but it would be difficult to erase in a genuine fossil."

"Then you think—"

"I think they may want us to believe that there are forests and swamps here with reptiles like that at large in them. If this is a museum our taking refuge in it would suit their purpose very well. The building could hardly have been moved here for that purpose, as part of their plan. It just happened to be here, in our line of flight, and they're taking full advantage of it. You don't always need to rig an advantage in a deadly game of skill and cunning. Chance, blind luck, may sometimes provide a loaded, dangerously destructive pawn."

He nodded, conviction strong in his voice. "The pawn's loaded and they're making it more destructive by a deliberate assault on our minds. They're hoping these skeletons will slow us up, demoralize us just enough to make us easy victims when that insect comes in here after us. If it's following our scent, it won't waste any time."

Janice shuddered and looked at him, fear rising in her eyes again. "But we'll be at its mercy anyway. How can we get out? We couldn't be more hopelessly trapped."

"There may be another entrance. We've got to look for it. We've got to keep moving."

Janice made no reply. She had turned and was staring back at the shadowed columns just inside the entrance through which they had passed. Something huge and long-legged was emerging into the hall, its bulk blending with the shadows, and making it seem even larger than it actually was.

For an instant it hovered just inside the entranceway, swaying hideously back and forth, a shape of nightmare horror with many-faceted eyes, its bloated scarlet abdomen half-raised, its rapier-sharp stinger darting in and out.

Then it was advancing toward them, slowly at first and then more rapidly, with a violent quivering of its entire bulk. Loring looked around him in search of a weapon, but saw nothing that he could clasp and hurl. The bones of the skeleton reptiles were embedded in mountings and were too massive to dislodge. No weapon-shaped fragment could be chipped from them without making use of a knife or saw, and there were no cutting instruments in the vast hall. He had thought for an instant there might be paleontological tools left scattered about. But it was an insane thought and he put it quickly from him.

Vain hopes now could be dangerous, could result in a lessening of his alertness, a lowering of his guard. He was unarmed and defenseless, completely at the swift-moving creature's mercy. He only knew that it had to be stopped. It could not be allowed to attack and destroy him first and be free to turn about and attack Janice, sinking its cruel stinger deep in her flesh.

She saw it coming, and screamed in utter panic. It had bypassed Loring and was darting straight toward her, as if a female of the human species had aroused in it some instinctive awareness of how much better nourishment a more rounded, full-fleshed body would provide for its grubs.

It was instinct solely that prompted Loring to strip himself naked at that instant. Not to convince the fly that his own body was in any way comparable as a source of nourishment, but solely to protect the woman he loved. He needed a weapon. And the strange, sash-like garment, which engirdled his loins, was a weapon of a sort. It was not a weapon that could save them for long. But if he used it as a net, hurling it directly at the fly and entangling the creature in its folds—

The fly was almost upon Janice when the skillfully flung garment swirled above it, descended upon its head and wrapped itself around the rearing insect's upraised forelegs.

Loring had not completely let go of the garment, and he jerked back on it relentlessly, so that it became both a net and a strangling whipcord. It cut cruelly into the fly's substance and tightened in a quite terrible way.

Suddenly Loring saw that the fly had no head. Its head was in a fold of the garment, an enshrouded and bulging horror, still squirming, the huge compound eyes visible through the almost transparent cloth. The completely decapitated body was sinking jerkily to the floor.

He was still gripping the end of the garment, but he flung it from him suddenly with a shudder of revulsion, and turned.

Janice had slumped to the floor in a dead faint.

"Wake up," a cold voice said. "It is over now. You have won your struggle and are in a garden of delight."

There was a drowsy hum in Loring's ears, as of bees in a woodland glade. Not the hum of long-bodied hornets, cruel and rapacious, but the gentler hum of golden, honey-seeking bumblebees. And bumblebees did not sting if you did not anger them. They did not paralyze their victims to provide food for their grubs.

He awoke to an awareness of sunlight and shadow, garlanded bowers, grassy slopes and the gleaming bright waters of a stream. He blinked sleep from his eyes and rose to a sitting position.

He saw the women by the stream first, bare to the waist, their ivory breasts dew-bright in the dawn glow, their hips voluptuously curved. Some of the women were bending above the stream, filling long-necked, delicately fashioned urns with water. Others were bathing in the stream and had removed their garments completely.

Then, quite suddenly, Loring realized that there was no need for him to watch the women bathing. Or even the women who were bending with such tantalizingly sensual grace on the banks of the stream.

There were women much closer to him, attired in the same way or wearing no clothes at all. One of them was embracing him now, her arms creeping up under his...

He remembered the strange garment that had been placed upon him before an earlier awakening and how he had flung it from him. And he realized now that he was not encumbered by a garment of any sort.

He had felt a little embarrassed before, to be even lightly clad in Janice's presence. But he experienced no such embarrassment now. The woman closest to him was whispering soft words in his ear.

"You were very brave. You did not flinch or draw back when the hornet attacked. I adore men who are very strong, as you are, and completely sure of themselves. What a lover you will make! I have claimed you first and the others can wait. There is no need for them to grow impatient. No one woman could hope to exhaust the capacity for love of a man like you. There will be enough love for all. But I have claimed you first and you I shall have. Now. Kiss me, lover! Hold me close!"

She moved in his arms, and it seemed to him that he was clasping not one woman, but a hundred, each different in her knowledge of the dedicatory arts that can be learned only at Eros' shrine, but each a woman passionate and responsive and by the same token eternally the same.

One woman blending with many, her loveliness dissolving and reforming, but her ardor remaining constant, a living flame.

He heard himself whispering: "I am more human than you seem to believe. The struggle was almost too much for me. Without the solace of love I would not have had the strength to endure."

"You have that solace now," she whispered. "Kiss me, lover. And do not be a fool. All men are little boys at heart. At least, there is a little boy in them, buried deep in their nature—the little boy they once were. In moments of stress and torment that little boy lives again. It does not make them less manly, less sure of themselves when they desire a woman as you now desire me. Make love to me."

It was no longer in Loring's power to resist or to care how completely he abandoned himself to the woman in his arms. His desire, in fact, had already surpassed hers and he could find no fault with her ardor.

It came to him then that this was a real woman. The passion of her had stirred him as he had never been stirred before. He was in a whirlpool of passion. His lips were on her breasts that had swollen with desire; warm, soft, round, dazzling, spheres made for man's pleasure.

Caressing them, he remembered as if from some pre-existence that man's first desire was for woman's breasts, to draw the sweet milk of motherhood. The breasts burgeoning under him now, were incomparable.

Her body, that had been virginal a moment before, was moving in frenetic appeal. The heat of her passion was burning him. Heavens, he thought in sudden panic, supposing she gets pregnant? Gosh what will I do, siring a child by this creature? It's a sin. I've got to stop. He tried to withdraw, but it was too late. The seed of his loins was already fighting its way into her quivering body.

She knew what had happened. "Wonderful, wonderful," she cried stiffening her entire body in physical ecstasy. "My beautiful brilliant man." Then, with a little moan that was half pain and half pleasure, she went limp in his arms. Their mating was complete. Loring lay dazed and exhausted.

It was at that moment that he heard Janice scream. It seemed to him that a white-hot shaft of dread went through him before a coldness fastened on his heart, and he began to tremble violently. He thrust the woman in his arms almost brutally from him, and struggled to rise. It was a struggle, because the arms of other women had instantly entwined themselves about his arms and shoulders and even about his legs. It was as if they had mistaken his blind, fear-inspired brutality for rejection of one woman in favor of many, and thought of the many as themselves.

He thrust their arms aside, forced them to release him by smiting them cheek and thigh. He did it unconsciously, thinking only of Janice and what the scream might mean. But they seemed to take the blows as compliments and murmured: "What a lover! What a man!"

He saw her then—saw her above the straining white arms and tumultuously heaving breasts of women who seemed suddenly Medusa-like, the shadowy Gorgons of some monstrous dream.

She was struggling in the arms of a man who seemed in all respects the exact opposite of a brute. He had the body of an Athenian athlete in the days of Grecian splendor and his head was aureoled in gold. He was young and lithe-limbed and the band of gold which encircled his light blond hair, worn long, above the classic manliness of his features, glittered in the sunlight, giving him an almost Apollo-like aspect as he stood by the stream. Apollo, the Sun god.

Damn him to hell, Loring thought.

He knew nothing about how a woman would feel, but from his knowledge of women he could hardly doubt or question the man's undisputed right to consider himself literally brimming over with male sex appeal. He was the kind of man it was hard to imagine any woman resisting for long and yet Janice was struggling violently in his arms!

Loring had freed himself completely now and he lost no time in reaching the man's side. Greek athlete or not, the man had no chance at all and he seemed to realize it the instant he looked into Loring's eyes.

He released Janice and started to move backwards, away from Loring. But Loring did not let him retreat far. He dropped the repulsed Apollo to the ground with a savage right to the jaw.

CHAPTER ELEVEN

Tragor sat facing the Chief Coordinator for the second time in four days, and if he had been shaken the first time he was infinitely more alarmed now. His shoulders were trembling so that he was sure the Coordinator would remark about it, and all of the color had drained from his face.

"Tragor," Kraii said, his eyes piercingly accusing, "your plan for Earth conquest has been a disastrous failure from first to last. Subject a man to struggle and hardship, you said—place his life in danger, and he will find an android woman impossible to resist! Well, did that fool of an artist find thirty android women irresistible? Did he? Answer me, Tragor."

It did not seem as though Tragor's face could have gone any paler. But suddenly it did. It seemed paler than pale, as if the receding blood had turned it into a thin tissue so clueless that the term "color" could not even be applied to it.

"His surrender would have been complete if the Earthwoman had not screamed," he said. "All of his resistance was gone."

"Tragor, have you lost your mind? Two-thirds of the men in high places on Earth have women they love just as compulsively. And if we put your miserable plan into operation a good many women would scream. Just the sight of us would start them screaming. You have proved conclusively that the Plan cannot work."

Tragor started to rise, appalled by the sudden fury which blazed in the Coordinator's eyes. He recoiled backwards and as he did so a handgun clattered on the chart stand before him. Kraii had whipped the handgun from beneath the stand so quickly that it seemed almost like a conjuring trick. But to deceive the eye of a Martian frozen with terror was no great feat and Kraii knew it.

He seemed to enjoy the sudden look of stricken disbelief in Tragor's stare. He seemed actually to relish inflicting such an irrevocable choice of evils on a Martian completely at his mercy.

"Do it now, Tragor," he said. "If you put it off even for a moment you'll waver and lack the courage to kill yourself. Then we shall have to execute you publicly. Think of the shame and disgrace of a public execution, Tragor. I am offering you the easiest choice first. Do it immediately. Right here and now. When it is over, I'll aerate the compartment thoroughly, so you need not worry on that score."

"No, I can't! You're asking too much of me!"

Tragor recoiled another step, looking at the Chief Coordinator with an almost childlike simplicity of appeal that would have moved a Martian with a heart of stone. But if Kraii had a heart, it was certainly not of stone. Stone can be splintered and shattered and even dissolved. Quite obviously the fierce, dangerous and obdurate metal of the Chief Coordinator's heart was not in the least like stone.

"Oh, I know, I know," Kraii said. "It's customarily done after a decent interval, in the privacy of the condemned's own compartment. Watching you kill yourself will be very painful to me. But I am prepared to endure it for your sake. It will be easier for you this way.

"Think, Tragor. I'll be right here, close to you, and if you imagine for a moment that I am not still your friend you do me a grievous injustice. My nearness right up to the end should be comforting to you. A fellow Martian, sharing every one of your life drives, every compulsive emotion you've every experienced from the cradle to the grave. I did not blunder as you did, but that is the only real difference between us. Do you imagine for a moment that I do not sympathize with you?"

"No, no. Give me a little time. Only a few minutes," Tragor pleaded. "That's all I ask. Then if you can't—"

Tragor's voice broke on a strangled sob.

"Tragor, listen to me. You have a choice of two alternatives. You can either kill yourself—and that is the honorable way—or you'll be shamefully executed. Which will it be?"

Tragor took a slow step forward. It was a short step and it hardly seemed to bring him much nearer to the handgun. But to the Chief Coordinator it seemed a step in the right direction and his features relaxed a little.

"I'm glad you've decided on the honorable way, Tragor. It would be humiliating to be publicly executed in full view of a wretch like Sull. You are right in distrusting him. He hates you and will try to step into your shoes. I may even be compelled to permit it as a necessary expediency."

"No," Tragor said, slowly. "No one is going to step into my shoes—or over them when I am lying dead. Not even you."

Tragor had the handgun before Kraii could grasp the implications of a statement so unbelievable.

Tragor held the weapon firmly. He drew himself up and just as resolutely stepped quickly back from the desk again. But he did not raise the handgun to his own brow. Instead he narrowed his eyes and pointed the weapon directly at Kraii. He fired three times, straight across the chart table, aiming at the Chief Coordinator's heart.

The bullets struck Kraii just above the heart and went right through him.

Blood spattered on the chart table. It spattered also on the Chief Coordinator's resplendent uniform, his out-flung arms, his vacantly staring face. He fell straightforward across the chart table, and as he collapsed upon it Tragor fired for the fourth and last time.

He stood for a moment with the still smoking weapon in his hand, a cold, triumphant smirk on his face. The terrible hatred that had been generated within him by the Chief Coordinator's final taunts had dispelled every vestige of his fear and he was no longer trembling. In working off his fury on the lump of cold clay before him he had forgotten the meaning of fright. It was that way with most Martians. They could be demoralized by terror until an outlet for vindictiveness presented itself with overwhelming force. Then they became exacters of vengeance, cold, deadly, precise.

The fact that the Chief Coordinator had died without speaking marred just a little the completeness of Tragor's triumph. But not seriously, and he immediately set about taking the precautions that would turn that triumph into permanent victory for himself.

He stepped to the chart table, raised the slain Martian's taloned right hand, and coiled the limp talons firmly around the handgun, having taken care to wipe all talon prints from the weapon first. He left just a little slack, to make sure that when rigor set in the resulting contraction would not appear excessive, or cause anyone to question the naturalness of the "suicide's" grip.

Then he stepped back and surveyed his handiwork. He was well pleased with himself. By a near miracle psychology had played directly into his hands, the very psychology Kraii had accused him of neglecting in his appraisal of Earthmen.

It was taken for granted that no one—*no one*—would dare oppose the judgment of a Chief Coordinator. It was taken for granted that a handgun sent clattering before a condemned Martian could be used in only one way. That it should be turned on the Chief Coordinator himself was against all reason. It went contrary to the most powerful of ingrained psychological compulsions: a Martian's need to feel himself completely a Martian until the moment of his death.

But for one incredible moment Tragor had not thought of himself as a Martian. He had thought of himself as an instrument of destiny, set apart from all other members of his race by a plan for conquest he had spent half a lifetime in perfecting. It was intolerable that the Great Plan should perish with him. It was intolerable that he should die in any case.

His love of life was greater even than the Martian hunger for inflicting death. In that respect he was unusual. Among Martians, he was, perhaps, unique.

Tragor looked briefly and for the last time at the slain Coordinator's hated features, reflecting with satisfaction that no one— not even a Chief Coordinator—could maintain his dignity in death.

Then he turned and walked resolutely from the compartment.

He was half way down the passageway outside when he saw the woman he had taken captive and would have died to possess. She was advancing slowly to meet him and saw with amazement that she was clasping a handgun similar to the one he had just used with such deadly accuracy of aim. How, he wondered with a swift intake of his breath, had she managed to secure it? Had she stolen it, from one of the warrior-caste brutes? There could be no other way of explaining it, but—

He had no time to puzzle it out, because she raised the weapon suddenly and blew off his head, splintering and shattering the skull and filling the passageway with a drifting spiral of smoke.

"You beast!" she whispered. "You monstrous beast!"

CHAPTER TWELVE

A change in command on any level, on any world, must have instant repercussions. Morale will sag or soar. New faces will appear and grow authoritative and forbidding and old faces will dim and vanish. When the change is limited in scope, only small thrones totter. When it is planet-wide a new world of power comes into existence.

On Mars, the death of the Chief Coordinator produced a social, political, economic and military earthquake; or what, on Mars, was the equivalent of an earthquake. The Martian social structure was shaken to its foundations. Political power became a plum ripe for the plucking. A dozen taloned hands reached for it, but the hands of Sull were the most adroit and experienced.

Sull grasped the plum and began steadily to squeeze it, until it began to remold itself to his satisfaction. But it was not a remolding which could take place overnight, and while power was changing hands, demoralization gained a momentary ascendancy.

On Mars there was famine, pestilence and widespread vandalism. There was a wavering, an uncertainty, in Martian military planning. Orders were delayed or garbled, and the commanders of the Martian ships did not quite know what course of action to follow or how much leeway between the golden heights of a soaring prestige and the deadly shoals of treason.

That uncertainty generated a need for solidarity in action, and the Martian commanders, though wary and suspicious of one another, were drawn more closely together in their hatred of the common enemy. They became defiantly reckless, and for the first time Martian ships took to traveling openly in mass formation, in a display of armored strength which they foolishly imagined might bring Earth to its knees.

While Loring and Janice stood alone on Mars, in a small room with one window, under constant guard and completely at Sull's mercy, five Martian ships moved westward across the Eastern United States, and began deliberately to court—Armageddon.

Colonel Richard Clegman of the United States Air Force awoke from a dream of coffee cups set in a row, each cup steaming and unstirred, and blinked sleep from his eyelids. In his dream it hadn't been just the coffee cups that had upset him with their tantalizing aroma, which seemed to hover just beyond the less appetizing aromas of drifting smoke, vaporized rocket fuels and burning rubber. He had been annoyed by the barking of a dog just outside the high wire fence where four Intercontinental Ballistic Missiles stood on their launching platforms with their nose cones pointing skyward, their silvery tail fins resplendent against the dawn sky.

Dogs at a guided missile and bombing plane base were an anomaly he strongly resented, but could do nothing about. Air Force personnel in general were not in the least allergic to mascots and dogs and cats were mascots, of a sort. But so were pin-up blondes, and as Clegman did not have the kind of mind which might have permitted him, under certain circumstances, to confuse the two they remained forever distinct and poles apart in his thoughts.

A blonde pin-up met with his full approval, and he even carried one himself, in a small gold locket beneath his meticulously laundered officer's shirt. Only—he would not have cared to admit to anyone that the girl in the photograph was his wife. To do so would have been a betrayal, because it was important that the members of his command should think of him as a devil of a fellow who could trade Rabelaisian jests with the salty freedom which can come only from a wide range of experience in all fields of human warfare, not excluding the amorous.

That sort of thing made for tough-fibered camaraderie in action, as every experienced soldier knew. In fact, Clegman was quite sure that even John Paul Jones and Lord Nelson had played down the fact that they'd been one-woman men to keep shipboard morale on a gusty, universally shared "I've a big-eyed doll in Tokyo" level.

He had only to think about it for a moment for Korean War memories to come roaring back, with the deck of the Flat Top awash in the dawn and the big bombing planes warming up. Not as big as the jets of today but big enough.

"If I live through this one, Commander, I won't just phone Maizie. It's six dolls for me, if I have to burn up the wires and run into debt getting them on long distance and paying their fares on a Borling Special. How about you, Commander? I'll bet you've got a dozen cuties from Miami to Tahiti you're keeping mum about. I don't blame you—with brunettes at a premium and blondes and redheads so scarce you've got to dazzle them with at least seven wound stripes. How about it Commander? I'm sort of curious."

"That's my business."

"Oh, sure, sure. You could get sore and pull rank on me. But you won't. You're too human a guy. Why don't we form a pool and trade a few phone numbers? We could make it a party to end all parties. A real bang-up night. This time tomorrow we may he pushing up daisies—or sea anemones. How do the jokers put it? The daisies hammer you home. And then you're in a pine box, Commander, you'll sure as hell wish you hadn't let a single day go by."

"You're right about that, Lieutenant," Clegman could hear himself replying, even though it wasn't strictly true in his case. "I can't complain exactly. But there was a girl in Paris—well, if I'd dated her properly I might have been less worried than I am right now about being blown apart."

"Real curves, eh, Commander?"

"Real curves. And not just curves alone. There was a sultry-eyed something about her—"

"Commander, how many dames do you figure there are in the world? Ever stop to count them? I've been too busy myself to add up the sum total of the really special ones I've just missed meeting."

"I know what you're trying to say. There'll be plenty of choices ahead for both of us if we're lucky enough to be alive this time tomorrow. You don't have to draw me a diagram. I've been thinking along the same lines."

It hadn't been true, of course. There was such a thing as loyalty, and when you've met the one and only girl and married her at an early age it kept your far-roaming Casanova impulses from making you even want to talk like that. But you had no right to think only of yourself. A sternly straight-laced Commander could weaken the fighting strength of even a big Flat Top, with twenty planes serving for the moment as a kind of woman-substitute.

Clegman wasn't Puritanic, of course. In fact, he was the exact opposite of a blue-nosed killjoy... But you didn't need a hundred blondes if there was just one you thought of night and day. People could laugh if they wished, but he considered himself a very lucky guy.

He had then, and he still did, because he'd been married for fourteen years to the same blonde, and every time he met her she seemed like a new woman to him, because she was always making adorable little changes in herself.

Only, for the sake of keeping up morale, it was something he couldn't let the members of his command suspect. The full truth would have made them feel like outcasts, standing before the locked gates of paradise. So he kept the locket well concealed, and only took it out to whisper, "My darling," thirty or forty times a day.

If someone had asked him he would have lied without hesitation and insisted that it was a picture of Jayne Mansfield.

He was awake now, fully awake and not even the cups of black coffee he'd dreamt about could make more supportable the harsh realities of his command, or keep them at arm's length any longer. Besides, he had merely sniffed the coffee without tasting it and all of the cups had been whisked away out of sight by a dozen agile-fingered memories. Agile-fingered at first and then iron-fisted, and dominated by a pair of silver eagles.

The eagles were on the shoulders of his uniform, which was draped across a chair on the opposite side of the room. He found himself wishing that the eagles were maple leaves or, better still, the silver bars of a lieutenant. Hell—why stop there? A private's uniform would have suited him fine.

He luxuriated in the thought for a moment, thinking of how nice it would be to hop in a jeep and go calling on his wife, not caring if he was docked a month's pay and given eight days in the guardhouse. If only he could forget for an hour that the IBMs were Top Secret and had to be zealously guarded by high ranking officers every hour of the day and night.

Well, he couldn't and that was that. He had eagles to remind him that his duty was an awesome one and that he ought to feel proud. Probably he did, but when you started thinking in terms of tomorrow you felt humble and unimportant. Target Moon, Target Mars,

Interplanetary Guided Missiles. Not yet, but soon. And if one of them exploded on takeoff it would tear out your guts, because you'd know exactly what the big babies cost.

You couldn't build them overnight.

In addition to the IBMs, there were eight land-based bombers groomed for instant takeoff just south of the missile launching area and the entire base was under the command of a two-star general who did his best to be everywhere at once, but couldn't quite manage it.

Clegman often found himself wondering if the general wouldn't have preferred the less complicated duties of a master sergeant if it wouldn't have meant giving up such a massive kind of prestige. A colonel could demote himself in his mind without undergoing quite such an emotional wrench, but it was probably too much to expect of a general. He'd have to suffer in silence and delegate as much authority as he safely could to Clegman, who had earned his eagles the hard way, on a twice almost bombed-out Flat Top.

Clegman had to admit that almost everyone in the Air Force had earned his insignia the hard way, whether West Pointers or not. He supposed that went for the other branches of the Service as well but the Air Force was an island universe in itself, and he was well content not to look beyond it.

He wouldn't have too much minded being a two-star general but the private idea appealed to him more. Privates had no major headaches at all until they stepped out of line, which they were certain to do sooner or later.

But the penalties for minor infractions were seldom severe and privates had more freedom of movement on a guided missile base than any officer from a captain on up. His, Clegman's, own day was restricted from dawn to dusk, for in ways that were mysterious the IBMs had taken over command. They were like big-eyed owls awake all night in a whispering forest, and still awake in the daytime.

If you were not careful, an Intercontinental Ballistic Missile could lean on you. IBMs seemed to know exactly how to lean and seemed always to be whispering: "We're powerful preventives, chum. You created us and now we have a life of our own. If you don't treat us with respect—awe, even—we may decide to blow up the world!"

Basically it was absurd, perhaps, to think of the IBMs as alive. But were not all the weapons of men a little like fertile ghosts that could walk the world at will, and give birth continuously to offspring more deadly and specialized than themselves?

Had not the rude stone flints of Dawn Man given birth to bows and arrows and arrows to steel-edged weapons? And did not a good many African tribesmen today still think of weapons as the opposite of inanimate?

All forms of animism were primitive perhaps, but just how primitive was the nuclear fission bomb giving birth to the hydrogen bomb? All right—it was only the belief itself that was primitive and the modern world took a dim view of Dawn Age Man's animism. But dim or not, the view could still be frightening.

Clegman was startled out of his somber reverie by a shout from outside the Administration Barracks. When a missile is traveling at the speed of sound its sides pick up all kinds of echoes, subsonic, sonic and supersonic. The shout sounded like that, the human voice distorted, shrill with excitement and then dwindling to just below the threshold of ear-perceptible sound and yet remaining somehow chillingly audible.

The same instant there was a buzzing at Clegman's elbow. He leapt up and clicked on the intercom. A voice said inflexibly: "I've just sent out an emergency alert, sir! Didn't dare wait to contact you. You might not have believed it and a delay of even half a minute—"

"Fraser! What the hell are you talking about? Are you drunk, Captain?" Clegman almost shouted the words, an angry flush creeping up over his cheekbones.

"I was never more sober," the voice said, with unruffled firmness. "Go to the window and look out. The south end of the missile area. You can see them from the barracks now, I think. A moment ago I might have had to talk you into going outside and we'd have wasted precious seconds. I'll take all responsibility for the alert, Colonel."

"You certainly will!" Clegman shouted, his shoulders shaking a little as he clicked off the intercom. "Remember that at the court martial!"

He crossed to the window in four long strides and looked out.

"Oh, Lord!" he breathed.

He had always been a doubter. The Air Force had insisted, as it had every right to do on the basis of available evidence, that flying saucers could be given no support at all in official quarters. It had never stated categorically that the numerous reported sightings could be all explained away in easy and facile fashion, but it had maintained a sound, sane and entirely justifiable attitude in regard to them. That attitude was everlastingly to the Air Force's credit. Even now Clegman could find no fault with it. It was just that—here at last was the evidence!

They were coming in over the southern tip of the missile area, still a half-mile or more from the base and flying at a very low altitude. Five immense silvery disks, their edges glinting in the dawn light, their summits slightly turreted.

Later, Clegman was never quite able to decide just what convinced him that the five UFOs had no intention of passing over the base without launching an attack upon it. But something did—a warning signal deep in his mind, a premonition that he had no right to delay a counter-decision for another half-minute. In the absence of the General—just where the General might be he did not even stop to ask himself—it was up to him.

The invading UFOs were committing an act of armed aggression by flying over an IBM base whether they knew it or not. And both consciously and unconsciously—deep in his mind—Clegman was overwhelmingly convinced that they did know it. It was a very big country. An IBM base was a mere pinpoint on the map and the presence of Unidentified Flying Objects in the sky above it could not possibly have been coincidental.

The long arm of coincidence could never stretch that far—not in a million years or anywhere in space or time.

It was up to Colonel Richard Clegman, who had earned his insignia the hard way on a smoke blackened Flat Top. Being a man of strength and a man of decision, Clegman acted without hesitation and with no feeling of guilt. He gave the signal for the launching of an all-out guided missile and jet bomber attack.

Corporal Thomas Walton would always think of it as a day to remember. But if anyone had told him that he would occupy a full page in the elementary school history books of the late twentieth century he would have refused to believe it, for he was an extraordinarily modest young man.

There can be no doubt, however, that a full page was no more than his due. Circumstances alone can create a legend, a hero-image and when a man risks his life in a hazardous undertaking it is not too important that he is merely carrying out orders and performing a duty which he might, with complete freedom of choice, prefer to avoid.

Corporal Thomas Walton was the first United States soldier to see a Martian face to face.

The Martian ship was a smoking, half-telescoped mass of wreckage and how a living Martian could have survived deep in the hull, in the midst of what must have been a raging inferno, was not an easy enigma for the scientists to unravel or the newspaper-reading public to grasp. The TV-viewing public would have liked very much to see that particular Martian but he died soon afterwards and was never televised. There were eight hundred Martian captives to question, and TV coverage remained so overburdened for days that viewers did not feel any pronounced sense of outrage until it was too late to rectify an official blunder that was tragic from a documentary point of view.

Fortunately Corporal Walton did see that first remarkable survivor—saw him close and saw him plain. He had been advancing cautiously toward the wreckage with a Geiger counter, which was not clicking, and a protective helmet that he had just started to take off. Neither the Geiger counter nor the helmet were of any particular value to him, for the wreckage was not radioactive and never had been.

The Martian ships had been attacked by both guided missiles and swooping jets. Three successive bombing attacks had been launched against them. But the small, intermediate-range ballistic missiles had not carried atomic warheads and neither had the jets. The towering, silver-finned IBMs had remained on their launching pads, their destructive potential quiescent and unchallenged. It had been a World War II-type bombing attack, but so sudden, fierce and unrelenting that two of the Martian ships had gone down in flames and another had been forced to land and disgorge its entire crew. The two remaining ships had flown lopsidedly westward, trailing clouds of smoke, too crippled to retaliate with more than a single blast of searing fire. The blast had struck far west of the missile base, blackening two acres of woodland, but missing the base completely.

A slender jet had gone in pursuit of the fleeing disks, and that one jet had been armed in a more formidable way—with a small, gray-nosed atomic projectile. The fleeing disks had not returned.

Corporal Walton was remembering all this as he drew near to the wreckage of the only ship that was still smoldering after five hours of exposure to fire-extinguishing vapor showers from two circling planes.

Precaution demanded that he follow decontamination unit procedures even if the Geiger failed to click, for there was always the danger that there might be unknown and hitherto unsuspected forms of radiant energy in proximity to an UFO which would not register on a G-Muller counter.

But Corporal Walton liked to think that he could determine such things for himself and had suddenly decided to lift his helmet to get a better view of the smoke-enveloped ship.

He did so, standing very still, letting the immense weight of Army discipline and tradition wash over him for an instant like a tidal wave, appalled by his own audacity in defying it and more than a little frightened.

He was taking a dreadful risk and he knew it. There *could* be unknown forms of radiant energy that might seep into his bones and remain undetected for years, a slow but deadly radioactive blight which would kill him before he was forty. He wanted to live to be ninety, but he wouldn't have a chance if he went on taking risks like this.

He saw the Martian before the Martian saw him. He saw the hideous, mask-like face, smoke-blackened, and the talons that were creeping toward him in a blind fumbling that might have moved him to pity if he had not been too terrified to do anything but recoil backwards with a scream.

The Martian shuddered convulsively, as if a human scream at such a moment was more than he could endure. Perhaps he had heard too many human screams. Perhaps he did not want to hear any more or perhaps it was just pain which caused him to shut his eyes quickly and just as quickly open them again and fasten them on the youth standing white-lipped and trembling before him.

"I did not want to come to Earth," the Martian said. "I am too young to die. I knew this would happen. We are cruel—and we are merciless. But I was never quite like that. There are a few of us who are not like that."

The Martian was silent for an instant and then he whispered: "It is your world again. We took some of it from you, and we would have taken it all. But the Plan is shattered forever now. We give back what we have taken. It is completely your world again."

EPILOGUE

Sull, wearing the resplendent garments which only a Chief Coordinator new to his high station and completely sure of himself would have dared to flaunt in the face of envious subordinates, stepped into the compartment where Loring and Janice stood waiting and slightly inclined his head.

"We are taking you both back to Earth," he said. "You have convinced me that you have a strong bargaining point. Five of our ships made the very stupid mistake of flying in mass formation within range of an air-alerted missile and bombing plane base in the Eastern United States. Three of the ships have been destroyed and eight hundred Martians have been taken captive. Our only desire now is to depart from Earth as quickly as possible and never return.

"But, as I have said, eight hundred Martians have been taken captive. We should like to see them released and returned to us. We should also like to have a man like yourself plead our cause with the men and women who are in a position to make decisions on Earth, and institute measures which will give us at least a reasonable assurance that those decisions will be carried out and remain binding."

Loring nodded and looked Sull straight in the eye. "We would be fools to trust you to keep any pledge," he said. "But if you withdraw your ships we will have won at least a temporary victory. When you return—and you will, with another dangerous plan—you may find that our resistance may still be more than you had bargained for.

"There is one supreme glory in life which men do not hold lightly. That glory is unknown to you. You will never understand it. It turns night into day for us and transforms every aspect of reality. If men and women could not love, they would be as crippled as Martians in body and mind, for what you call love is a hollow mockery. A surrender to passion is only the beginning. It must grow and brighten until it fills the world with its creative splendor."

THE END

STRANGERS ON A STRANGE WORLD...

The ship had crash landed on an alien world, burning to death the two parents of two small children on board. Although thoroughly jostled and bruised, Dee and her little brother Petey had somehow survived. Comprehending their horrible situation wasn't easy for a child of eight! But, gathering up all the courage she could muster, she set off exploring the area near the ship. What she found, was a large garden, and a lot of very big, ugly, and overly curious, bugs!

Veteran science fiction author Judith Merril has presented here a fascinating and convincing picture of the thought-processes of a different species on a far-off world. It's a tale filled with unusual adventure and thought-provoking situations.

ABOUT JUDITH MERRIL

Judith Merril…

…was born Judith Josephine Grossman on January 21, 1923 in Boston, Ma. In 1936, Judith m oved to New York City, where she pursued Zionism and Marxism. She took the pen-name Judith Merril about 1945, and began writing professionall y, speci alizing in short stories about sports. She publi shed her first sci ence-fiction story, "That Only a Mother," in John Campbell's *Astounding Science Fiction* in 1948. A short time later, Merril began editing science fiction short story anthologies in 1950—especiall y a popular "Year's Best" story-anthology series that ran from 1956 to 1967—and published her last in 1985. In her editorial introductions, talks and other writings, she actively argued that science fi ction should no longer be i solated, but become part of the literary mainstream. In the late 1960s, Merril moved to Canada, and was an active organizer and promoter of science fiction. She became a Canadian citizen in 1976. From 1978 to 1981 Merril introduced Canadian broadcasts of *Doctor Who*. She passed away on Sept. 12, 1997.

HOMECALLING

By
JUDITH MERRIL

ARMCHAIR FICTION
PO Box 4369, Medford, Oregon   97501-0168

*For more information about Armchair Books and products, visit our
website at…*

www.armchairfiction.com

Or email us at…

armchairfiction@yahoo.com

CHAPTER ONE

THERE WAS no warning. Deborah heard her mother shout, *"Dee! Grab the baby!"*

Peter's limbs hung loose; his pink young mouth fell open, as he bounced off the foam-padded floor of the play-space, hit more foam on the sidewall at a neat ninety-degree angle, and bounced once more. The small ship finished upending itself, lost the last of its spin, and hurled itself surfaceward under constant acceleration. Wall turned to ceiling, ceiling to floor and Petey landed smack on his fat bottom against the foam-protected toy-bin. Unhurt but horrified, he added a lusty wail to the ever-shriller screaming of the alien atmosphere, and the mighty reverberations of the rocket's thunder.

"...the bay-*beeee...Dee!"*

"I got him." Deborah hooked a finger finally through her brother's overall strap, and demanded: "What do I do now?"

"I don't know; hold on to him. Wait a minute." Sarah Levin turned her head with difficulty toward her husband. "John," she whispered, "what's going to happen?"

He gnawed at his lower lip, tried to quirk a smile out of the side of his mouth nearest her. "Not good," he said, very low.

"The children?"

"Dunno." He struggled with levers, frantically trying to fire the tail rockets—now, after their sudden space-somersault became the forward jets. "Don't know what's wrong," he muttered fiercely.

"Mommy, it hurts..."

Peter was really crying now, low and steady sobbing, and Dee whimpered again, "It hurts. I can't get up."

"Daddy's trying to fix it," Sarah said. "Dee...listen..." It was hard to talk. "If you can, try to...kind of wrap yourself around Petey..."

"I *can't*..." Deborah too broke into sobs.

Seconds of waiting, slow eternal seconds; then incredibly, a gout of flame burst out ahead of them.

The braking force of the forward rocket eased the pressure inside, and Dee ricocheted off a foamed surface—wall, floor, ceiling? She didn't know—her finger still stuck tight through Petey's strap. The ground, strange orange-red terrain with towering bluish trees, was close. Too close. There was barely time before the crash for Sarah to shout a last reminder.

"...*right around him!*" she yelled. Dee understood; she pulled her baby brother close to her chest and wound her arms and legs around his body. Then there was crashing splintering, jagged noise through all the world.

IT WAS too warm. Dee didn't want to look, but she opened an eye.

Nothing to see but foam-padded sides of the play space, with the toys scattered all over.

A bell jangled, and a mechanical voice began: "Fire...Fire...Fire...Fire...Fire..." Dee knew what to do. She wondered about letting go of Petey, but she'd have to, she couldn't ask her mother, because the safety door was closed. Her mother and father were both on the other side in front—that was where the fire would be. She wondered if they'd get burned up, but let go of Petey, and worked the escape lock the way she'd been taught. While it was opening, she put on Petey's oxy mask and her own. She didn't know for sure whether they would be needed on this planet, but one place they'd been, called Carteld, you had to wear a mask all the time because there wasn't enough oxygen in the air.

She couldn't remember the name of this planet. They'd never been here before, she knew that much; but this must be the one they were coming to, or Daddy wouldn't have started to go down, and everything wouldn't have happened.

That meant probably, at least the air wasn't poisonous. They had spacesuits and helmets on the ship, and Dee had space-suit drill every week; but she was pretty sure she didn't need anything more than the mask here. And there wasn't time for space-suits anyhow.

The lock was all the way open. Deborah went to the door and recoiled before the blast of heat; it was burning *outside*. Now she had to get away, quick.

She picked up Petey, looked around at all the toys, and at the closet where her clothes were; at the blackboard, the projector, and the tumbled pile of fruit and crackers on the floor. She bent down and stuffed the pockets of her jumper with the crumbly crackers and smashed sticky fruit. Then she looked around again, and felt the heat coming through the door, and had to leave everything else behind.

SHE CLIMBED out, and there were flames in back. She ran, with Petey in her arms, though she'd been told never to do that. She ran straight away from the flames, and kept going as long as she could; it was hard work, because her feet sank into the spongy soil at every step. And it was still hot, even when she got away from the rocket. She kept running until she was too tired, and began to stumble, then she slowed down and walked—until Petey began to be too heavy, and she couldn't carry him any more. She stopped, and put him down on the ground and looked him over. He was all right, only he was wet—very wet—and the whole front of her jumper was wet too, from him.

Deborah scowled, and the baby began to cry. She couldn't stand that, so she smiled and tried playing games with him. Petey wasn't very good at games yet, but he always laughed and stayed happy if she played with him. Sometimes she thought he liked her better than anybody else, even Mommy. He acted that way. Maybe it was because she was closer to his size—a medium size giant in a world full of giant-giants; that's how people would look to Petey.

When he was happy again, she gave him half a cracker from her pocket, and a piece of fruit for his other hand. He tumbled over backwards, and lay down, right on the muddy grounds, smearing the food all over his face and looking sleepy.

Sooner or later, Dee knew, she was going to have to turn around and look back, meanwhile, she sat on the ground, cross-legged, watching Peter fall asleep. She thought about her ancestors, who were pioneers on Pluto, and about her father and how brave he was. She thought once, very quickly, about her mother, who was maybe all burned up now.

She had to be brave now—as brave and strong as she knew, in her own private self, she really was. Not silly-brave the way grown-ups expected you to be, about things like cuts and antiseptics, but deep-down *important brave*. She was an intrepid explorer on an alien planet, exposed to unknown dangers and trials, with a helpless infant under her wing to protect. She turned around and looked back.

HER OWN footsteps faced her, curving away out of sight between two tall distant trees. She looked harder in the direction they pointed to, if the fire was still burning, she ought to be able to see it. The trees were far enough apart, and the ground was clear between them—clearer than any ground she'd ever seen before. There were no bushes or branches near the ground, higher than a rocket-launch—tall yellow orange poles with whispering foliage at the top.

The overhead canopy was thick and dark, a changeable ceiling with grey and green and blue fronds stirring in the air. She couldn't see the sky through it at all, or see beyond it to find out whether there was any smoke. But that made it dark here, underneath the trees, so Dee was sure she would be able to see the fire, if it was still going.

She got up and followed her own footsteps back, as far as she could go without losing sight of Petey that was the spot where the trail curved away in a different direction. It curved away she saw farther on; that was strange, because she was sure she'd been going in a straight line when she ran away. The trees all looked so much alike, it would have been hard to tell. She'd heard a story once about a man who went around and around in circles in a forest till he starved to death. It was a good thing that the ground was so soft here, and she could see the footprints so clearly.

Petey was sound asleep. She decided she could leave him alone for a minute. She hadn't seen any wild beasts or animals, or heard anything that sounded dangerous. Deborah started back along her own trail, and at the next bend she saw it, framed between two far trees: the front part of the rocket, still glowing hot, bright orange red like the persimmons Daddy had sent out from Earth one time. That was why she hadn't been able to see it before, the color was hardly different from the ground on which it stood: just barely redder.

Nothing was burning any more.

"Mommy!" Deborah screamed, and screamed it again at the top of her lungs.

Nothing happened.

She started to run toward the rocket, still calling; then she heard Peter yelling, too. He was awake again and she had to turn around and run back, and pick him up. Then she started the trip all over again, much slower. Petey was dripping wet now, and still hollering. And heavy. Dee tried letting him crawl, but it was too slow. Every move he made, he sank into the soft ground an inch or so; then he'd get curious and try to eat the orange dirt off his fingers, so she had to pick him up again.

By the time they got back to the rocket, Dee was wet all over, plastered with the dirt that Petey had picked up, and too tired even to cry when nobody answered her call.

CHAPTER TWO

THE LADY OF THE HOUSE sat fat with contentment on her couch, and watched the progress of the work. Four of her sons—precision masons all—performed deft maneuvers with economy and dispatch; a new arch took place before her eyes, enlarged and redesigned to suit her needs.

They started at the floor, sealing the jagged edges a full foot farther back on either side than where the frame had been before. They worked in teams of two, one to stand by and tamp each chip in place with sensitive mandibles, smoothing and firming it into position as it set; the other stepping off to choose a matching piece from the diminishing pile of hardwood chips, coating it evenly with liquid plastic from his snout and bringing it, ready for placement in the arch, just at the instant that his brother completed the setting of the preceding piece.

Then the exchange in roles: the static partner moving off to make his choice; the second brother setting his new chip in perfect pattern with the rest. Two teams, building the two sides of the arch in rhythmic concert with each other. It was a ritual dance of function, a mosaic of color and motion and form, chips and plastic, workers and work, each in its way—an apparently effortless inevitable detail of the whole. Daydanda gloried in it.

The arch grew taller than ever before, and the Lady's satisfaction grew enormous, while her consort's fluttering excitement mounted. "But *why?*" he asked again, still querulous.

"It is pleasant to watch."

"You will not use it?" He was absurdly hopeful.

"Of course I will!"

"But, Lady...Daydanda, my dearest, Mother of our children, this whole thing is unheard of. What sort of example...?"

"Have you ever," she demanded coldly, "had cause to regret the example I set to my children?"

"No, no, my dear, but..." She withdrew her attention entirely, and gave herself over to the pure esthetic delight of watching her sons—the two teams of masons—working overhead now on the final span of the arch, approaching each other with perfect timing and matched instantaneous motions, preparing to meet and place the ceremonial center-piece together.

Soon she would rise, take her husband's arm and experience— for the first time since her initial Family came to growth—the infinite pleasure of walking erect through her own door into the next chamber.

Even the report, shortly afterwards, of a fire spreading on the eastern boundary, failed to diminish her pleasure. She assigned three fliers to investigate the trouble, and dismissed it from her mind.

CHAPTER THREE

FOR A LONG, long time Deborah sat still on the ground, hugging Petey on her lap, not caring how wet he was, nor even try- ing to stop his crying—except that she rocked gently back and forth in a tradition as ancient as it was instinctive. After a while, the baby was asleep; but the girl still sat cross-legged on the ground, her shoulders moving rhythmically, slower and slower, until the swaying was almost imperceptible.

The rocket—the shiny rocket that had been new and expensive a little while ago—lay helpless on its side. The nozzles in the tail, now quiet and cool, had spouted flame across a streak of surface that stretched farther back than Dee could see, leaving a Halloween trail of scorched black across the orange ground. Up forward, where the fire in the ship had been, there was nothing to see but the still-red glow of the hull.

Deborah tried to figure out what flames she had seen when she left the ship with Peter; but it didn't make sense, and she hadn't looked long enough to be sure. She'd been taught what to do in case of fire: *get out!* She'd done it; and now...The lock was still open where she'd climbed out before. Very very carefully, not to wake him, she laid her baby brother on the soft ground, and step by reluctant step she approached the ship. Near the lock, she could feel heat; but it was all coming from one direction—from the nose, and not from inside. She touched a yellow clay stained finger to the lock itself, and felt the wall inside, and found it cool. She took a deep breath, ignored the one tear that forced its way out of her right eye, and climbed up into the rocket.

IT WAS QUIET in there. Dee didn't know what kind of noise she'd expected, until she remembered the last voice she'd heard when she left, saying calmly, "Fire...fire...fire..."

She thought that out, and knew the fire had stopped: then it was all right to open the safety door to the front part. Maybe...maybe they weren't hurt or anything; maybe they just couldn't hear her call. If there was just a *little* fire in there, it might have damaged the controls so they couldn't open the door, for instance.

She knew where the controls on her side were, and how to work them. Her hand was on the knob when she had the thought, and then she was afraid. She knew from T.Z.'s how a burning body smelled; and she remembered how hot the outside of the hull was.

Her hand withdrew from the knob, returned, and then withdrew again, without consulting her at all.

That wasn't any *little* fire.

If they were all right, they'd find some way to open the door themselves; Daddy could always figure out something like that.

If people ask, she told herself, *I'll tell them I didn't know how.*

"Mommy," she said out loud. "Mommy, *please...*"

Then she remembered the tube. She ran to it and took the speaker off the hook, fumbling with impatience so that it fell from her hand and dangled on its cord. It buzzed—the way it should; it was working!

She grabbed at it, and shouted into it. "Mommy! Daddy! Where are you?" That was a silly thing to say. "Please answer me. Please. *Please!*" I'll be good all the rest of my life, she promised silently and faithfully, all the rest of my life, if you answer me.

But no one answered.

She didn't think about the door controls again. After a while she found she could look around without really seeing the locked safety door. She had only to try a little, and she could make-believe it was a wall just like the sidewalls, that belonged there.

EIGHT AND a half years is a short span of time to an adult; no one seriously expects very much of a child that age. But almost nine years is a long time when you're growing up, and more than time enough to learn a great many things.

Besides the sealed-off control room, and the bedroom-play-space, the family rocket had a third compartment, in the rear. Back there were the galley, bathroom facilities, and the repair equipment, with a tiny metals workshop. Only this last section held any mysteries for Deborah. She knew how to find and prepare the stored food supplies for herself and the baby; how to keep the wate-reuser and air-fresher operating; where the oxy tanks were, and how to use them if she needed them.

She knew, too, how to let the bunks out of the wall in the play space, and how to fasten Petey in so he wouldn't smother or strangle himself, or fall out, or even get uncovered in the night. And she knew where all the clean clothes were kept, and how to change the baby's diapers.

These things she knew as naturally and inevitably as a child back on Earth would have known how to select a meal on the push-panel, how to use the slide-walks, how to dial his lessons.

For five days, she played house with the baby in the rocket.

The first day it was fun; she made up bottles from the roll of plastic containers, and mixed milk in the blender from the dried supply. She ate her favorite foods, wore all her best clothes, dressed the baby and undressed him, and took him out for sun and air in the clearing blasted by the rocket jets. She discovered the uses of the spongy soil, and built fabulous mud castles while Petey played. Inside, when he was sleeping, she read films, and colored pictures, and left the T.Z. running all the time.

The second day, and the third, she did all the same things, but it wasn't so much fun. Petey was always crying for something just when she got interested in what she was doing. And you couldn't say, "Soon as I finish this chapter," because he wouldn't understand.

Deborah got bored; then she began to get worried, too.

AT FIRST, she had known that help would come; the people who lived on this planet would come looking for them. They'd rescue her and Petey; she'd be a heroin, and perhaps they'd never even ask if she knew how to open that door.

The third day, she began to think that perhaps there weren't any people on the planet at all—at least not on this part of it. There always had been a few people at least, whenever they went any place. The Government didn't send out survey engineers or geologists, like John and Sarah Levin, until after the first wildcat claims began to come in from a new territory. But this time maybe nobody knew they were coming. Or perhaps nobody had seen the crash. Or maybe this wasn't even the right planet.

She worried about that for a while and then she remembered that her father always sent back a message-rocket when they arrived anyplace. He'd told her it was so the people on the last planet would know they were safe; if it didn't come at the right time, somebody would come out looking, to see what had happened to them.

Dee wondered how long it would take for the folks back on Starhope to get worried and come and rescue them. She couldn't even figure out how long they'd been in space on the way here. It was a long trip, but she wasn't sure if it had been a week, or a month, or more. Trips in space were always long.

THE FOURTH day, she got tired of just waiting, and decided to explore.

She wasn't bothering with the masks any more. The dials still said *full* after the first three times they went out, and that meant the air had enough oxygen in it so that the masks weren't working. So *that* was no problem.

And she could take along plenty of food. The only thing she wasn't sure about was Petey. She was afraid to leave him by himself, even in the play space, and he was too heavy to carry for very long. She took his stroller out and tried it, but the ground was too soft to push it when he was inside.

The next morning, early, Deborah packed a giant lunch, and took the stroller out again. She found out that, though it wouldn't push, it could be *pulled*, so she tied a rope to the front, and loaded it up with bottles and diapers and her lunch and Petey. Then she set off up the broad black avenue of the rocket jets; that way she could always see the ship, and they wouldn't get lost.

CHAPTER FOUR

DAYDANDA was tired. Truthfully, all this walking back and forth between chambers was a strain. Now she submitted gratefully to Kackot's fussing anxiety as he plumped the top mat here and pulled it there, adjusting the big new dais-couch to conform to her swollen body.

"I told you it was too much," he fumed. "I don't see why you want to do it anyhow. Now you rest for a while. You..."

"I have work to do," she reminded him.

"It can wait; let them think for themselves for once!"

She giggled mentally at the notion. Kackot refused to share her amusement.

136

"There's nothing that can't wait half an hour anyhow." He was almost firm with her; she loved to have him act that way sometimes. Contentedly, she stretched out and let her weight sink into the soft layers of cellulose mat. Her body rested, but her mind and eye were as active as ever. She studied the new shelves and drawers and files, the big new desk at the head of the bed. Everything was at hand; everything in place; it was wonderful. The old room had been unbearably cluttered. Now she had only the active records near her. Everything connected with the departed was in the old room, easy to get at on the rare occasions when she needed it; but not underhand every time she turned around.

Daydanda examined the perfect arch her sons had built, and exulted in the sight of it. When she wanted anything on the other side, all she had to do was *walk right through.*

She was aware of Kackot's distress. Poor thing, he did hate to have her do anything unconventional. But no one had to know, no one who wasn't really *close* to them..."

"Lady! Mother Daydanda!"

KACKOT'S image blanked out. This was a closed beam, an urgent call from an elder daughter, serving her turn in training as relay-receptionist for messages from the many less articulate children of the household.

"What's wrong?"

"Mother! The Stranger Lady has left her wings at last! She came out from *inside* them! And with a babe in arms! She...oh, Mother, I do not know how to tell it; I have never known the like. She is *not* of our people. The wings are not proper wings. She has no consort. A Family of *one!* I do not understand..."

"Be comforted, child. There is no need for *you* to understand." With her own mind seething, Daydanda could still send a message of ease and understanding to her daughter. "You have done well. She is *not* of our people, and we must expect many strange things. Now I want the scout."

The daughters mind promptly cleared away; in its place, Daydanda felt the nervous tingling excitement of the winged son who had been sent out to report on the fire in the east, and then to keep watch over the Strange Wings he had found there.

"Mother! I am frightened!" The message was weak; the daughter through whom it came would be struggling with her curiosity. She was of the eighth family, almost mature, soon to depart from the Household and already showing signs of individualism and rebelliousness. She would be a good Mother, Daydanda thought with satisfaction, even as she closed the contact with the scout and shut the daughter out with a sharp reprimand for inefficiency.

"There is nothing to fear," she told her son sharply. "Tell me what you have seen."

"The Strange Lady has left her Wings. She has not enough limbs, and she uses a Strange litter to carry her babe. She..."

"She is a Stranger, son! And you have already quite adequately described her appearance. If you fear Strangeness for its own sake, you will never pierce the treetops, nor win yourself a Wife. You will remain in the Household till your wings drop off, and you are put to tending the corral..."

AS SHE HAD expected, the familiar threat reassured him as nothing else would have done. She listened closely to his detailed report of how the Stranger had left her Wings, and set off down the blackened fire-strip, pulling behind her a litter containing the Strange babe and some Strange, entirely unidentifiable, goods.

"She has not seen you?" the Mother asked at last.

"No."

"Good; you have done well. Keep her in sight, and do not fear. I shall assign an elder brother to remain near the Wings, and to join you when the Stranger chooses her new site. Do not fear; your Mother watches over all." But when the contact was broken, she turned at once in perturbation to her consort: "Kackot, do you suppose...please, now, try to use a *little* imagination...do you suppose...?" She caught his apprehensive agreement, even before the thought was fully articulated; clearly that was the case. "The little one is no babe, but her consort!"

That put a different complexion on the whole matter. The flames of landing clearly could not be considered an act of deliberate hostility, if the Strange Lady's consort were so small and weak that he could not walk for himself, let alone assist in the clearing of a House-site. The fire thus assumed a ritual-functional aspect that made good sense.

If the explanation were correct, there need be no further fear of fire. And since the Strangers' march now was in a direction that would carry them toward the outer boundary of Daydanda's Houseland—or perhaps over it, into neighboring territory—there was no need either for immediate conflict of any kind.

Daydanda wondered that she did not feel pleased. As long as one assumed the smaller creature to be a babe, it would have meant that a fully-developed Mother was capable of leaving her home, and walking abroad...

Kackot, pacing restlessly across the big room, sputtered with derision. "A Mother," he reminded her irritably, "of a *very* Strange race!"

"Yes," Daydanda agreed. In any case, they had been wrong in assuming the smaller one to be a babe, simply because of size. Still, as she lay back to rest and think, the Lady was bemused by a pervading and inexplicable sense of disappointment.

CHAPTER FIVE

IT WAS VERY hot. After half an hour of sweat and glare, Deborah compromised with her first plan of staying out in the open, and began following a path just inside the forest edge. She kept one tree at a time—and only one—between herself and the "road." That way she had shade and orientation both.

Lunch time seemed to come quickly, judging from her own hunger. She stepped out from under the trees, and tried to look up at the sun to see how high it was. It was too bright; she couldn't look at it right. Then she realized she was fooling herself. You didn't need a clock if you had Petey. He would want his bottle before it was time for her to eat. She trudged on, dragging the ever-heavier stroller behind her. Petey just sat there, quiet and content, gurgling his approval of the expedition, and refusing to show any interest in food at all.

Dee might have been less concerned with her insides if the exterior were any less monotonous. It didn't seem to matter where she was, or how far she walked: the forest went on endlessly, with no change in appearance except the random situation of the great trees.

After a while, she stepped out again and sighted back to the rocket; then off the other way. The end of the blasted road was in sight now; but as far as Dee could see, there was nothing beyond it but more trees—exactly the same as the ones that stretched to left and right: tall straight dirty-yellow trunks, and a thin dense layer of grey-blue fronds high up on top.

At last Peter cried.

Dee was delighted. She tilted him back in his seat, and adjusted the plastic bottle in the holder, then fell ravenously on her own lunch.

When she was finished, she looked around again, more hopefully; at least they'd come this far in safety. Tomorrow, maybe, she'd try another direction, through the woods, away from the road. While Petey napped, she raised a magnificent edifice of orange towers and turrets in the soft dirt; when he woke, she pulled him home again, content.

Maybe nobody lived here at all; maybe the planet had no aborigines. Then there was nothing to be afraid of, and she could wait safely with Petey till somebody came to rescue them. She was thinking that way right up to the time she stepped around the tail-jets of the rocket, and saw tracks.

There were two parallel sets of neat V-prints, perhaps two feet apart; they came from behind a tree near the ship, went almost to the open lock, and curved away to disappear behind another tree.

Two not-quite-parallel sets of tracks; nothing else.

Dee had courage. She looked to see what was behind the tree before she ran. But there was nothing.

THAT NIGHT was bad. Dee couldn't fall asleep, even in the foam bunk, even after the long walk and exercise. She twisted and turned, got up again and walked around and almost woke Petey, and got back in bed and tried to read. But when she got tired enough to sleep, and turned the light out, she'd be wide awake again, staring at shadows, and she'd have to turn the light on and read some more.

After a while she just lay in her bunk, with the night light on, staring at the closed safety door to the control room, where her mother and father were. Then she cried: she buried her face in the pillow and cried wetly, fluently, hopelessly, until she fell asleep, still sobbing.

She dreamed, a nightmare dream with flaming V-shaped feet and a smell of burning flesh; and woke up screaming, and woke Petey too. Then she had to stay up to change and comfort him; by the time she got him back to sleep again, she was so tired and annoyed that she'd forgotten to be scared.

Next morning, she opened the lock cautiously, expecting to see…almost anything. But there were only giant trees and muddy orange ground: no mysterious tracks, no strange and horrifying beasts. And no glad crew of rescuers.

Maybe the V-tracks had never existed, except in that nightmare. She spent most of the morning trying to decide about that, then looked out again, and noticed one more thing. Her own footsteps were also gone; the moist ground had filled in overnight to erase all tracks. There was no way to know for sure whether she had dreamed those tracks or seen them.

THE NEXT two days, Dee stayed in the rocket. She was keeping track of the days now. She'd looked at the chrono right after they crashed, so she knew it was seven Starhope days since they came to the planet. She knew, too, that the days here were different, shorter, because the clock was getting ahead. The seventh day on the chrono was the eighth Sunday here; and at high noon the dial said only nine o'clock. She could still tell noon by Petey's hunger, and she wondered about that: his hunger-clock seemed to have set itself by the new sun already. Certainly, he still got sleepy every night at dusk, though the clock told three hours earlier each time.

Deborah spent most of one day working out the difference. She couldn't figure out any kind of arithmetic she'd been taught to do it with, so she ended up by making little marks for every hour and counting them. By evening, she was sure she had it right. The day here was seventeen hours instead of twenty. And then she realized she didn't know how to set days on the chrono anyhow; all that work was useless.

THE NEXT morning she went out again. Two days of confinement had made Petey cranky and Dee brave.

Nothing happened; after that, they went out daily for airings, as they had done at first. Dee made a calendar, and marked the days on that; then she started checking the food supplies.

They had enough of almost everything, too much to figure out how long it would last. But she spent one afternoon counting the plastic bottles on Petey's roll, and figured out that they'd be gone in just three weeks, if he kept on using four a day.

Someone would come for them before that; she was sure of it. Just the same, she decided that the baby was old enough to learn to drink from a glass and started teaching him.

Eight days became nine and ten, eleven and twelve; still nothing happened. There was no sign of danger nor of help. Dee was sure now that she had dreamed those tracks, but somewhere on this planet she knew there were people. There *always* were; always had been, whenever they came to someplace new. And if the people didn't come to her, she'd have to find them. Deborah began to plan her second exploratory expedition.

There was no sense in covering the same ground again. She wanted to go the other way, into the woods. That meant she'd need to blaze a trail as she went; and it meant she couldn't use the stroller.

She added up the facts with careful logic, and realized that Petey would simply have to stay behind.

CHAPTER SIX

THE BABY crawled well now, and he could hold things; he could pick up a piece of cracker and get it to his mouth. He couldn't hold the bottle for himself, of course, but...

She tried it, closing her ears to the screams that issued steadily for an hour before he found his milk. But he did find it: her system worked. If she hung the bottle in the holder while his belly was still full, he ignored it: but when he was really hungry, he found it, and wriggled underneath to get at the down-tilted nipple. That gave her, really, a whole day to make her trip.

The night before, she packed her lunch, and for the first time, studied the contents of her father's workshop. There was a small blowtorch she had seen him use; and even in her present restless state Deborah was not so excessively brave that the thought of a weapon, as well as tree-marker, didn't tempt her. But when she found the torch, she was afraid to try it out indoors, and had to wait till morning.

At breakfast time, she stuffed Petey with food till he would eat no more. Then she clasped a bottle in the holder she'd rigged up, set the baby underneath to give him the idea once again, and went outside to try her skill with the torch. She came back, satisfied, to finish her preparations. When she left, a second bottle hung full and tempting in the play space; Petey's toys were spread around the floor; and a pile of the crackers in the corner would keep him happy, she decided, if all else failed. There was no way to solve the diaper-changing problem; he'd just have to wait for her return.

AT FIRST, she tried to go in a straight line, marking every second tree along the way. After just a little while, she realized that it didn't matter which direction she took; she didn't know where she was going, anyway.

She walked on steadily, a very small girl under the distant canopy spread by the tall trees; very small, and insignificant, but erect and self-transporting on two over-alled legs; a small girl with a large hump on her back.

The hump disappeared at noon, or somewhat earlier. She stuffed the remaining sandwich and a few pieces of dried fruit into her pockets, and tied the emptied makeshift knapsack more comfortably around her waist where it flopped rhythmically against her backside at every step.

Never did she forget to mark the trees, every second one along the way.

Nowhere did she see anything but more trees ahead, and bare ground underfoot.

She had no way of knowing how far she'd gone, or even what the hour was, when the silence ceased. Ever since she'd landed, the only noise she'd heard had been her own and Peter's. It was startling; it seemed impossible by now, to hear anything else.

She stopped with one foot set ahead of the other in mid-step and listened to the regular loud ticking of a giant clock.

It was impossible. She brought her feet into alignment and listened some more, while her heart thumped sympathetically in time to the forest's sound.

It was certainly impossible, but it came from the right, and it called to her; it promised warmth and haven. It was just an enormous alarm clock, mechanically noisy, but it was somehow full of the same comfort-and-command she remembered in her mother's voice.

Deborah turned to the right and followed the call; but she didn't forget to mark the trees as she passed, every other one of them.

IF IT WEREN'T for the trail-blazing, she might have missed the garden entirely. It was off to one side, not directly on her path to the ticking summons. She saw it only when she turned to play the torch on one more tree: a riot of colors and fantasy shapes in the near distance, between the upright trunks.

Not till then did the ticking frighten her: not till she found how hard it was to move crosswise, or any way except right toward it. She wanted to see the garden. She had to see it. Most likely it was just wild, but there was always a chance...

And when she tried to walk that way, her legs didn't want to go. Panic clutched at her, and failed to take hold. She was an intrepid explorer on an alien planet, exposed to unknown dangers. Also, she was a Space Girl.

"I pledge my honor to do everything in my power to uphold the high standards of the human race," she intoned, not quite out loud, and immediately felt better. "A Space Girl is brave. A Space Girl is honest. A Space Girl is truthful. A Space Girl..."

She went clear down the list of virtues she had learned in Gamma Troop on Starhope, and while she mumbled them, her legs came under control. The ticking went on, but it was just a noise—and not as loud as it had been, either. She dodged scoutwise from behind one tree trunk to another, approaching the garden. If, indeed, it was a garden. Two trees away, she stopped and stared.

Every planet had strange new shapes and sights and smells; the plants in each new place were always excitingly different. But Dee was old enough to know that everywhere chlorophyll was green, as blood was red. Oh, blood could seem almost black, or blue, or pale pink, or even almost white; and chlorophyll could shade to dark grey, and down to faint cream-yellow. But growing gardens had green-variant leaves or stems. And everywhere she'd been, the plants, however strange, were unified. The trees here grew blue-green-grey on top. The flowers should not grow, as they seemed to do, in every random shade of color.

THERE WAS no way to tell the leaves from seeds from stems from buds. It was just…growth. A sort of arched form sprouted bright magenta filaments from its ivory mass. A bulbous some-thing that tapered to the ground showed baby blue beneath the many-colored moss that covered it. Between them on the ground, a series of concentric circles shaded from slate grey on the outside to oyster white in the center, only it was so thin that a tinge of orange showed through from the soil below. Dee would not have thought it lived at all, until she noticed a slow rippling motion outward toward the edges.

Farther in, one form joined shapeless edges with another; one color merged haphazard with the next. Deborah blinked, confused, and walked away, following the call of the great ticking clock, then mumbled to herself, "I pledge my honor to do every-thing…" She turned back to the puzzling growths again, aware now that the calling power of the sound diminished when she said the words aloud.

The colors were too confusing. She had to concentrate, and couldn't think about the garden while she talked to herself. Maybe the Pledge wasn't the only thing that would do it. She said under her breath: "That one is purple, and the other's like a pear…"

It worked. All she had to do was make her thoughts into words. It didn't matter what she said, or whether she whispered or shouted. As long as she kept talking, the summoning call would turn to a giant clock again, with no power over the movements of her legs. She went up closer to the baffling colored shapes, and made out a fairy-delicate translucent spiral thing and then a large mauve mushroom in the center.

Mushroom! At last she understood. They were so big, she hadn't thought of it at first: it was all fungus growth, and that made sense in the dim damp beneath the trees.

Strange it isn't every place, all over, she thought, and realized she was moving away from the garden again, and remembered this was one time it was all right to talk to herself out loud. "There must be some people here. Some kind of people or natives. That noise is strange, too. It couldn't just happen that way; somebody lives here…"

SHE DIDN'T want to touch the fungus, but she went up close to it. "Things don't just happen this way. That stuff would grow all over if it was wild; somebody planted it." She peered through the arch-shape to the inside, and jumped back violently.

The thing was lying on its side, sucking a lower follicle of the arch, its livid belly working as convulsively as its segmented mouth, its many limbs sprawled out in all directions.

Dee jumped away in horror, and crept back in fascination. "It doesn't know I'm here," she remembered to whisper. From around the other side of the bulbous growth she watched, and slowly understood.

"It's like some kind of insect." It couldn't really be an insect, of course, because it was two feet long—much too large for an insect. An insect this size, on a planet as much like Earth as this was, wouldn't be able to breathe. They'd explained about why insects couldn't be any larger than the ones you found on Earth in Space Girl class. But men had found creatures on other planets that did look a lot like insects, and acted a lot like them, too. And even though people knew they weren't really insects, they still called such creatures "bugs…"

Well, this thing was as close to an insect as a thing this size could be, Deborah decided. It was two feet long, and that made sense when you stopped to think about it, what with the tall trees and the giant mushrooms. She counted six legs, and then realized that the other two in front, resting quietly now, were feelers. The two front legs clutched at a clump of hairy shoots on the arched moss, almost like Petey holding his bottle. The back leg that was on top was longer than the front ones; it was braced against the arch for steadiness. The lower leg was tucked underneath the body; its lower middle leg also lay still on the ground, stretched straight out. The upper middle leg was busily scratching at a small red spot on the belly, acting absurdly independent of the rest of the feeding creature.

There was really, Dee decided, nothing frightening except the mouth. She looked for eyes, and couldn't see them, then remembered that some bugs on other planets had them on the backs of their heads. But that mouth...

It worked like Petey's on a nipple; but not like Petey's, because this one had six lips, all thick and round-looking instead of like people's lips, and all closing in toward each other at the same time. It was horrible to watch.

DEE BACKED off silently, and found herself walking the wrong way again. She tried the multiplication table while she made a circuit of the "garden," examining it for size and shape, and looking for a clear part that would let her see into the center.

She found, at last, a whole row of the jelly-like translucent things, lying flat and low, so she could look inside. The ground beneath them was scattered with flashing jewel-like stones...

No, black stones, with the bright part in the middle, she thought in words. *No, not the middle. At one end...*each stone was lying partly on an edge of the jelly-stuff...*about as big as my foot,* she thought, and saw the tiny feet around the edge of every stone.

Eyes on the backs of their heads, she thought, *and they have car...carpets? ...carapaces!* These bugs were smaller than the first one, and not frightening at all. Bugs only looked bad from the bottom, she realized, and instantly corrected that impression.

Something walked into the garden, and picked up four of the little ones. Something as tall as Dee herself when it went in, and half again as high when it left. It entered on four legs, and walking upside-down, head carried toward the ground, and looking backward...no, *facing* backward, *looking* forward. It entered calmly, moving at a steady even pace; approached the edge of the garden where Deborah watched the infants feeding...and froze.

An instant's immobility, then the big bug erupted into a frenzy of activity: scooped up the four closest little ones—two of them with the long hairy jointed arms (or legs? back legs?), and two more hurriedly with two front legs (or arms?)—and almost *ran* out, now on just two legs, the center ones, its body neatly balanced fore and aft, almost perfectly horizontal, the heavy hooded head in front, the spiny rounded abdomen in back.

It scuttled off with its four tiny wriggling bundles, and as it left, Dee registered in full the terror of what she had seen.

She fled...and by some miracle, fled past a tree she'd marked, so paused in flight to find the next one, and the next, and followed her blazed trail safely back. The ticking of the forest followed for a while, then stopped abruptly. But while it lasted, it *pushed* away as hard as it had pulled before.

CHAPTER SEVEN

DAYDANDA made the last entry in her calendar of the day, and filed it with yesterdays and all the others. Things were going well. The youngest Family was thriving; the next-to-youngest—the Eleventh—was almost ready to start schooling; ready, in any case, for weaning from the Garden. Soon there would be room in the nurseries for a new brood.

Kackot was restless. She hadn't meant the thought for him at all, but he was sensitive to such things now, and he moved slightly, eagerly, toward her from his place across the room—perhaps honestly mistaking his own, desire for her summons.

She sent a thought of love and promise, and temporary firm refusal. The new Family would have to wait. Within the Household, things were going well; but there were other matters to consider.

There was the still-unsolved puzzle of the Strangers, for instance. For a few hours, that mystery had seemed quite satisfactorily solved. When the Strange Lady left her Wings with babe-or-consort—now it seemed less certain which it was—to travel the path the flames had cleared for her, the whole thing had assumed a ritual aspect that made it easier to understand. Whatever strange reasons, motives, or traditions were involved, it all seemed to fit into a pattern of some kind, until the next report informed Daydanda that the two Strangers had returned to their Wings—an act no less, and no more, unprecedented than their manner of arrival, or their strange appearance.

They had not since departed from the—

The House? she wondered suddenly. Could a House be somehow made to travel through the air?

SHE FELT Kackot's impatient irritation with such fantasizing, and had to agree. Surely the image of—*it*—relayed by the flier-scout who had approached most closely, resembled in no way any structure Daydanda had ever seen or heard of.

But neither was it similar in any way, she thought—and this time guarded the thought from her consort's limited imagination—to ordinary, Wings, except by virtue of the certain knowledge that it had descended from the sky above the trees.

Today there had been no report. The Fliers were all busy on the northern boundary, where a more ordinary sort of nesting had been observed. When the trouble there was cleared up, she could afford to keep a closer watch on the apparently not hostile Strangers.

Meantime, certainly, it was best to let a new Family wait.

Laying was hard on her; always had been. And with possible action developing on two fronts now...

Kackot stirred again, but not with any real hope, and the Lady barely bothered to reply. It was time to bring the young ones in. Daydanda began the evening Homecalling, the message to return, loud and strong and clear for all to hear: a warning to unfriendly neighbors; a promise and renewal to all her children in the Household, young and old.

"LADY! OH, MOTHER!" Daydanda sustained the Homecalling at full strength, through a brief surge of stubborn irritation; then, suddenly worried—the daughter on relay knew enough not to interrupt at this time for anything less than urgent—

she allowed enough of her concentration to be distracted so as to permit a clear reception.

"*Lady!* ...nurse from east garden very frightened, confused message unclear...she wishes..."

"Send her in!" Daydanda cut off the semi-hysterical outburst, and terminated the Homecalling abruptly, with extra emphasis on the last few measures.

The nurse dashed through the archway, too distraught to make a ritual approach, almost forgetting to prostrate herself in the presence of the Lady, her Mother. She opened communication while still in motion, as soon as she was within range of her limited powers. Daydanda recognized her with the first contact: a daughter of the fifth family—not very bright, even for a wingless one, but not given to emotional disturbance either, and a fine nurse, recently put in charge of the east garden.

"The Stranger, Mother Daydanda! The Strange Lady...! She came to the *nursery*...she would have stolen...killed...she would have..."

To the nursery!

The Mother had to quell an instant's panic of her own before she could commence the careful questioning and reiterated reassurance that were needed to obtain a coherent picture from the nurse. When at last she had stripped away the fearful imaginative projections that stemmed from the daughter's well-conditioned protectiveness, it appeared that the Strange Lady had visited the Garden, had spied on the feeding babes, and then had departed with haste when the Nurse came to fetch them home for the night.

"The babes are all safe?" the Mother asked sternly.

"Yes, Lady. I brought them to the House quick as I could, before I came to you. I would not have presumed to come, my Lady, but I could not make the winged one understand. Will my Mother forgive..."

"There is nothing to forgive; you have done well," Daydanda dismissed her. "You were right to come to me, even during the Homecalling."

Breathing easy again, and once more in full possession of her faculties, the nurse offered thanks, and farewell, and wriggled backward out of sight under the arch, quite properly apologetic.

The Lady barely noticed; she was already in contact with the flier-scout who had been reassigned from the North border by the daughter on relay, as soon as the nurse's first wild message was connected with the Strange Wings.

It was a son of the eighth Family the same scout who had approached the Wings before a well-trained, conscientious, and devoted son, almost ready to undertake the duties of a consortship. Daydanda could not have wished for a better representative through whose sense to perceive the Strangers.

YET THERE was little she could learn through him. The Strange Lady had returned to the Wings...the *House?* More and more it seemed so...where the small Stranger presumably awaited her. Now they were both inside, and the remarkable barrier that could be raised or lowered in a matter of seconds was blocking the entranceway.

Perception of any kind was difficult through the dense stuff of which the...whatever-it-was: Wings? House? ...was made. The scout was useless now. Daydanda instructed him to stay on watch, and abandoned the contact. Then she concentrated her whole mind in an effort to catch some impression—anything at all—from beyond the thick fabric of...whatever-it-was.

Eventually, there was a flash of something; then another. Not much, but the Lady waited patiently, and used each fleeting image to build a pattern she could grasp. One thought, and another...a wave of feeling...a hope of some kind...another thought, and...

To Kackot's astonishment, the Lady relaxed suddenly with an outpouring of amusement. She did not communicate to him what she knew, or thought she knew, but abruptly confirmed all his worst fears of the past weeks with a single command: "I will go to the Strange Wings, oh Consort. Prepare a litter for me."

When she addressed him thus formally, he had no recourse but to obey. If she noticed his sputtering dismay at all, she gave no sign, but lay back on her couch, thoroughly fatigued, to rest through the night while her sons and daughters prepared a litter, and enlarged the outer arches sufficiently to accommodate its great size.

CHAPTER EIGHT

DEE WAS scared, and she didn't know what to do. She wanted her mother; it was no fun taking care of Petey now. She made him a bottle to keep him from screaming, but she didn't bother with his diaper or fixing up his bunk or anything like that. It didn't matter any more.

There were no people on this planet.

Nobody was going to rescue them; nobody at all.

It wasn't the right planet, at all. If anybody on Starhope got worried and went to look for them, it was some other planet they'd look on. It had to be, because there were no people here. Just *bugs!*

Petey fell asleep with the bottle still in his mouth, sprawled on the floor, all wet and dirty. Deborah didn't care; she sat on the floor herself and fell asleep and didn't even know she slept till she woke up, with nothing changed, except that the clock said it was morning.

And she was hungry after all.

She started back to the galley, but first she had to open the outer lock. She actually had her hand on the lever before she realized she didn't want to open it. She was hungry; the last thing in the world she wanted to do was look outside again. She went back and got a piece of cake and some milk.

Milk for Petey, too. If she got it fixed before he woke up, she wouldn't have to listen to him yelling his head off again. She started to fix a bottle, but first she had to open the lock.

This time, she stopped herself halfway there.

It was silly to think she had to look out; she didn't want to.

Petey was awake, but he wasn't hollering for once. She went back and got the bottle, and brought it into the play space.

"Open it," Petey said. "Come out. Mother."

"All right," Dee told him.

She gave him the bottle, went over to the lock, and then turned around and looked at him, terrified.

He was sucking on the bottle. "Come on," he said. "Mother waiting."

She was watching him while he said it. He didn't say it; he drank his milk.

She didn't think she was crazy, so she was still asleep, and this was a dream. It wasn't really happening at all, and it didn't matter.

She opened the lock.

CHAPTER NINE

ONCE SHE HAD flown above the tree-tops, silver strong wings beating a rhythm of pride and joy in the high dry air above the canopy of fronds. Her eyes had gleamed under the white rays of the sun itself, and she had looked, with wild unspeakable elation, into the endless glaring brilliance of the heavens.

Now she was tired, and the blessed relief from sensation when they set her down on the soft ground—after the lurching motion of the forest march—was enough to make her momentarily regret her decision. A foolish notion, this whole trip...

Kackot agreed enthusiastically.

The Lady closed her thoughts from his, and commanded the curtain at her side to be lifted. Supine in her litter, safely removed from the Strangers under a tree at the fringe of the clearing, her vast body embedded on layers of cellulose mat, Daydanda looked out across the ravaged black strip. And the sun, in all its strength, collected on the shining outer skin of the Strange Wings, gathered its light into a thousand fiery needles to sear the surface of her eyes, and pierce her very soul with agony.

Once she had flown above the trees themselves...

Now her sons and daughters rushed to her side, in response to her uncontained anguish. They pulled close the curtain, and formed a tight protective wall of flesh and carapace around the litter. And from the distance, came a clamouring bloodlust eagerness: the Big heads, waking in answer to her silent shriek of pained surprise. She sent them prompt soothing, and firm command to be still; not till she was certain they understood, and would obey, did she dare turn any part of her mind to a consideration of her own difficulties. Even then she was troubled with the knowledge that her stern suppression of their rage to fight would leave the entire Bighead brood confused, and useless for the next emergency. It might be many days before their dull minds could be trained again to the fine edge of danger-awareness they had just displayed. If any trouble should arise in the meanwhile...

SHE SENT instructions to an elder daughter in the House to start the tedious process of reconditioning at once, then felt herself free at last to devote all her attention to the scene at hand. Tomorrow's troubles would not have to take care of themselves till tomorrow. For now, there was disturbance, anxiety, and mortification enough.

That she, who had flown above the trees, higher and farther than any sibling of her brood, that she should suffer from the sunlight now...

"It was many years and many Families ago, my dear, my Lady."

Daydanda felt her consort's comforting concern and thought a smile. "Many years indeed..." And it was true; she had not been outside her chamber till this day—since the first Family they raised was old enough to tend the fungus gardens, and to carry the new babes back and forth. That was many years behind her now, and she had grown through many chambers since that time: each larger than the last, and now, most recently, the daring double chamber with the great arch to walk through.

The Household had prospered in those years, and the boundaries of its land were wide. The gardens grew in many places now, and, the thirteenth Family would soon outgrow the nursery. The winged sons and daughters of Seven Families had already grown to full maturity, and departed to establish new Houses of their own...or to die in failure. And through the years, the numbers of the wingless ones who never left the Household grew great; masons and builders, growers and weavers, nurses and teachers—there were always more of them, working for the greater welfare of the House, and their Mother, its Lady.

Through all those building, growing, widening years, Daydanda had *forgotten*...forgotten the graceful wings and the soaring flight; the dazzling sunlight, and the fresh moist air just where the fronds stirred high above her now; the bright colors and half-remembered shapes of trees and nursery plants. Not once, in all that time, had she savored the full sensory sharpness of *outside...*

She thought longingly of the nursery garden, the first one that she and Kackot had planted together when they lost their wings, while they waited for the first Family to come. She thought of it, determined to see it again one day, then put aside all thoughts, hopes, and regrets of past or future.

DAYDANDA directed that her litter be moved so that the opening of the curtain would give her a view of the forest interior. Then, while her eyes grew once again accustomed to their former functioning, she began to seek—with a more practiced organ of perception—the mind-patterns of the Strangers inside that frighteningly bright structure in the clearing.

It was hard work. Whether there was something in the nature of the dense fabric of the Wings, or whether the difficulty lay only in the Strangeness of the beings inside, she could not tell, but at the beginning, the Lady found that proximity made small difference in her ability to perceive what was inside.

Strangers! One could hardly expect them, after all, to provide familiar friend-or-enemy patterns for perception. Yet that very knowledge made the brief flashes of contact that she got all the more confusing, for they contained a teasing familiarity that made the Strange elements even less comprehensible by contrast.

For just the instant's duration of a swift brush of minds, the Mother felt as though it were a daughter of her own inside the Strange structure; then the feeling was lost, and she had to strain every effort again simply to locate the image.

A series of slow moves, meantime, brought her litter gradually back round to where it had been at first; and though she found it was still painful to look for any length of time directly at the blazing light reflected from the Wings, the Lady discovered that by focusing on the trees diagonally across the clearing, she could include the too-bright object within her peripheral vision.

That much assured, she ceased to focus visually at all. Time enough for that when—*if*—the Strangers should come forth. Once more she managed to grasp, briefly, the mental image of the

Strangers, or of one of them; and once again she felt the unexpected response within herself, as if she were in contact with a daughter of the Household…

She lost it then; but it fitted with her sudden surmise of the night before.

Now, in the hopeful certainty that she had guessed correctly, she abandoned the effort at perception entirely; she gathered all her energies instead into one tight-beamed communication aimed at penetrating the thick skin of the Wings, and very little different in any way from the standard evening Homecalling.

IT TOOK some time. She was beginning to think she had failed: that the Strangers were not receptive to her call, or would respond only with fear and hostility. Then, without warning, the barrier at the entranceway was gone.

No…not actually *gone*. It was still there, and still somehow attached to the main body of the Wings, but turned around so it no longer barred the way. And the opening this uncovered turned out to be, truly, the double-arch she had seen—but not quite credited—through her son's eyes.

Two arches, resting on each other base-to-base, but open in the center: the shape of a hollowed-eye. Such a shape might grow, but it could not be *built*. Half-convinced as she had been that the Wings, or House, or whatever-it-was, was an artificial structure rather than a natural form, Daydanda had put the relayed image of the doorway down to distortion of communication the night before. Now she saw it for herself: that, and the device that moving like a living thing to barricade the entrance…

Like a living thing…

It could fly; it was therefore, by all precedent of knowledge, alive. Reluctantly, the Lady discarded the notion that the Wings had been built by Strange knowledge. But even then, she thought soberly, there was much to be learned from the Strangers.

And in the next moment, she ceased to think at all. The Stranger emerged—the bigger of the two Strangers—and at the first impact of full visual and mental perception, Daydanda's impossible theory was confirmed.

CHAPTER TEN

DEBORAH STOOD outside, on the charred ground in front of the rocket, earnestly repeating the multiplication table: "Two two's are four. Three two's are six. Four two's..."

She was just as big as any of these bugs. The only one that was bigger was the one inside the box that she could only see part of—but that one had something wrong with it. It just lay there stretched out flat all the time, as if it couldn't get up. The box had handles for carrying, too, so Dee didn't have to worry about how big that one was.

All the rest of them were just about her own size, or even smaller, but there were too *many* of them. And when she thought about actually touching one, with its hairy, sticky legs, she remembered the sick crackling sound a beetle makes when you step on it.

She didn't want to fight them, or anything like that; and she didn't think they wanted to hurt her specially, either. She didn't have the knotted-up, tight kind of feeling you get when somebody wants to hurt you. They didn't *feel* like enemies, or act that way, either. They were just too...

"Four four's are sixteen. Five four's are twenty. Six four's are twenty-four. Seven..."

...too *interested!* And that was a silly thing to think, because how could she tell if they were interested? She couldn't even see their faces because all the ones in front were bending backwards-upside-down, like the one she'd seen in the garden...

"...four's are twenty-eight. Eight four's are thirty-two. Nine four's are..."

...just standing there, the whole row of them, with their back legs or arms or whatever-they-were sticking up in the air, and their heads dipped down in front so they could stare at her out of the big glittery eye in the middle of each black head...

"...thirty-six. Ten four's are forty. Eleven..."

What did they want, anyhow? Why didn't they *do* something?

"...four's are forty-four. Twelve four's..."

The Space Girl oath was hard to remember if you were trying to think about other things at the same time; but Deborah knew the multiplication tables by heart, and she could keep talking while she was thinking.

DAYDANDA was fascinated. She had guessed at it, in her chamber the night before...more than guessed really. She would have been *certain* if the notion were not so flatly impossible in terms of all knowledge and experience. It was precisely that conflict between perception and precedent that had determined her to make the trip out here.

And she was right! These two were neither Lady and consort, nor Mother and babe, but only two children—a half-grown daughter and a babe in arms. Two young wingless ones, alone, afraid, and...*Motherless?*

Eagerly, Daydanda poured out her questionings:

Where did they come from?

What sort of beings were they?

Where was their Mother?

"TWELVE four's are forty-eight. One five is five. Two five's are ten. Three..."

The important thing was just to keep talking—Dee knew that from when she had so much trouble at the garden. As long as she was saying *something*, anything at all, she could keep the crazy stuff out of her head.

"...five's are fifteen. Four five's are twenty. Five five's..."

It was harder this time, though. At the garden, with the drumbeat-heartbeat sound that felt like Mommy's voice, all she had to do was *think* words. But now, it was stuff like thinking Petey was saying things to her—or feeling like somebody else was asking her a lot of silly questions. And every time she stopped for breath at all, she'd start wanting to answer a lot of things inside her head that there wasn't even anybody around to have asked.

"...are twenty-five. Six fives are thirty."

THE ACHING soreness in her body from the jolting journey through the forest…the instant's agony when the sunlight seared her eye…the nagging worry over the disturbed Big-heads…all these were forgotten, or submerged, as the Lady experienced, for the first time in her life, the frustration of her curiosity.

Every answer she could get from the Strange child came in opposites. Each question brought a pair of contradictory replies…if it brought any reply at all. Half the time, at least, the Stranger was refusing reception entirely, and for some obscure reason, broadcasting great quantities of arithmetic—most of it quite accurate, but all of it irrelevant to the present situation.

Would they remain here? the Lady asked. Or would they return to their own House? Had they come to build a House here? Or was the Wing-like structure on the blackened ground truly a House instead?

The answers were many, and also various.

They would not stay, the Stranger seemed to say, nor would they leave. The structure from which she had, emerged was a House, but it was also Wings: Unfamiliar concept in a single symbol—Wings—House? *Both!*

Their Mother was nearby—inside—but—dead? *No!* Not *dead!*

How could the child possibly answer a sensible question sensibly if she started broadcasting sets of numbers every time anyone tried to communicate with her? *Very rude,* Daydanda thought, *and very stupid.* Kackot eagerly confirmed her opinion, and moved a step closer to the litter, as if preparing to commence the long march home.

The Lady had no time to reprimand him. At just that moment, the Strange child also broke into motion—perhaps also feeling that the interview was over.

"…THIRTY. Seven five's are thirty-fi…"
One of them moved!
Just a couple of steps, but Dee, panicked, forgot to keep talking and started a dash for the rocket; her head was full of questions again, and part of her mind was trying to answer them, without her wanting to at all, while another part decided not to go back inside, with a mixed-up kind of feeling, as if Petey didn't want her to.

And *that* was silly, because she could hear Petey crying now. He wanted her to come in, all right, or at least to come and get him. She couldn't tell for sure, the way he was yelling, whether he was scared and mad at being left alone—or just mad and wanting to get picked up. It sounded almost more like he thought he was being left out of something, and wanted to get in on the fun.

If he thinks this is fun...!

"We're lost, that's what we are," she said out loud, as if she were answering real questions someone had asked, instead of crazy ones inside her own head. "I don't know where we are. We came from Starhope. That's a different planet. A different *world.* I don't know where... One five is five," she remembered.

"Two sixes are seven. I mean two seven's are twenty-one... I can't think anything right!"

It *really* didn't matter what she said; as long as she kept talking. If she answered the silly questions right out loud, that was all right too, because they couldn't understand her anyhow. How would *they* know Earthish?

IT WAS POSSIBLE that the Stranger's sudden move to return to the Wings-House was simply a response to Kackot's gesture of readiness to depart. The Lady promised herself an opportunity to express her irritation with her consort—soon. For the moment, however, every bit of energy she could muster went into a plea-command-call-invitation to the Strange child to remain outside the shelter and continue to communicate.

The Stranger hesitated, paused—but even before that, she had begun, perversely, now that no questions were being asked, to release a whole new flood of semi-information.

More contradictions, of course!

These two, the Stranger children, were—something hard to comprehend—not-aware-of-where-they-were.

They were in need of help, but not helpless.

The elder of the two—the daughter who now stood wavering in her intentions, just beside the open barrier of the Wings-House—was obviously acting in the capacity of nurse. Yet her self-pattern of identity claimed reproductive status!

Certainly, the girl's attitude toward her young sibling was an odd mixture of what one might expect to find in nurse or Mother. Possibly the relationship could be made clearer by contact with the babe himself. There was little enough in the way of general information to be expected from such a source, but here he might be helpful. Tentatively, with just a small part of her mind, Daydanda reached out to find the babe, still concentrating on her effort to keep the older one from departing…

"Food…mama…suck…oh, look!"

The Lady promptly turned her full attention to the babe.

After the obstructionist tactics, and confused content of the Strange girl's mind, the little one's response to a brushing contact was doubly startling. Now that she was fully receptive to them, thoughts came crowding into the Mother's mind, thoughts unformed and infantile, but buoyantly eager and hopeful.

"Love…food…good…mama… suck…see…see…"

"THREE seven's are twenty one!" Dee remembered triumphantly, and began feeling a lot better. They were all standing still again, for one thing; and her head felt clearer, too.

She moved a cautious step backward, watching them as she went, and not having any trouble now remembering her multiplication.

"Four seven's are twenty-eight…"

Just a few more steps. If she could just get back inside, and get the door closed, she wouldn't open it again for *anything*. She'd stay right there with Petey till some *people* came…

"…MAMA…SUCK…see…see…good…love…"

It might have been one of her own latest brood, so easy and familiar was the contact. Just about the same age-level and emotional development, too. Daydanda was suddenly imperatively anxious to see the babe directly, to hold it in her own arms, to feel what sort of strange shape and texture could accommodate such warmly customary longings and perceptions.

"The babe!" she commanded. "I wish to have the babe brought to me!" But the nurse to whom she had addressed the order hung back miserably.

"The babe. I said!" The Lady released all her pent-up irritation at the Stranger child, in one peremptory blast of anger at her own daughter. *"Now!"*

"Lady, I cannot...the light...forgive me, my Lady..."

With her own eye still burning in its socket, Daydanda hastily blessed the nursing daughter, and excused her. Even standing on the fringes of the bright-lit area must be frightening to the wingless ones. But whom else could she send? The fliers were unaccustomed to handling babes...

"Kackot!"

He was good with babes, really. She felt better about sending him than she would have had she trusted the handling of the Stranger to a nurse. Kackot himself felt otherwise; but at the moment, the Lady's recognition of his discomfiture was no deterrent to her purpose; she had not forgotten his ill-advised move a little earlier.

The consort could not directly disobey. He went forward, doubtfully enough, and stood at the open entranceway, peering in.

"Oh, *look!*...love...look!"

The babe's welcoming thoughts were unmistakable; Kackot must have felt them as Daydanda did. Stranger or no, the near presence of a friendly and protective entity made it beg to be picked up, petted, fondled, loved—and hopefully, though not, the Mother thought, truly hungrily—perhaps also to be fed.

Meantime, however, there was the older child to reckon with. The babe was eager to come; the girl, Daydanda sensed, was determined not to allow it. Once more, the Mother tried to reach the Strange daughter with empathy and affection and reassurance. Once again, she met only blankness and refusal. Then she sent a surge of loving invitation to the babe, and got back snuggling eagerness and warmth—and suddenly, from the elder one, a lessening of fear and anger.

Daydanda smiled inside herself; she thought she knew now how to penetrate the strange defenses of the child.

CHAPTER ELEVEN

DEE STOOD still and watched it happen. She saw the nervous fussy-bug—the one that had scared her when he moved before—go right over to the rocket and *look inside*. He passed right by her, close enough to touch; she was going to do something about it, until Petey started talking again.

He said, "Baby come to mama."

At least, she *thought* he said it. Then she *almost* thought she heard a Mother say, "It's all right; don't worry. Baby wants to come to mama."

"Mother's *dead!*" Deborah screamed at them all, at Petey and the bugs, without ever even opening her mouth. "Five seven's are thirty-five," she said hurriedly. She'd been forgetting to keep talking, that's what the trouble was. "Six seven's are forty-two. Seven..."

And still, she couldn't get the notion out of her head that it was her own mother's voice she'd heard. "Seven seven's..." she said desperately, and couldn't keep from turning around to look at the part of the rocket where Mommy was—would be—had been when—

The smooth gleaming metal nose looked just the same as ever, now it was cool again. There was no way of knowing anything had ever happened in there. *If anything had happened...*

Deborah stared and stared, as if looking long enough and hard enough would let her see right through the triple hull into the burned-out inside: the wrecked control room, and the two charred bodies that had been Father and Mother.

"...seven seven's is forty-seven? ...eight...?"

She floundered, forgetting, she was too small, and she didn't know what to do about anything, and she wanted her mother.

"It's all right. Stand still. Don't worry. Baby *wants* to come to mama."

IT WASN'T her own mother's voice, though; that wasn't, the way Mommy talked. If it was these bugs that were making her hear crazy things and putting silly questions in her head...seven seven's...seven seven's is...just stand still...don't worry...everything will be all right...seven seven's...*I don't know*...don't worry, all right, stand still, seven's is...

"Forty-nine!" she shrieked. The fussy-bug was all the way inside, and she'd been standing there like any dumb kid, hearing thoughts and voices that weren't real, and not knowing what to do.

"Forty-nine, fifty, fifty-one, fifty-two," she shouted. She could have been just counting like that all along, instead of trying to remember something like seven times seven. *Get out of there, you awful hairy horrible old thing!* "Fifty-three, fifty-four. You leave my brother alone!"

The fussy-bug came slowly crawling its way out of the airlock, with Petey—soft little pink-and-wet Petey—clutched in its sticky arms.

"Fifty-five," she tried to shout, but it came out like a creak instead. *You leave him alone!* her whole body screamed; but her throat was too dry and it felt as if somebody had glued it together, and she couldn't make any words come out at all. She started forward to grab the baby.

"Come to Mama," Petey said. "Nice Mama...Like. Good."

SHE WAS looking right at him all the time, and she knew he wasn't *really* talking. Just drooling the way he always did, and making happy-baby gurgling noises. He certainly didn't act scared—he was cuddling up to the hairy-bug just as if it was a *person*.

"Come to Mama," the baby crooned inside her head; she should have made a grab for him right then, but somehow she wasn't *sure*...

The fussy-bug walked straight across the clearing to the tree where the big box was, and handed Petey inside.

"Oo-oo-ooh, Mama!" Petey cried out with delight.

"Mommy's *dead!*" Deborah heard herself shouting, so she knew her voice was working again. "Dead, she's dead, can't you understand that? Any dope could understand that much. She's *dead!*"

Nobody paid any attention to her. Petey was laughing out loud; and the sound got mixed up with some other kind of laughter in her head that was hard to not-listen to, because it felt *good.*

CHAPTER TWELVE

HOLDING the babe tenderly, Daydanda petted and patted and stroked it, and made pleased laughter for them both. Cautiously she experimented with balancing the intensities of the two contacts, trying to gage the older child's reactions to each variation. Reluctantly, as she observed the results, she came to the conclusion that the Strange daughter had indeed been consciously attempting to block communication.

It was unheard-of, therefore, impossible—but impossibilities were commonplace today. The Mother's own presence at this scene was a flat violation of tradition and natural law.

Nevertheless:

The child had emerged from the Wings-House, in response to a Homecalling pattern.

Therefore, she was not an enemy.

Therefore, she could not possibly feel either fear or hostility toward Daydanda's Household.

These things being true, what reason could she have for desiring to prevent communication?

Answer: Obviously, despite the logic of the foregoing, the Strange child was *afraid.*

Why? There was no danger to her in this contact.

"Stupid," Kackot grumbled; "just plain stupid. As much brains as a Bighead. Lady, it is getting late; we have a long journey home…"

Daydanda let him rumble on. A child a likely to behave stupidly when frightened. She remembered, and sharply reminded her consort, of the time a young winged one of her own, a very bright boy normally—was it the fifth Family he was in? No, the sixth—had wandered into the Bigheads' corral, and been too petrified with fear to save himself, or even to call for help.

The boy had been afraid, she remembered now, that he would call the Bigheads' attention to himself if he tried to communicate with anyone, so he closed off against the world. Of course, he knew in advance that the Bigheads were dangerous, if the Stranger here had somehow decided to be fearful *in advance,* perhaps her effort to block contact was motivated the same way...

"The Homecalling," Kackot reminded her; "she answered a Homecalling."

"She is a Stranger," Daydanda pointed out. "Perhaps she responded to friendship without identifying it...I don't know..."

But she would find out. Once again she centered her attention on the babe, keeping only a loose contact with the older child.

DEE KEPT watching the box on the ground that had the big bug inside it. She couldn't see much of the bug, and she couldn't see Petey at all, after the other bug handed him in. But it wasn't just Petey she was watching for.

It was that big bug that was—talking to her. Well, anyhow, that was making it sound as if Petey talked to her and putting questions in her head and...

She didn't know *how* it did it, but she couldn't pretend any more that it wasn't really happening. Somebody was picking and poking at her inside her head, and she didn't know how they did it or why, or what to do about it. But she was sure by now that the big bug in the box was the one.

"Let's see now—seven seven's is forty-nine." Just counting didn't seem to work so well. "Seven eight's is...I mean, *eight seven's* is...I don't *know* I can't *remember*...We came for Daddy and Mommy to make reports. That's what they always do. Daddy's a Survey Engineer, and Mommy's a Geologist. They work for the Planetary Survey Commiss...I mean they *did...*"

It was none of their business. And they did know Earthish!

If they didn't, how could *they* talk to *her?*

"Seven seven's is forty-nine. Seven seven's is forty-nine. Seven seven's..."

AT THE FIRST exchange, the Lady had put it down to incompetence, but she could no longer entertain that excuse. The

Strangers had no visible antennae, yet the ease of communication with the babe made it clear that they could receive—as well as broadcast readily—if they wished.

The perception appeared to be associated with an organ Daydanda had at first mistaken for a mouth: small and flat, centered toward the bottom of the face, and enclosed by just two soft-looking mandibles.

In the babe, the mandibles were almost constantly in motion, and there was a steady flow of undirected, haphazard communication, such as was normal for the little one's apparent level of development. With the older child, it was apparent that the messages that came when the mandibles were moving were stronger, clearer, and more purposeful in meaning than the others. Unfortunately, the content of these messages was mostly nothing but arithmetic.

Yet even when the "mouth" was at rest, Daydanda noticed that there was a continuous trickle of communication from the Strange daughter—a sort of reluctant release of thought, rather like the babe's in that it was undirected and largely involuntarily, but with two striking differences: the eagerness of the babe to be heard, and the fact that the content of the older one's thoughts were not at all infantile, but sometimes startlingly mature.

Daydanda repeated her questions, this time watching the mandibles as the answers came, and realize that the thin stream of involuntary communication went on even while mandible messages were being sent—and that the "opposite" answers she'd been receiving were the result of the differences between the purposeful broadcasts and the background flow.

The Strangers' Mother and her consort, it appeared, (gradually, the Lady learned to put the two answers together so that they made sense) had come here to survey the land (to look for a House-site, one would assume), and they had techniques as well for determining before excavation what lay far underground. However, they were now dead...perhaps...and...

More arithmetic!

"What is it that you fear child?" the Mother asked once more.

"I'm not afraid of those(unfamiliar symbol—something: small and scuttling and unpleasant)," the daughter addressed her sibling, mandibling. "Scared, scared, *scared!*" came the running edge of thought behind and around it.

"DON'T BE scared," Petey told her.

"I'm not afraid of those old bugs! she told him.

But it wasn't Petey, really; it was that big *Mother-bug* in the box. *Mother-bug?* What made her think that? That was what *Petey* thought…

Deborah was all mixed up. And she *was* scared; she was scared for Petey, and scared because she didn't know how they put things in her mind, and scared…

Scared all the time except when that good-feeling laughing was in her head; and then, even though she knew the—the *Mother-bug* must be doing that too, she *couldn't* be scared.

Deborah stood still, trembling with the realization of the awfulness of destruction she would somehow have to visit upon this bunch of bugs, if anything bad happened to Petey. She didn't understand how she had come to let them get him out of the ship at all and now that they had him, she didn't know what to do about it. The first large tear slid out of the corner of her eye and rolled down her cheek.

"MAKE FOOD for sibling?" the Mother inquired, as she watched the clear liquid ooze out of the openings she had at first thought to be twin eyes.

The Strange daughter was apparently receiving all communication as if from the babe, for her answer was addressed to him: a reassurance, a promise, "I will prepare (unfamiliar symbol) inside the…Another unfamiliar symbol there—*ship*—but with it came an image of an interior room of Strange appearance; and Daydanda safely guessed the symbol to refer to the Wings-House. The first symbol—*bottle*, she found now, in the babe's mind—was a great white cylinder, warm and moist, and connected with the sucking concept…but no time to classify it further, because the older child was mandibling another message, this time directly to the Mother.

"Return the babe to me. The babe is hungry. I must prepare his food."

"You have food for the sibling now," Daydanda pointed out patiently. "Come here to the litter and feed him."

"SURE THERE'S milk," Dee said. "There's lots of milk, Petey. I'll give you a bottle soon as we get back inside," she promised, and warned the big bug hopefully: "That baby's hungry; he's awful hungry...you wait and see. He'll start yelling in a minute, and then you'll see. You better give him back to me right now, before he starts yelling."

"THERE IS much food inside the ship," the child told the babe, but all the while a background-message trickled out; "There isn't; there really isn't. It won't last much longer." And even as the two conflicting thoughts came clear in her own mind, Daydanda saw a large drop of the precious fluid roll off the girl's face and be lost forever in the ground.

"Come quickly!" she commanded. '*Now!* Come to the Mother, and give food to the babe. Quick!"

But the doltish child simply stood there rooted in her fears.

MAYBE IF she just walked right over and lifted him out of the big box, they wouldn't even try to stop her...but there were too many of them, and she didn't dare get much further away from the rocket.

"You better give him back to me," she cried out hopelessly.

IT TOOK a while to sort out the sense from the nonsense. Of course, the child believed the babe to be hungry because the message about feeding came to her through him. Actually, the little one was warm and happy and content, with no more than normal infantile fantasies of nourishment in his mind. His belly was still half-full from earlier feeding.

But half-full meant also half-empty. If the older child was now producing food, and could not continue to do so much longer—as seemed clear from the contradictory content of her messages—the babe should have it now, while it was available. The daughter's reluctance to provide him with it seemed somehow connected with the *bottle* symbol. It was necessary to go into the Wings-House to get the *bottle*...

DAYDANDA searched the babe's mind once again. *Bottle* was food...? No...a *mechanism* of some sort for feeding. Perhaps the flat mandibles were even weaker than they looked; perhaps some artificial aid in nourishment was needed...

And that thought brought with an equally startling notion in explanation of the Wings-House...a Strange race of people might possibly need artificial Wings to carry out the nuptial flight...

That was beside the point for now. Think about it later. Meantime...she had to reject the idea of artificial aid in feeding; the babe's repeated sucking image was too clear and too familiar. He nursed as her own babes did; she was certain of it.

Then she recalled the Strange daughter's earlier crafty hope of finding some way to return to the Wings-House with the babe, and emerge no more. Add to that the child's threat that the babe, if not immediately returned to her, would start *yelling*—would attempt to block communication as the girl herself did. It all seemed to mean that *bottle* was not a necessity of feeding at all, but some pleasurable artifact inside the *ship,* somehow associated with the feeding process, with which the daughter was trying to entice the babe.

"You wish to feed?" Daydanda asked the little one, and made a picture in his mind's eye of the girl's face with liquid droplets of nourishment falling unused to the ground.

"NOT FOOD," came the clear response. "Not food. *Sad.*" Then there was an image once again of the tubular white container, but this time she realized the color of it came from a cloudy fluid inside...milk. "Milk-food. Tears-crying-*sad.*"

Tears-crying was for the face-liquid. It was useless, or rather useful only as emotional expression. It was a waste product... (and she had been right in the first guess about twin eyes!)...and then the further realization that the great size she had at first attributed to the *bottle* was relative only to the babe. The thing was a reasonably-sized sensibly-shaped storage container for the nutrient fluid the babe and child called *milk;* and it was furthermore provided with a mechanism at one end designed to be sucked upon.

Out of the welter of freshly-evaluated information, one fact emerged to give the Lady an unanticipated hope.

There was food—*stored, portable* food inside the winged structure. The Strangers were *not biologically tied* to the Wings; there was no need to return the babe in order to satisfy its hunger. Babe and Strange daughter both could, if they would, return to Daydanda's House, there to communicate at leisure.

It remained only to convince the daughter...and Daydanda had not forgotten that the child was susceptible to the Homecalling and to laughter both.

CHAPTER THIRTEEN

DEBORAH walked behind the litter where Peter rode in state with...with *the Mother*...and all around her walked a retinue of bugs; dozens of them. They walked on four front legs, heads carried down and facing backward, eyes looking forward. The tallest of them was just about her own height when it stood up straight. Walking this way, none of them came much above her waist; they weren't so awful if you didn't have to look at their faces.

Certainly they were smart—so smart it scared her some—but not as much as it would have scared her to keep on staying in the rocket. She was just beginning to realize that.

Dee still didn't know how they made her think things inside her head; or how they made Petey seem to talk to her; or how they knew what she was thinking half the time even if she didn't say a word. She wasn't sure either, what had made her decide to do what *the Mother* wanted, and pack up food to take along back to their house. She didn't even know what kind of a house it was or where it was. But she was pretty sure she'd rather go along with them than just keep waiting in the rocket alone with Petey.

Wherever they were going, it was a long walk. Dee was tired, and the knapsack on her back was heavy. They'd started out right after lunch time, and now the dimness in the forest was turning darker, so it must be evening. It was hot, too. She hoped the milk she'd mixed would keep overnight; but she had crackers and fruit, too, in case it didn't. It wasn't the food that made the knapsack so heavy, though. It was the oxy torch she'd slipped into the bottom underneath the clean diapers.

These bugs were smart but they didn't know *everything*, she thought with satisfaction. They never tried to stop her from taking along the torch.

IT WAS HOT and damp and the torch in the knapsack made a knobby hard spot bouncing against her back. But the bugs never stopped to rest; and Dee walked on in their midst, remembering that she was a Space Girl, so she had to be brave and strong.

Then suddenly, right ahead, instead of more trees, there was a bare round hill of orange clay. Only when you looked closer, it wasn't just a hill, because it had an opening in it, like the mouth of a cave. Only it wasn't a natural cave, because the edges of the arch were smooth. It was even on both sides, and perfectly round on top; it had little bits of rock or wood set in cement around the edges to make it keep its shape.

She couldn't tell what was inside. It was dark in there. *Too dark.* Deborah paused inside the entranceway, oppressed by shadows, aghast at far dim corridors. One of the bugs tried to take her hand to lead her forward. The touch was sticky. She shuddered back, and stood stock-still in the middle of the arch.

"*I hate you!*" she yelled at all of them.

"Not hate," said Petey, laughing. "Fear."

"I'm not scared of anything," she told him; "you're the one who's scared, not me. Petey's afraid of the dark," she said to the big bug. "You give that baby back to me right now. That's not your baby. He's *my* brother, and I want him back."

THE ROCKET, lying helpless on its side in the bare black clearing, seemed very safe, and very far away. Dee didn't understand how she could have thought—even for a little while— that this place would be better. Everything back there was safety: even the burned-out memory of the control room was sealed off behind a *safety* door. Everything here was strange and dark, and no doors to close on the shadows—just open arches leading to darker stretches beyond...

172

"'Fraid of a *door!*" said Petey.

"I'm not afraid of any old door." Deborah's voice was hoarse from pushing past the choke spot in her throat that was holding back the tears. "You give me back my brother, that's all; we're not going into your house. He is too, afraid of the dark; and he hates you too!" *A Space Girl is brave,* she thought, and then she said it out loud, and walked right over to the shadowy outline of the big bug's box, and reached in and grabbed for Petey.

Only he didn't want to come. He yelled and wriggled away; held on tight to the Mother-bug, and kicked at Dee.

She didn't know what to do about it, till she heard that good laughing in her head again. Petey stopped yelling, and Dee stopped pulling at him. She realized that she was very tired, and the laughing felt like home, like her own mother, like food and a warm room, and a bed with clean sheets—and maybe even a fuzzy doll tucked in next to her as if she were practically a baby again herself.

She was tired, and she didn't feel brave any more. She didn't want to go inside, but she didn't want to fight any more, either—especially if Petey was going to be against her, too. She sat down on the ground under the arch to figure out what to do.

"Light?" a voice like Mother's asked gently inside her head. "You want a light inside?"

"I've got a light," Dee said, before she stopped to think. "I've got a light right here."

She dragged the knapsack around in front of her and dug down into it. She was going to have to go on in after all, there wasn't anything else to do. She got the torch out, and turned it on low, so it wouldn't get used up too fast. Then she started laughing, because this time it was the bugs who were scared. They all started running around like crazy, every which way, and half of them ran clear way, inside.

THE CHILD was certainly resourceful, Daydanda thought ruefully, as she issued rapid commands and reassurances, restoring order out of the sudden panic that the light had caused among the sensitive unpigmented wingless ones.

No daughter of mine, she thought angrily, with admiration, *no daughter of mine would ever dare to act this way!*

173

"So you begin to see, my dear Lady…" Kackot was obviously irritated and not impressed. "They have no place in the Household. Useless parasites… Why not admit…?"

"*Quiet!*"

Useless parasites? No! *Dangerous* they might well be; *useless* only if you counted the acquisition of new knowledge as of no use. The child would certainly have to be watched closely. This last trick with the light was really quite insupportable behavior: rudeness beyond belief or toleration. Yet the bravado of the Stranger's attitude was not too hard to understand. Still unequipped for Motherhood, she had already acquired the instincts for it; she was doing, in each case, her inadequate best to protect both sibling and self from any possible dangers. And each new display of unexpected—even uncomfortable—ingenuity left Daydanda more determined than before to make both Strangers a part of her Household.

There was much to be learned. And…

DAYDANDA was many things:

As a Mother, she felt a simple warm solicitude for two unmothered creatures.

As the administrative Lady of her Household, it was her duty first to make certain that the Strangers were so established that they could do no harm; and then to learn as much as could be learned from their Strange origins and ways of life.

As a person—a person who had flown, long ago, above the treetops—a person who had only a short time ago walked through the enlarged archway in defiance of all precedent and tradition—a person who had just this day dared the impossible, and ventured forth from her own House to make this trip—Daydanda chuckled to herself, and wished she knew some way to make the Stranger understand the quite inexplicable affection that she felt.

The child said the babe feared darkness; this was manifestly untrue. The Mother still held the soft infant in her arms, and she knew there was no fear inside that body. As for the older one—it was not lack of light that she feared, either. Yet if the presence of accustomed light could comfort her—why, she should have her light!

"Come, child," Daydanda coaxed the girl gently through the mind of the babe. "Inside, there is a place to rest. You have done much, Strange daughter, and you have done well; but you are tired now. Inside, there is safety and sleep for the babe and for you. Come with us, and carry your light if you will. But it is time now to sleep; tomorrow we will plan."

At the Lady's command, the litter-bearers picked up her stretcher once more, and the lurching forward motion recommenced. The child on the ground stood up slowly, holding her light high, and followed after them. All down the dim corridors, Daydanda's warning went ahead, to spare those whom the little light might hurt from the shock of exposure.

CHAPTER FOURTEEN

DEBORAH lay on her back on a thick mat on the floor. It had looked uncomfortable, but now that she was stretched out on it, it felt fine. She had no blanket, and no sheets, and she'd forgotten to bring along pajamas. At first she tried sleeping in all her clothes, but then she decided they were only bugs after all, and they didn't wear anything; so she took off her overalls and shirt. The room was warm, anyhow—almost too warm.

She got up and went across the room to the other mat, where Petey was, and changed his diaper and took off the rest of his clothes, too. She didn't know what to do with the dirty things; there was no soil-remover here. Finally, she folded them up neatly—all except the dirty diaper, which she wadded up and threw in a far corner. The rest of the things they'd have to wear again tomorrow, dirty or not.

Then she propped up Petey's almost empty bottle, and went back to her own mat, lay down again, and turned the oxy torch as low as she could, without letting it go out altogether. She could barely see Petey across the room, still sucking on the nipple, though he was just about asleep.

They hadn't really been captured, she told herself. Nobody tried to hurt them at all. It was...the way she felt now, it was more like being *rescued*. She didn't know what would happen tomorrow, except one thing—and that was that she would have to go back to the rocket to get some clothes, at least. It was a long walk, though. Right now, she felt warm and safe and sleepy.

These bugs were smart, but there were plenty of things they didn't know at all...

She was pretty sure they wouldn't understand anything about the safety door, for instance. Unless...

Maybe they could find out about it in—her mind. But even if they did, they wouldn't *understand*...

And they couldn't even find out anything, if she just didn't *think* about it any more...

That was the best way. *I'll just forget all about it*, she decided.

She felt very brave. The Space Girl Troup Leader on Starhope would be proud of her now, she thought, as she reached out and turned the light all the way off before she fell asleep.

PETEY was crying again. "Shut up," Dee said crossly; "why don't you shut up a minute?"

Her eyes felt glued together. She didn't want to wake up. She was warm and comfortable and still very sleepy; and now that it was all over, why didn't Mommy come, and...?

She opened one eye slowly, and couldn't see anything. It was pitch dark in the room; no lights or windows...

She reached out for the oxy torch, her hand scraping across the smooth clay floor, and it wasn't there. The bugs had taken it away. They had come in while she was sleeping and taken it...

Her hand found the torch, fumbled for the switch, and she had to close her eyes against the sudden bright flare of light. Petey, startled, stopped crying for a minute, then started in again just twice as loud.

The knapsack was in the corner, back of the light, and there was a bottle all ready for him inside it, but Dee still didn't want to get up. If she got up, it would be admitting once and for all that this was real, and the other part had been a dream—the part where she'd been waking up in a real bed, with Mommy in the next room ready to come and take care of them and give them breakfast.

It still felt that way a little bit, as long as she lay still with her eyes closed. *Mother in the next room...* Dee didn't want the feeling to stop, but she couldn't help it if the food was in this room.

Mother can't feed me... That was a silly thing to think. She was a big girl; nobody had to *feed* her...

Dee got up and got the bottle for Petey, and some fruit and crackers for herself. She was wide awake now and she knew she wasn't dreaming; but when she was all done eating, she didn't know what to do. There was still some food left, but she wasn't really hungry. She knew she might need it later on, so she just sat around listening to Petey making sucking noises on his bottle, and wondering what was going to happen next.

CHAPTER FIFTEEN

THE MORNING pattern of the Household was a familiar and punctilious ritual: a litany of instruction and response, of order and affirmation. Each member of each Family knew his role and played it with conditioned ease; the sum of the parts produced a choreography of timing and motion, such as had delighted the Mother on that day when she watched her mason sons construct the new arch in her double chamber.

Daydanda's great body rested now, as then, on the couch of mats from which she had once thought she would never rise again; but her perceptions spread out of the boundaries of her Household, and her commands and reprimands were heard wherever her children prepared for the day's labor.

Some of the pattern was set and unvarying: the nurses to care for the babes, and the babes to the gardens to feed; the growing sons and daughters to their classrooms, workrooms, and the training gardens; those whose wings are sprouting to instruction in the mysteries of flight and reproduction.

The winged ones whose nuptial flight time has not come as yet wait in their quarters for assignments to scouting positions for the day; the builders breakfast largely to prepare cement, and gather up clay and chips for work in some new structure of the House; the growers, gardeners, and harvesters spread out across the forest, clearing the fallen leaves and branches, sporing the fungi, damming or redirecting a flow of water to some more useful purpose, bringing back new stores of leaf and wood and brush to fill the storage vaults beneath the House.

IT WAS NEVER precisely the same. There was always some minor variation in the combination of elements: a boundary dispute today on this border, instead of the other; a new room to add to the nursery quarters, or an arch to repair in the vaults; a garden to replant into more fertile soil. And on this particular morning, two matters of special import claimed the Lady's attention.

The most urgent of these was the reconditioning of the disturbed Bigheads. Two of the eldest winged daughters—both almost ready for nuptial departures from the Household—had been assigned to work with the nurses who ordinarily tended to the needs of the corral. Under different circumstances, Daydanda would have considered the process worthy of her own direct supervision.

Now, however, she contented herself with listening in semi-continuously on the work being done. The program was proceeding slowly—too slowly—but as long as some progress was being made, she refrained from interfering, and concentrated her own efforts on a matter of far greater personal interest: the Strangers in the House.

Or, rather, the Strange daughter. The babe was no great puzzle; his wants were familiar, and easy to understand. Food and love he needed. The latter was easy; the former they would simply have to find some way to provide...

She pushed aside the train of thought that led to making these new arrivals permanent members of the Household. No telling how much longer their supply of their own foods would last; nor whether it would be desirable to keep them in the House. For the time being, Daydanda could indulge her curiosity, and concentrate on the unique components of the Strange daughter's personality.

THE CHILD was a conglomeration of contradictions such as the Mother would not previously have believed possible in a sane individual—in one who was capable of performing even the most routine of conditioned tasks, let alone initiating such original and independent actions as those of the Stranger.

And yet, the confusions that existed in the child's thought patterns were so many, and so vital, it was a wonder she could even operate her own body without having to debate each breath or motion in her neurons first.

Fear! The child was full of fear. And of something else for which there was no proper name at all: *I should—I shouldn't.*

Impossible confusion, resulting even more impossibly in better-than-adequate responses!

Hunger...Mother...hunger...Mother...?

The drifting thoughts merged with the Lady's reflections, and for a moment she was not certain of the source. Too clearly-formed in pattern to be the babe...and then she realized it was the older one, just waking from sleep, and still stripped of defenses.

"I cannot feed you, child," she answered the Strange daughter's unthinking plea. "Not yet. You brought food with you from your...*ship*. Eat now, and feed the babe; then we will make plans for tomorrow."

But in her own mind, Daydanda knew, there was no question of what plans to make. If there were any way to do so, she meant to have the Strangers stay within her House. She meant to have the secrets of the Strange Wings-House explored and uncovered and to learn the Strange customs and knowledge. It remained only to determine whether it was possible to feed them and care for them adequately within the Household...and to convince the strange daughter to stay.

The Mother opened her mind once more to her sons and daughters, at their tasks, and found that all was well throughout the Families. Then she waited patiently till the Strangers were done feeding.

PETEY WAS sleeping. All he ever did was drink milk and go to sleep and yell and act silly. Dee got up and walked around the room, but there was nothing to see and nothing to do.

She didn't even remember which way they had come to get to this room last night, and she didn't know whether they'd let her go out if she wanted to. There was no door closing the room off from the corridor—just another open archway. But outside there was only dimness and darkness.

Abruptly, she picked up the torch and walked to the doorway, flared brilliance out into the hall, and peered up and down. After that she felt better, at least they weren't being *guarded.* She had seen half a dozen other open arches along the corridor, but not even a single bug anywhere.

When Petey woke up, she decided they'd just start walking around until they found some way to get out. She'd have to wait for him to get up, though, because she couldn't carry the lighted torch and the baby both; and even if she didn't need it to see with, she had to have the torch turned up real bright, because that's what they were afraid of. They wouldn't bother her…

They're not all scared of the light, she thought. *Just the white-colored ones are.* She wondered how she knew that, and then forgot about it, because she was thinking: *If we did get out of here, I don't know how we could get back to the rocket.*

It was a long way, and she'd have to carry Petey most of the time; and she didn't know which way it was, and…

I'm going to go find the Mother-bug! she decided. For just an instant after that she hesitated, wondering about leaving Petey, but somehow she felt it was all right. He was asleep, and she figured if he woke up and started yelling, she could hear him; any place in here she'd be able to hear him because there weren't any doors to close in between.

She picked up the torch again, and turned it down low, so there was just enough light to see her way. *Don't scare them.* she thought. *They're friends.* But it was comforting to know anyhow, that she *could* scare them just by turning it up. The white ones were the only ones who couldn't *stand* it, but none of them were used to bright light.

She wondered again how she knew that, and tried to remember something from last night that would have let her know it, but by that time she was too busy trying to figure out which corridors and archways would take her to the Mother-bug's room.

CHAPTER SIXTEEN

A TREMENDOUS excitement was building up inside Daydanda's vast and feeble bulk, while she guided the Strange child through the labyrinth of the House from the visitor's chamber near the outer walls to her own central domain.

Yesterday, for the first time in many years of Motherhood, she had experienced once more—with increasing ease and pleasure through the day—the thousand subtly different sensations and perceptions of direct vision. Through all the years between, she had known the *look* of things outside her chamber—and of beings outside her own Families—only through the distortions and dilutions of the minds of her sons and daughters, travelling abroad on missions of her choosing, and reporting as faithfully as they could, all that they saw and touched and felt for her appraisal.

But no image filtered through another's brain emerges quite the same as when it entered…and no two beings, not even those as close as Mother and daughter. can ever see quite the same image of an object. Certainly, Daydanda had perceived both more and less of the winged object in the clearing when she viewed it with her own eye, than when she had watched it through the mind of her scouting son.

And now she was to have the Strange child here before her eyes again, to watch and study! The thought was so far-removed from precedent and past experience, it would not have occurred to her at all to have the girl come to her chamber. But when she tried to make the child aware of her desire to converse, to exchange information, the prompt and positive response had come clearly: *I want to see the Mother. I want to try and talk to her.*

And behind the response was a pattern Daydanda dimly perceived, in which two-way communication was commonly associated with visual sensation. The girl seemed to assume that an exchange of information would occur only where an exchange of visimages was also possible!

AND NOW the child was standing in the entrance to the new chamber, and the background patter of her mind was a complaint about the difficulty of seeing clearly.

"You may have more light, child, if you wish to see me more clearly," the Mother assured her. "I told you before, it is only the ones unpigmented who are harmed by the brightness, and only the wingless who fear it at all."

An instant later, she realized she had been boasting. The flaring-up of the light caused her no agony, such as she had experienced the day before; but it was quite sufficient to cause her to turn her face abruptly toward the stranger, so as to shield her eye.

And then there was a far worse pain than anything her eye could feel. The Mother's vanity was almost as carefully fed, and quite as much enlarged, as her great abdomen; certainly it was far more vulnerable to attack.

DEBORAH stood in the open archway between the two big rooms, and peered intently at the great bulk of the Mother-bug on the couch of mats against the far wall. Then she decided it was all right now to turn the torch up high, so she could see something more than her own feet ahead of her.

The shadows jumped back, and the gently heaving mass on the cot sprang suddenly into full view. Deborah stood still, and gawped at ugliness beyond belief.

The big bug's enormous belly was a mound of grey-white creases and folds and bulges under the sharp light, reflecting pinpoints of brightness from oily-looking drops of moisture that stood out all over the dead-looking mass.

And up above the incredible belly, a cone-shaped bulbous lump of the same whitish grey that must have been a face despite its eyeless lack of any expression, tapered into six full thick lips just like the ones of the baby bugs in the fungus garden.

It was a good thing, Dee thought, that she hadn't seen the Mother-bug this close the day before. She never could have made herself believe that anything that looked … that looked like *that* …could possibly be friendly.

SHE TRIED now to believe it was true, tried to remember that good-feeling laughter that she was certain had come from the big bug; but the inside of her head had begun to prickle, just as if somebody was sandpapering in back of her eyes. She shook her head, rubbed at her stinging eyes, sniffled, and the feeling went away as suddenly as it had come.

Then she got mad. "You did that on purpose!" she gasped. And then a moment later, she had a crazy thought come through her head that the Mother-bug wanted her to feel better, like sometimes Mom...the way a mother, maybe, would feel bad after she'd spanked a child.

The idea of being a big fat bug's little girl was too silly, and she couldn't help laughing. Then she felt the same kind of *patting* inside her head that she remembered from last night, and she knew what the Mother-bug thought.

Nobody had ever thought her anything but beautiful before. The Stranger child, at the first clear look, thought she was *ugly and awful, and frightening and fat!*

It was the clearest, sharpest message she had had at any time from the Strange daughter...that she was *hideous!*

SHAME and disappointment both receded before a sudden access of fury. Reflexively, Daydanda shot out a spanking thought: and in the very, next instant, regretted it.

"I am sorry, child. I should not have punished you for what you could not help thinking, but I am not *used* to such thoughts."

"You did that?" the child demanded, and angrily: "You *meant* to do it?"

"I did not *plan* to do it; but it was done with volition, yes."

The Stranger, Daydanda felt, had no clear concept in her mind to understand that distinction. A thing was done either—*on purpose* was the child's symbol, or, else involuntarily. Nothing, in between. Well, it was a common enough childish confusion, but not one the Mother would have expected in this uncommon child.

"It was a punishment," she tried to explain, "which I had no right to administer. You are my guest, and not my daughter. I offer apology."

"I AM laughing, came a mandible message; but the background was a quick shiver of fear. Daydanda tried to soothe the fright away, and the laughing stopped, to be replaced by a sturdy mandibled denial of the fear that was, truthfully, already considerably lessened. And then an apology! "I am sorry," the child said. "It was most improper of me to laugh." And the background message was not different, but only more specific: "It was very rude of me to be frightened at the idea of being your daughter."

This time Daydanda repressed her reflexive irritation. "Laugh when you like, child," she said; "perhaps it is a good way to release your fear."

"I AM NOT scared," she said emphatically. "What do you think I do? *Laugh* when I get scared?" Then she thought it over and decided it wasn't very nice of her to laugh at an idea like that—about being the Mother-bug's child—if the big bug really *could* read her mind, so she apologized.

"I'm sorry," she said. "I guess it wasn't very nice of me to laugh at you." And she had a feeling as if the Mother-bug knew she had apologized, and was telling her it was all right.

The big old bug was ugly, all right, Dee thought, but so were a lot of *people* she'd seen…and the bug was really pretty nice. *Good*, sort of, the way a mother ought to be…

Promptly, Daydanda was rewarded by a clear, unmandibled, but strong reply: "You're good; I like you. I don't care what you look like."

THE WOMAN'S vanity quivered, but her curiosity triumphed. The child, at long last, was receptive to communication. Daydanda withdrew from contact entirely, to calm her wounded feelings, and to formulate carefully the question now uppermost in her mind: how to gain more knowledge of the Wings-House in which the Strangers had arrived.

JUST THE same, Dee realized, she didn't want to stay here. She didn't want to stay in the rocket either, though. *I don't know which is worse*, she thought mournfully; then she decided *this* was worse—even though a lot of ways it was better—just because she didn't know whether she could get out if she wanted to.

She had to find that out first. She had to get back to the rocket. Once she was safe inside again, with Petey, she could make up her mind.

CHAPTER SEVENTEEN

"I HAVE TO go back to the rocket," Dee said out loud. "I have to go back and get us some clothes, anyhow, if we're going to stay here."

Then she thought she felt cold, but there was a question-y feeling in her mind; she decided the Mother-bug must be *asking* her if she was cold, and finally realized that that was because she had said they needed clothes.

"No, I'm not cold," she said. "We have to have some clothes, that's all. The ones we wore yesterday are dirty. Unless..." Unless they had a soil-remover. Then she'd have to think of some other reason to go back to the rocket. "Unless you have some old clothes around," she finished up craftily. But it sounded silly, and her voice sounded too loud anyhow, every time she said anything, as if she were talking to herself...and how did she know she wasn't, anyhow? How did she know she wasn't making it all up?

The feeling she got was so exactly like the sound of her own mother's little impatient sigh when Dee was being stubborn, that it was suddenly impossible to go on doubting at all.

When the Mother-bug laughed, it tickled in her mind; when the Mother was angry, it prickled. When the Mother called to her, it was a feeling that came creeping; when she didn't want to hear, it came seeping anyhow.

Tickle-prickle; creep-seep. I spy. I speard you. It was like seeing and hearing both, if you let it be, or just like knowing what you didn't know a minute before. It could be without the seeing part, as when she thought she heard Petey's voice; or it could be without hearing, just a picture full of meaning, without any words. You didn't *really* see or hear; you really just *found out.*

AND IF you let yourself know the difference, you could tell what your own idea was, and what was coming from the Mother-bug...such as thinking she was cold for a minute a little while ago. You could tell, all right, if you wanted to...

It was a lot smarter to make sure you knew the differences to watch for when the Mother-bug was putting something in your head, so you wouldn't get mixed up and start thinking you wanted something yourself, when it was really what *she* wanted. Or like thinking *Petey* wanted her to open the door in the rocket, where it was really the Mother-bug.

No it wasn't either. Petey *did* want her to, because he heard the Mother-bug calling them from outside, before Dee heard it...or he understood better what it was, or...*she's telling me all this; I'm not thinking it for myself!* Up to that part about Petey being the one who wanted her to open the door, she *had* been thinking for herself; after that, it was the bug. It was getting easier, now, to tell the difference.

"How do you know Earthish?" she asked out loud, but there wasn't any kind of answer except the question-y feeling again. "I mean the language we use. I mean how do you know the words to put in my head...?" She stopped talking because her head was hurting; then she realized the Mother-bug was trying to explain, only it was too complicated for her to understand. Part of it was that the bugs *didn't* know Earthish, though. She understood that much well enough, and lost the hope she'd had for just an instant that other *people* were here already. She didn't try to understand the rest. "How do you make Petey put things in my head?" she asked instead.

IT FELT as if the Mother was smiling. She didn't *make Petey say things at all.* He was always saying things, only mostly Dee didn't know how to listen—except, somehow, when the Mother-bug was around, it was easier...

Her head was starting to hurt again, so she stopped asking questions about that. "Listen," she said; "I still have to go back to the rocket."

She didn't know whether she wanted to come back here or stay there. No—that was true, all right, that she didn't know; but right now it was the Mother-bug *asking* her what she wanted to do.

"I don't know," she said, not trying to pretend anything, because the Mother-bug would have spy-heard that part already. "Only, I have to get back there anyhow; so I'll wait till I get there to decide."

She'd leave Petey behind, and return at least for a visit?

"No!" she said. That was one thing at least she was sure about. Even if she was sure she was coming back, she couldn't leave Petey all alone here with these bugs. Mommy would...*anybody* would get mad at a kid for doing a thing like that!

"No!" she said again. "I've got to go, and Petey has to go with me; that's all there is to it." She thought she sounded very firm and grown-up, until she felt the Mother smiling again in the way that made her remember her...somebody she used to know.

CHAPTER EIGHTEEN

THE MORE she learned, the less she seemed to know. The Strange child, though still inexplicably frightened, was at last being communicative and cooperative. Yet each new piece of information acquired during the morning's interview had only served to make the puzzle of the Strangers more complex or more abstruse.

How and why they had come here...even *whence* they had come...their habits, customs, biology, psychology...the nature of the *ship* in which they lived, and flew...the very fact of the existence of the older child's continuing fear and doubt...and Strangest of all, perhaps, the by-now irrefutable fact that *neither of the children knew whether their Mother was alive, inside the Ship, or had departed...*

None of these matters were any easier to comprehend now than they had been the day before; and most of them were more confusing.

However, there was now at least some hope of solving some parts of the puzzle...two parts, in any case. The Strange daughter had agreed, after only slight hesitation, to allow a flying son to come inside the *ship* with her, and to explain to the Mother, watching through her son's eyes, as much of what was to be found there as she could. The child apparently had felt that by permitting the exploratory visit, she was securing the right of the babe to accompany her on the trip…a right she would in any case have had for the asking. And there was some further thought in the girl's mind of perhaps not returning…but Daydanda was not seriously concerned about it. She had refrained carefully from proffering any insistent hospitality, since the daughter's fear of remaining alone with her sibling seemed even greater than that of remaining with the Household, provided only she did not feel herself to be a *captive* in the House.

IT STILL remained to be seen, of course, whether it would be possible to provide for the two Strangers within the biological economy of the Families. That, however, was the other part of the puzzle that was already on the road to a solution. The daughter had most fortuitously, before leaving the Lady's chamber, expressed an urgent need to perform some biological functions for which, apparently, a waste receptacle of some sort was required. Daydanda had issued rapid orders to one of the more ingenious of the mason sons, to manufacture as best he could a receptacle conforming to the image she found in the child's mind. Then she had seized the opportunity to ask if she might have a nursing daughter take some samples of the *milk* and other food that had come with them from the *ship*, and of such other bodily by-products as she had already observed the Strangers to produce; the tears that came from the eyes in the release of grief, and the general bodily exudation for which the child's symbol was *sweat*, but whose purpose or function she seemed not to understand herself.

ONCE AGAIN, as she had had occasion to do many times before, the Lady regretted the maternal compulsiveness of her own nature that had stood in the way of producing a Scientist within the Household. As matters now stood, the samplings she had secured from the Strange children would have to be flown two full days journey away, to the Encyclopedic Seat, for analysis. If she had been willing—just once in all these years—to inhibit the breeding of a full Family in order to devote the necessary nutrient and emotional concentration to the creation of a pair of Scientists, she would be able to have the answer to the present problem in hours instead of days, and without having to forego the services of two of her best fliers for the duration of the trip there and back. Then, if it appeared necessary to utilize the more varied facilities of the Seat, she could submit her samples with the security of knowing that her own representative there would keep watch over her interests; and that everything learned about the Strange samples would be transmitted instantly and fully from the brother at the Seat to the twin in the Household. Daydanda knew only too well how often in the past the Seat had seen fit to retain information for its own use, when the products for analysis came from an unrepresented House...

No use in worrying now, either about what might be, or about what had not been done. *One* matter, at least, would be resolved before the day was done...the baffling question of what lay inside that double-arched opening in the wall of the Wings-House...and along with it, the answer, perhaps, to the puzzle of the Strange children's Mother.

CHAPTER NINETEEN

THIS TIME, they rode in the litter; and the trip that had taken a long afternoon the day before was accomplished in a short hour of trotting, bouncing progress. Yesterday the pace had been slowed as much by the litter-bearers' efforts to spare their Lady any unnecessary jostling, as by the shortness of Dee's leg; today Daydanda's laboring sons were inhibited by no such considerations.

At the edge of the clearing they paused, their eyes averted from the shiny hull.

Dee laughed out loud, and ran out into the sunlight. It felt good. She knew she was showing off, but it made her feel better just to stand there and look straight *up*, because she knew there wasn't one of them that would dare to do it.

"Sissies!" she yelled out, there was no answer...not even a scolding-feeling from the Mother-bug.

She went back to the litter, got Petey out, and parked him on the muddy ground near the airlock, wondering if it was safe to leave him out there while she went inside. They wouldn't do anything like grabbing him and running off, she decided. The Mother-bug wanted to know about the rocket too much; and the Mother-bug wanted *her* to come back, too—not just Petey.

Still, she didn't make any move to go inside. It was good standing there in the sun, even without the showoff part of it. She watched Petey grab big chunks of yellow mud and plaster himself with them, and felt the sun soak into her shoulders and warm the top of her head.

This place wouldn't be so bad, she thought, if it wasn't for the trees everyplace, cutting out the sun. Inside the forest, it was always a little bit drippy and damp, and the light was always dimmed. But when you got out into it, the sun here was a good one—better than on Starhope. It felt like the sun used to feel, she thought she remembered, when she was almost as little as Petey, before they went away from Earth.

SHE WISHED she could remember more about Earth. Mommy always told her stories about it, but Mom…
Don't think about that!
She wished she could remember more about Earth. It was green there. Green like in the forests here, where the treetops lent their color to everything? That wasn't what Mom…what the stories meant, she was sure. For just an instant, there was a picture in her mind; and because it came so suddenly, she suspected at first that the Mother-bug put it there, but it didn't *feel* that way. Then she wasn't sure whether it was something she remembered, from when she was very little, or whether it was truly a *picture*—one she'd seen at school, or on the T-Z. But she was sure that that was how Earth was supposed to look, wherever she was remembering it from.

The trees there were called Apple trees, for a kind of fruit they had, and they grew separated from each other on a hillside, with low branches where the children could climb right up to the tops of them like walking up steps. Then you'd sit in the top, and the breeze would come by smelling sweet and fresh like Mom…the way lavender looked. And you would eat sweet fruit from the swaying branch, and…

SHE JUMPED as a hairy arm brushed her hand. It was the one with wings who was supposed to go with her into the rocket. It...*he,* the Mother said it was her *son,* pointed to the air-lock, and Dee got the question-y feeling again. Then there were words to go with it.

"Go inside now?"

It was surprising at first that his "voice" "sounded" just like the Mother-bug's. Then she realized it *was* the Mother-bug, talking through his mind. Dee understood by now that the words she "heard" were supplied by herself to fit the picture or emotions the other person—*that was silly, calling a bug a person!*—"sent" to her; but she was pretty sure that the words or the sort-of-a-voice sound she'd make up for one person—bug—would be different from the way she'd "hear" another one.

Anyway, the Mother wanted her to go inside. She decided against leaving Petey outdoors by himself, and picked him up and lifted him in before she climbed through the air lock, the bug with wings came right behind her...

The playroom was a mess.

Living in there all the time, Dee hadn't realized how everything was thrown around; but now, when she had a visitor with her—even if he was just a bug—she felt kind of ashamed about the way it all looked. Maybe he wouldn't know the difference...but he would. She remembered how the inside of their big House was neat and clean all over; and not just the inside...even the woods were kept tidy all the time. She'd seen a bunch of bugs out picking up dead branches, and gathering leaves off the ground on the way over here.

THIS BUG didn't seem to care though. He looked around at everything, with his head bent down backwards so he could see, and Dee got the idea he wanted to know if it was all right to touch things. She picked up a toy and some clothes, and put them into the hands on his front legs. After that, he went around looking and touching and handling things all over the playroom, while Dee hunted up some clothes to take back with them.

She couldn't find very much that was clean, so she took a whole pile of stuff from the floor, and went in back to put them into the soil remover. The bug followed her. It—*he*—watched her put the clothes into the square box; he jumped a little when she turned the switch on and it started shaking, as it always did, a little. Dee laughed. Then she went around turning on all the machines that she knew how to work, just to show the bug. She wished she knew how to use the power tool, because that made a whole lot of noise, and did all kinds of different things; but Daddy never let...but she didn't know how to, that's all.

The bug just stood still in the middle of the room, looking and listening. He didn't even *want* to touch anything in here, Dee figured; so she asked him out loud, didn't he want to feel what the machines were like? And then she found out she *could* tell the difference in one bug's voice and another's, because the Mother said a kind of eager, "Thank you—are you sure it will do no harm?" But the son-bug said at the same time, kind of nervous-sounding, "No, thank you; these devices are very Strange..." and then he must have realized what his Mother wanted, because he said, "I am afraid I might damage them."

DEE FELT the Mother's smiling then, and with the smile, a question: "Where do they breathe? With what do they eat?"

"Who?" Dee said out loud.

"Those others...*the machines*, is your symbol for them." And at the same time, she saw inside her head a sort of twisty picture of the room all around her. She saw it with her own eyes, the way it really was; and at the same time, she was seeing it the way the Mother-bug must be seeing it—which was the way her son was seeing it, and "sending" the picture to her. It wasn't *much* different, mostly just the colors weren't as bright. And somehow, all the machines, the way the Mother-bug saw them, were *alive*.

Dee laughed. Those bugs were pretty smart, but there were lots of things she knew that they didn't.

"They *don't* breathe," she said scornfully; "they're just machines, that's all."

"?????"

"They're machines: they do things for people. You turn 'em on and make them work, and then when you're done, you turn them off again. They run on electricity."

"?????"

She couldn't explain electricity very well. "It's like...lightning."

But the Mother didn't know what she meant by that either. "Don't talk," the big bug told her; "make a picture in your head. Stand near the machine-that-cleans, and make pictures, not words, in your own head, to show how it works for you."

DEBORAH tried, but she'd never seen what the machinery looked like inside the soil remover. There wasn't very much of it anyway. Da...somebody had explained it to her once. There was just a horn—or something like a horn—that kept blowing, without making any noise; at least not any noise that you could hear. The blowing shook all the dirt out of the clothes, and there was a u-v light inside to sterilize them at the same time. That was all she knew, and she didn't know what it really *looked* like, except for the u-v bulb; and she didn't even know what made *that* work, really.

"I'm sorry," she said. "I'd make a picture for you if I could."

"Is there one of these creatures...machines...you have *seen* inside?"

She'd seen the inside of the freeze unit when it was being fixed once. She tried to remember just how that looked; but it was complicated, and the Mother still didn't seem to understand.

"The little pipes?" she asked, and Dee wasn't sure whether she meant the freezing coils or the wires; but then she was sure it was the wires. "They bring food to the creature so it can work?"

"No. I *told* you. It's not a 'creature.' It doesn't even *ever* eat. The wires just have electricity in them, that's all. Don't you even know what an electric wire is?"

"Where do the pipes...wires...bring the *electric* from?"

Dee looked around. The generator was...it was in... "There's a generator someplace," she said carelessly. "It makes electricity; that's what it's for. I can show you how the T-Z works, because somebody I know showed me once." She went out to the playroom, and started talking, describing her favorite toy, and making pictures in her mind to show the Mother-bug how it worked, and what some of the stories looked like. She talked fast, and kept on talking till she had to stop for breath; but then she realized she didn't have to talk out loud to the Mother, so she went on thinking about stories she'd seen on T-Z, and she decided she'd take it back with some of the film strips, so the Mother could see for herself how it worked.

MACHINE! An entity capable of absorbing energy in one form, transmuting it to some other form, and expending it in the performance of work…work requiring judgment, skill, training…and yet the Strange child said these things were not alive! Daydanda rested on her great couch, but felt no ease, and wished again that she had had the fortitude to go out with the small group. To *see for herself*…

But she could never even have gotten through the narrow double-arch entrance to the *ship*. The ship…that too, then, was a machine! It was a structure; a builded thing; *not-alive;* yet it could fly…

These two Strangers were very different creatures from a very different race; she began to understand that now. The striking similarities were purely superficial. The differences…

The thought of the babe tugged at her mind, asking warmth, asking food, and she could not think of him as Strange at all. There were differences; there were samenesses. No need now to make a counting of how many of which kind. Only to learn as much as could be learned, while she determined whether it was possible or desirable to keep the two Strange ones within the Household.

Very well then: these *machines* are not alive…not all the time. They live only when the Strange daughter permits it, in most cases by moving a small organ projecting from the outside. Not so different, if you stopped to think of it, from the Bigheads, who might be counted not-alive most of the time. It was hard to adjust to the notion of working members of a Household existing on that low level, but…these were Strangers.

And still the child maintained the *machines* were not alive at all, not members of her Household, merely structures, animated by…

...By what? The things absorbed energy from somewhere, through the little pipes...apparently almost pure energy, the stuff the child called *electric*. What was the source of the *electric*?

THE STRANGE daughter had a symbol and not-clear picture in her mind: a thing with rotating brushes, and a hard core of some kind. A thing kept under a round shelter, made of the same fabric as the ship...*metal*. From under this *metal* housing came *wires* through which *electric* flowed to the machines...much as cement flowed from the snout or a mason, or honey from the orifice of a nurse.

Into this machine, food was...no, the child's symbol was a different one, though the content of the symbol was the same; food designed for a *machine* was *fuel*. Very well: *fuel* was fed only to the...the *Mother-machine!*

Now the whole thing was beginning to make sense. The *machines* were comparable—in relationship to the Stranger's Household—to the winged or crawling creatures that sometimes co-existed with the Household of Daydanda's own people, sharing a House in symbiotic economy, but having, of course, a distinct biology and therefore, a separate Mother and separate reproductive system.

The *generator*, said the child, supplied warmth and nourishment and vital power to the other *machines;* the *generator* was fed by the *humans* (the child's symbol for her own people); the *machines* worked for the *humans.*

"Is the generator of machines alive?" the Lady asked.

"No. I told you before..."

"Am *I* alive?"

"Yes. Of course."

The wonder was not that the Strange daughter failed to include the symbiotes in her semantic concept of "life," but rather that she *did* include Daydanda, and Daydanda's Household; The Lady abandoned the effort to communicate such an abstraction and asked if she might be shown the Mother-machine.

Wavering impression of willingness, but...

THE THING was on the other side of a door. The daughter went through one doorway into the room she had first entered, approached the far wall, and turned sideways, to demonstrate in great detail a mechanism of some sort (not one of the *machines;* no *wires* connected it to the Mother-machine) whose function apparently was educational. It created visual auditory, and olfactory hallucinations, utilizing information previously registered on strips of somehow-sensitized fabric inside it...roughly analogous to the work of a teaching-nurse, who could register and retain for instructive purposes information supplied by the Mother, and never fully available to the nurse in her own functioning, nor in any way necessary for her to "know." Thus an unwinged nurse could give instruction in the art of flying, and the biology of reproduction. But, once again, the Strangers' mechanism was—or so the child said—simply an artifact, a *made* thing, without life of its own and this time it was even more puzzling than before, because the object in question was self-contained—had its own internal source of *electric,* and needed no connecting wires with the Mother--machine.

Mother-machine...*Mother!*

Daydanda reacted so sharply to the sudden connection of data that Kackot asleep in the next chamber, woke and came rushing to her side. Smiling, she shared her thoughts with him.

Machine-Mother and Stranger-Mother both...behind a door! The same door?

"THE SOURCE of *electric* is behind the other door?" The Mother-bug's question formed clearly in her mind this time. Dee looked up from the T-Z. There wasn't any other door. She looked all around but she couldn't see one. There was just the airlock, and the door to the workroom and kitchen in back, but the Mother didn't mean either of those.

"I don't know what you're talking about," she said, and went back to get the clothes out of the soil-remover, and thawed out a piece of cake from the freeze.

DAYDANDA looked at one and the same time through the eyes of her son in the Strange ship, and through those of the Stranger. Both focused on the same part of the same wall. Through the son's eyes, the Lady saw a rectangular outline in the surface of the wall, and a closure device set in one side. Through the child's eyes, she could see only a smooth unbroken stretch of wall.

"There is no door," the child informed her clearly...then turned around and left the room, once more broadcasting meaningless symbols, and accurate, but inappropriate, arithmetic.

DEE MADE sure she had enough clothes for a while. She didn't want to come back here right away. Maybe later on. She'd have to come back later on, of course. She couldn't really *stay* with the bugs. But...

She took a long strip off the roll of bottles, and a lot of milk, and all the powdered stuff she could find that looked any good. They probably had water there, anyhow. Things out of the freeze would spoil if she took them, so she left them for later, when she came back to the rocket.

She had to make a couple of trips to get everything out to the litter: the clothes and food and the T-Z and Petey and some toys for Petey; and the Mother-bug or the son-bug, one of them, kept trying to say things at her, but she wouldn't listen. She just started saying the Space Girl oath again; and when she couldn't remember it, even some of the silly multiplication, because she didn't feel like talking right now.

CHAPTER TWENTY

DAYDANDA was short of time, and entirely out of patience. The Strange child's antics had gone from the puzzling to the incomprehensible, and the Lady of the House had other concerns...many of them now aggravated by inattention over the preceding days. She simply could not continue to devote nearly all her thought, nor nearly so much of her time, to any one matter.

The children had brought back with them provisions sufficient for a few days at least, and the Mother was satisfied that their presence in the Household for that period represented no menace to the members of her own Families.

There was no purpose to thinking about their continued stay until the Encyclopedic Seat completed a biological analysis. Nor could she determine how much responsibility she was willing to take for possible damage to the Wings-House in further exploration and examination, until she knew for certain that she could offer the Strange children a permanent home in her own Household.

The flying son who had accompanied the two of them on their trip to the *rocket,* had informed her that the barrier on which the daughter's fear seemed centered was, like the rest of the Strange structure, composed of *metal,* and that this *metal* was the hardest wood he had ever seen. It could be cut through, he thought, but not without damage to the fabric that might not be repairable. As for discovering the secret of the mechanism that was designed to hold the *door* closed or allow it to open, he was pessimistic.

There was nothing to do, then, but put the matter from her mind until she had more information.

Accordingly, the Mother gave instructions—when all her children were in communion after the evening Homecalling—that every member of the Household was to treat the Strange guests with kindliness and respect; to guard them from dangers they might fail to recognize; to cooperate with their needs or wishes, insofar as they could express them; and to offer just such friendship—no more and no less—as the young Strangers themselves seemed to desire. She then assigned a well-trained elder daughter (a nurse might have done better in some ways, but she wanted a written record of any information acquired, and that meant it had to be a winged one) to maintain full-time contact with the Strange daughter, so as to answer the visitors' questions and to keep the Household informed of their activities.

With that, she turned her mind to more familiar problems of her Household.

DEE WAS glad she'd decided to come back. Of course, they couldn't really stay here, but just for a little while, it was interesting.

The bugs were really pretty nice people she thought, and giggled at the silly way that sounded...calling bugs *people.* But it was hard not to, because they thought about themselves that way, and *acted* that way; and once you got used to how they looked, (And how they looked at you, too: it still felt funny having them turn their backs to you when you talked to them, so they could see you.) it was just natural to think of them that way.

Anyhow, they were all nice to her, and especially nice to Petey. She could "talk" to them pretty easily now, too; but she had an idea she wasn't really doing it herself. There was a…*big-sister?*…bug who was sort of keeping an eye on her, she thought. Not a real eye, of course; she giggled again. Just the kind of an eye that could see pictures in somebody else's head. But any time she wanted to know something, such as whether it was all right to go out, and where could she find some water to mix the food with, and—as now—how to get to one of those gardens—the big-sister-bug would start telling her almost before she asked. And Dee thought that probably most of the other bugs she talked to were at least partway using the big-sister's mind—the way the Mother-bug had helped her "hear" what Petey "said"—because now they all seemed to have pretty much the same kind of "voice." But it was different from the Mother's, or from the one who went to the rocket with her.

THAT GAVE her a strange feeling sometimes…thinking that maybe the big-sister one was *listening* in on her all the time, but at least it wasn't like with the Mother-bug, who'd make that prickly hurting if you thought something she didn't like. The big-sister-bug didn't try to tell her what to do or what not to do, or put ideas in her head, or anything like that. So if she wanted to just listen all the time, Deborah supposed it didn't matter much. And it certainly was useful.

Petey was stuck in the mud again; Dee helped him get loose. She couldn't carry him around all the time, so she'd finally settled for not putting any clothes on him except a diaper, and just letting him get as gucky as he wanted to. He'd learned to crawl pretty well on the soft surface; it was just once in a while that he'd put an arm in too deep, or something like that. But he didn't mind, so she didn't either.

She still couldn't see any garden; just the trees and the mud. "How far is it?" she asked…or wondered.

"Not much more," Big-sister told her. "Walk around the next tree, and go to…to your *right.*"

Just a little farther on, after she turned, Dee saw the sudden splurge of color. It was a different garden from the one she'd seen the first time; at least the big-sister-bug said it was. The other one was for the tiny babies—the ones who were really about the same age as Petey, but about half his size. This one was for the next oldest bunch, but they were all just about Petey's size, so maybe he could play with them.

IT LOOKED just the same, though; the same kind of crazy combinations of colors and shapes. Everything was just as she remembered, except for not being scared now; and when she got right up to it, she saw these bugs weren't nursing on the. plants the way the others had been doing. Once in a while, one of them would stop and suck a little while on a tendril; mostly, though, they were chasing each other around, and kind-of playing games—just like kindergarten kids anyplace.

There were two big bugs—the kind that had dark-colored skins, and had eyes, but didn't have any wings. These ones were nurses, Dee figured. There were others just like these, with different kinds of noses—and some with different kinds of hands—who did other things; but these ones had to be nurses, because they were watching the kids. They were sitting outside the garden, not doing anything, and Dee felt funny about going inside, partly because it was supposed to be for *little* kids, partly because she was afraid she'd step on one of the plants or something like that. So she let Petey crawl right on inside, by himself, and she sat down next to the nurses, and just watched.

IT WAS WARM in the forest. It was always warm there, but she was getting to like it. She wasn't wearing anything except shorts now, and the only thing she minded was always feeling a little bit *damp,* because the air was so wet. But altogether, she had to admit it was better at least than being in the rocket all by themselves; shut up in there as they had been, Petey was always cranky and fussing about something. Now he was having a good time, so he didn't keep bothering her. And she had the T-Z set back in their room, now, and you didn't even need a light on to work that. Of course, she didn't have very many filmstrips for it; she'd have to go back to the rocket pretty soon and get some more.

They'd need some more food, too, and she'd have to get Petey's diapers clean again. She wished there was some way to take along frozen food; then she wouldn't have to fuss around with mixing things with water, and all that, but...

The big-sister-bug was asking her what she meant by "frozen food," but she'd tried to explain that before.

Anyhow, she had to go back there pretty soon, if she and Petey decided to stay here for a while, because she had to leave a message, so that when somebody came to rescue them, they'd know where to look.

"You wish to visit the Wings-House *now?*" Big-sister asked.

"It's kind of late today," Dee said; "tomorrow, I guess." Sometimes she talked out loud like that, even though she knew it didn't make any difference. All she had to do was *think* what she meant, but sometimes she just talked out loud from habit.

"The litter goes swiftly," said Big-sister. "If you wish to make the visit now..."

"Tomorrow!" This time she didn't say it... just thought it extra hard. Big-sister stopped bothering her about it and she sat still and watched Petey crawling around and grabbing at the pretty colors.

CHAPTER TWENTY ONE

DAYDANDA received the report personally, and trusted not even her own memory to retain it all, but relayed to three elder daughters, so that whatever errors anyone might make in transcription, the records of the others could correct. There was so much technical symbology throughout the message—even though the clerk at the Seat tried to keep it intelligible—that she could not try to comprehend it entirely as it came. She would have to study and examine the meaning of each datum, before she could fully determine what it meant in terms of the questions she had to answer for her Household and the Strangers.

If she had *only* had a pair of Scientists! Communicating with each other, they would have known the purpose of the analysis;

communicating with her, Mother and sons, there would have been no problem of translation of symbols. But it was hardly possible to give full information to the Scientists at the Seat, when many of them were from neighboring or nearby Households, whose best interests were by no means identical with her own. Of course, they vowed impartiality when they took up Encyclopedic work, but...

The next breeding, *definitely....!* (Kackot, daily more sensitive, came to the archway and peered in. He had taken to working and napping in the other room these past few days. She sent a gentle negative.) The *very next* breeding would have to be limited to a pair of Scientists! Though now that she had put it off so long, and the youngest babes were already growing too big for fondling...

Scientists it would be! The Household needed them. All very well to follow easily along the drive to procreate, but it was necessary, also, to safeguard those already born. And right now, the problem was not one of breeding, or breeding inhibition, but of making enough sense out of the message so that she could come to some decision about the Strangers.

SHE HAD the three daughters bring her their copies, and lay for a long while on her couch, studying and comparing, and making rapid notes. Finally, she called to Kackot, and thought as she did so that it would perhaps do something to soothe his wounded feelings, if he felt she was unable to make this decision without his help.

He listened, soberly, and did what she knew she could count on him to do: reformulated, repeated, and advised according to what she wished. Since the report clearly established that the Strangers represented no biologic danger to the Household—their exudations were entirely non-toxic, and some of the solid matter was even useable containing large quantities of semi-digested cellulose—it was clearly her duty to keep them in the Household, and learn as much as possible from them. Since the report further indicated that normal food would be non-toxic to the Strangers (and Mother and consort both tended to avoid the question, unanswered in the report, of whether normal feeding would supply *all* the nourishment the two Strange children needed), it was possible to extend indefinite hospitality to them.

(After all, if there were elements of nourishment they required beyond what the fungus-foods and wood-honey offered, they could continue to make use of their own supplies...which would last longer if supplemented by native food. So Daydanda eased her conscience.)

The question of how far to go in examining the *rocket* was more complicated. The ethic involved...

"There is no ethic," Kackot reminded her stiffly, "above the duty of a Mother to her Household. The obligations to a Stranger in the House are sacred, but..." He dropped his formality, and ended, smiling and once more at ease "...*non-biologic!*" So, again, Daydanda soothed her conscience.

Still, it would be better at least to try to get the child's agreement, even though it was a foregone conclusion that they could not expect her cooperation. The Lady summoned the Strange daughter once more to her chamber.

"I COULD write the message here, I guess," Dee said thoughtfully. "If you're going to send somebody to the rocket anyhow, there's no reason for me to go." It wasn't as if she couldn't trust them; they wouldn't hurt anything. And anyhow, the Mother said she wanted to keep showing Dee what the son was doing, so they could ask questions whenever they didn't understand something.

Right now, the Mother-bug was feeling a question. "Write a message?" Dee stopped thinking herself, and then she understood. The bugs only used writing for keeping *records* of things. When they wanted to tell somebody something, it didn't matter how far away the person was; so they didn't write things down for other people. Just for themselves, and to make a kind of history for other bugs later on. The Mother wanted to know: wouldn't she "be aware" of the rescue party when it came.

She shook her head, and didn't try to explain anything, because it was just too *different*. "I've got some crayons in my room," she told the Mother-bug, "but I used up all the paper already."

"We have paper." The funny jumpy Father-bug jumped up in his funny way, and went over to a kind of big table full of cubby holes, even before the Mother was done "talking," and got a piece of their kind of paper, and gave it to Dee. The Mother was asking about crayons, what they were and how they worked, but Dee was asking *her* at the same time for something to write with, and what kind of paper was this?

THE PAPER was made out of tree bark, and covered with a kind of waxy stuff that they made in their bodies. They seemed to make everything right inside themselves—as if each bug was a kind of chemicals factory, and you could put in such and such, and turn some switches inside, and get out so-and-so. It was certainly useful, Dee thought, with vague distaste, and then realized nobody had given her a pencil or anything yet.

But you wouldn't use a pencil on this kind of paper. You'd use a stylus, or something sharp.

"Very soon," the Mother-bug said. "My daughter brings you a sharp thing to write with." Then she raised her arm to show Dee where a little sharp horny tip was, on the back of her elbow, that she used herself.

"But how can you see what…?" Dee started to ask, and then she felt the Mother-bug laughing, and then she laughed herself. It was so hard to get used to people with eyes in the *backs* of their heads.

One of the nurse-type bugs came in, bowing and crawling the way they always did if they got near the Mother-bug, handed Dee a pointed stick, and crawled out again.

"I am staying with some bugs in a big house," Dee scratched as clearly as she could through the wax. The bark underneath was orangey-colored, and the wax was white, so it showed through pretty well. "My baby brother Petey is with me. Please come and get us." Then she signed it, "Deborah (DEE) Levin." And then realized she hadn't put anything in about how to find them. She tried to ask the Mother, but so far they hadn't been able to get together on that kind of thing at all. The bugs didn't use measurements or distances or directions the same way; they just seemed to *know* where to go, and how far they were.

"We will know if Strangers come," the Mother promised her; "we will go to them."

Dee thought that over, and added to her message; "P.S. if some big bugs come around, don't shoot. They're friends; they're taking care of Petey and me." And put her initials at the end, the way you're supposed to do with a P.S.

"WHEN IS he going?" she asked. "I mean, should I stay here, so you can ask me questions, or do you want me to come back later?" Petey was getting kind of restless, and he wanted something, but she wasn't sure what.

"The brother wishes to return to the garden," the Mother explained. "He understands what I told you about the food. He wanted to suck on the sweet plants before, but was afraid. Now he desires to return to the garden and to the other children, and suck as they do." Then she said her son was going to the ship right away; but if Dee wanted to go to the garden with Petey, that was all right; the Mother-bug could talk to her just as well that way.

"I'd rather...I'd kind of rather *look* at you when we talk," Dee said. She knew it seemed silly to them, because they weren't used to it, but she couldn't help it. Anyhow, she got a kind of good feeling being in the Mother-bug's room. The first time she came in here it was *awful*, but right now she felt nervous or something. She didn't know why, but she *did* know she'd feel better if she stayed here with the big old bug.

"Stay then, my child."

One of the ones with wings came in; this kind just bowed, they didn't crawl. He took the message from Dee, and went back to the garden; then they just waited for a while.

THE MOTHER was busy, thinking someplace else, and the Father-bug gave her a funny feeling when she tried to talk to him, because he wasn't like a Daddy at all. Not the way the big fat bug was like a real Mother. The skinny, jumpy one was nervous and fussy and worried; and Dee thought he probably didn't like her very much. So she just sat still, squatting on the floor with her back against the wall, and thought maybe she'd go get her T-Z set and look at something till the Mother-bug was ready. But it was warm and comfortable and she didn't want to go away, out of this room, where the Mother was just like a Mother was a Mother—so she sort of rolled over a little bit, and curled up right on the floor and closed her eyes. If she didn't *look* at the piled-up mats and the ugly old belly on top, it felt more like a Mother than ever before for a long time since it was so warm, hot, glowing red, and the voice said, *fire...fire...fire...*

That was on Halloween, all black and orange, witches and ghosts, and the witch said, "Fire! Fire! Run! Run!" but the ghost looked like a big fat bug, only white, except the white ones don't have eyes; and this one had two great big hollow eyeholes; and it was crying because it couldn't find the little girl who should have opened...opened her eyes, so she could see, why didn't she open her eyeholes, so she could see the little girl? Because the little girl had no eyes, only it didn't matter as long as the door was closed, the ghost couldn't get through a safety safety safe; the little girl is safe, on Halloween when the ground is black and behind the door is black, black, black you can't see, and black it's all burned up, and the ghost is white; so there's no ghost there in the black, only a great big ugly bugley belly all swoll up with white dead long time...*No!* ...all black for Halloween, black, black...

CHAPTER TWENTY TWO

THE LADY heard; and by her lights, she understood. It was a sick and ugly thing to hear, and a terrible sad thing to comprehend.

A Mother of fourteen Families is, perforce, accustomed to grief and fear and failing; she has suffered time and again the agonies of flesh and spirit with which her children met the tests of growth; the fears of battle, terror of departure, pains of hunger, the awful skrinking from death. The time they almost lost their House to swarming hostile Families; the time the boy died in the ravenous claws of their own Bigheads; the time the rotten-fungus-sickness spread among them...time after time; but never, in all the crowded years of life-giving and life-losing had Daydanda known a sickness such as now shouted at her from the Strange girl's dream.

Even her curiosity would have faltered before this outpouring, but she could not turn away. One listens to a troubled child's dream to diagnose, to find a remedy...but *this!* If it were possible to invade the barriers of a full-grown Mother of crime, one might find sorrow and fear and torment such as this.

As the sunlight had seared her eyeball, so the hell-fires of the childish dreaming burned her soul.

The girl desired that they should find her Mother dead!

There was no other way to make sense of it. Daydanda tried. Everything in her fought against even the formulation of such a statement. It was not only evil, but impossible...*unnatural.* Non-biologic.

The child wanted to know that her Mother had been burned to death.

WITHIN THE shining rocket, Daydanda's son moved curiously, feeling and touching each Strange object cautiously, examining with his eager eye each Strange and inexplicable shape. He waited there, unable to be still in the presence of so much to explore; too fearful of doing damage to explore further till his Mother's mind met his. But the Lady could not be disturbed, the sibling at relay duty said; the Lady was refusing all calls, accepting no contact.

Wait!

He waited.

NON-BIOLOGIC...But what did she know of the biology of a Stranger? Even as much as the clerk at the Seat had told her, from the analysis of scrapings and samplings—even that much she did not fully understand, and that could not be more than a fractional knowledge in any case.

She could not, would not, believe that the Strange daughter's Strange complex of feelings and fears and desires was as subjectively sick as it seemed, by her own standards and experience, to be. A different biologic economy—which most assuredly they had—or a completely different reproductive social organization...

It *was* possible. The child's independence and resourcefulness...her untrained awareness of self and others...her lack of certainty even as to whether her Mother still lived...the very existence of two siblings of such widely divergent age and size, without even a suggestion of others who had departed, or been left behind...

207

Till now, the Mother had been trying to fit these two Strange children somehow into the patterns of her own world. But she remembered what she had considered at the time to be childish over-statement, or just a part of the confusion of the girl's mind as to place, time, and direction.

From another world...

FROM ABOVE the treetops, but that had not been startling. A nesting couple always descended from above the trees, after the nuptial flight. From above the treetops, *but not from below them. From another world...!*

Kackot was hovering nervously above her. The daughter on relay was asking again on behalf of the Son at the Strange ship. The daughters in the corral wished to report...

To Kackot and the son both, imperative postponements. She clamped control on her seething mind long enough to determine that it was no emergency in the corral, then closed them all out again, and tried to think more clearly.

The dream was still too fresh in her mind. And now there was more data to be had. Don't think, then...just to regain one's sanity, detachment, ability to weigh and to consider. One cannot open contact with the child while looking upon her as a monster.

(A monster! That's *how I* seemed to her!)

Perspective returned slowly. She groped for Kackot's soothing thoughts, refusing to inform him yet, but gratefully accepting his concern. Then the son, waiting relatively inside the Strange Wings-House. And last, the child... Strange child of a Strange world.

"Very well," she told them all calmly, or so she hoped. "Let us commence."

DEE WAS getting tired of it. For a while, it was sort of fun, looking at things the way the son-bug saw it, and watching how clumsy he was every time he tried to do anything the way she told him. Even if these bugs didn't have any machines themselves, you had to be pretty dumb not to be able to just turn a knob when somebody explained it to you.

She realized she was being rude again. It was hard to remember, sometimes, that you shouldn't even *think* anything impolite around here. It would be pretty good for some kids she knew, to come here for a while.

"Other children others like yourself?" the Mother felt all excited. "Of your own Family?"

Dee shook her head. "No; just some of the kids who were in the Scout Troup on Starhope."

"Others...brothers and sisters...from your Household then?"

She had to think about that, to figure out the right answer. A town or a dome or a city was kind of like the Household here...but of course, the other kids weren't brothers and sisters, just because you played with them and went to school together. "Petey's the only brother I have," she said.

She didn't think she'd made it very clear, but she had a feeling that the Mother was kind of glad about the answer. She didn't know why; and anyhow, it had nothing to do with the rocket. The son-bug was waiting for his Mother to pay attention to him again.

For a minute, everybody seemed to go away. *Telling secrets!* Dee thought irritably. She was beginning to get very bored now, just sitting here answering a lot of silly questions. They'd already put the message on the wax-bark up where anybody who came in could see it, and the son-bug had a batch of diapers cleaned for Petey, and a lot of food picked out of the dry storage cabinet. She hoped it was stuff she liked. She couldn't read the labels when she was looking through his eye; anyhow they didn't need her around any more.

"DON'T BE silly," she said out loud. "There isn't any door to open; they're both open." *Now what did I say that for?* "Listen, I better go see how Petey's getting along. I don't like him trying out that fungus food all by himself. I better..."

She started to stand up, but the Mother said quietly, "Soon. Soon, child. Just a little more. You did not understand; we wish to know how to *close* the door...just how to operate the mechanism. My son is eager to try his skill at turning knobs to make machines work."

"You mean the airlock?

You can't close that from outside. But if he just wants to try it out while he's inside, I guess that's all right. It's kind of complicated, though; he might get stuck in there or something, and…"

"No child. The airlock is the double-arch opening in the outer wall, is it not?"

"…yes, and I don't think he better…"

"He does not wish to experiment with that one. My son is brave, but not foolish. Only the other, the inner door. If you will…"

"Okay, but then I want to go see Petey, all right?"

"As you please."

"Okay. Well, you have to turn the lever on the right hand side…"

"No, please…make a picture in your mind. Move your own hand. Pretend to stand before it, and to do as you would do yourself. Think a picture."

No! It won't open again! That was a silly thing to think. *But all the food's in there!*

"He will not close it then, child. Only show him *how* it works, how he *would* close it if he did. He will not; I promise he will not."

She showed him. She pretended to be doing it herself, but she felt strange; and when she was done showing him, she took a good look through the Mother and through him to make sure he hadn't really done it. The door was still open though.

"Thank you, my child. You wish to go to the garden now?"

Dee nodded, and felt the Mother go away, and almost ran out. She felt very strange.

WEARILY, the Lady commended her son for his intelligent perception, and queried him about his ability to operate the mechanism. He was a little doubtful. She reassured him: such work was not in his training; he had done well. She ordered two of her mason-builder sons to join their winged sibling in the ship, and left instructions to be notified when they were ready to begin.

She tried to rest, meanwhile, but there was too much confusion in her mind: too much new information not yet integrated. And more to come. Better perhaps to wait a bit before they tried that door? *No!* She caught herself with a start, realized that she had absorbed so much of the Strange daughter's terror of…of what lay beyond…

What lay beyond? Because the child feared it, there was no cause for her to fear as well. It was all inside the girl's subjective world, the thing that was not to be known, the thing that made the door unopenable. It was all part and parcel of the child's failure to be aware of her own Mother's life or death, of…

Of the *sickness* in the dream. She, Daydanda, had brought that sickness into her Household. It was up to her now, to diagnose and cure it—or to cast it out. Such fears were communicable; she had seen it happen, or heard of it at least.

WHEN A MOTHER dies, there is no way to tell what will happen to her sons and daughters. Even among one's own people, strange things may occur. One Household she had heard of, after the sudden death of the Mother, simply continued to go about the ordinary tasks of every day, as though no change were noticed. It could not last, of course, and did not. Each small decision left unmade, each little necessary change in individual performance, created a piling-up, confusion that led at last to the inevitable result: when undirected workers no longer cared for the food supplies; when the reckless unprepared winged ones flew off to early deaths in premature efforts to skim the treetops; when nurses ceased to care for hungry Bigheads, or for crying babes, the starving soldiers stormed the corral fences, swarmed into the gardens and the House, and feasted first on succulent infants; then on lean workers, and at last—to the vast relief of neighboring Households—on each other.

For a time, Daydanda had thought the Strange child's curious mixture of maternal and sibling attitudes to be the product of some similar situation—that the girl was simply trying not to *believe* her Mother's death, and somehow to succeed in being daughter and Mother both in her own person. But the dream made that hopeful theory impossible to entertain any longer.

Nor was it possible now to believe that the two children were the remnants of any usual Household. The girl had been too definite about the lack of any other siblings, now or in the past.

WHAT THEN? Try to discard all preconceptions. These are Strange creatures from *another world.* Imagine a biology in which there is no increase in the race-only replacement. The Lady recalled, or thought she did, some parasitic life in the Household of her childhood wherein the parent-organism had to die to make new life...

The parent had to die!

Immediately, her mind began to clear. Not sickness then...not foul untouchable confusion, but a natural Strangeness. Daydanda remembered thinking of the fires of the landing as a ritual...and now more fire...the Mother must be burned before the young one can mature? Some biologic quality of the ash, perhaps? Something...if that were so, it would explain, too, the child's persistent self-reminder that she *must* return to the *rocket,* even while she yearned to stay here where safety and protection lay.

It was fantastic, but fantastic only by the standards of the familiar world. Mother and consort bring the young pair, male and female, to a new home; and in the fires of landing, the parent-creatures die...*must* die before the young pair can develop.

She thought a while soberly, trying this fact and that to fit the theory, and each Strange-shaped piece of the puzzle fitted the next with startling ease.

Perhaps, if a world became too crowded, after many Households had grown up, some life-form of this kind might evolve, and...yes, of course! ...that would explain as well the efforts at migration over vast distances across the glaring sky.

The Lady was prepared now to discover what lay behind the door; her sons were waiting on her wishes.

CHAPTER TWENTY THREE

PETEY WAS chasing a young bug just a little bit bigger than he was round and round a mushroom shape that stood as high as Dee herself. Out of the foot-wide base of the great plant, a lacy network of lavender and light green tendrils sprouted. Deborah watched them play, the bug-child scampering on all sixes, Petey on all fours; and she didn't worry even when they both got tired and stopped and lay down half-sprawled across each other, to suck on adjoining juicy tendrils.

One of the nurses had already told her that Petey had tried some of the fungus juice when he first came out to the garden. That must have been a couple of hours ago, at least. Dee wasn't sure how long she'd been asleep, there in the Mother-bug's room, but she thought it was getting on toward evening now. And she knew that a baby's digestion works much more quickly than a grown-up's; if the stuff was going to hurt him, he'd be acting sick by now.

Probably she shouldn't have let him try it at all, until she tested some first herself. She still didn't really want to, though; and when the Mother said it was all right for him, she hadn't thought to worry about it.

She couldn't keep on fussing over him every minute, anyhow. Besides, that wasn't good for babies either. You have to let them take chances or they'll never grow up...*where did I hear that?* ...somebody had said that...

She shook her head, then smiled, watching the two kids, Petey and the bug, playing again. Petey was chortling and laughing and drooling. She decided it was probably pretty safe to trust what ever the Mother-bug said.

THE STRANGE Mother and her consort were indeed inside the ship, behind the door the child wouldn't see; and they were most certainly dead.

"It is...they look..." Her son had not liked it, looking at them. "I think the fire's heat did as the teaching-nurse has told us might happen when we go above the treetops, if we fly too long or too high in the dry sun's heat." He had had trouble giving a clear visimage to her, because he did not like to look at what he saw. But the skin, he said, judging by that of the children, was darkened, and the bodies dehydrated. They were strapped into twisted couches, as though to prevent their escape. That and the locked door...the *taboo* door?

Each item fitted into the only theory that made sense. For some biologic reason, or some reason of tradition on an overcrowded home-world, it was necessary that the parents die as soon as a nesting place for the young couple was found. And the curious conflict in the Strange daughter's mind—the wish, that her Mother was burned, with refusal to accept her Mother's death...

After all, many a winged one about to depart forever from the childhood home—not knowing whether happiness and fertility will come, or sudden death, or lonely lingering starvation...many a one has left with just such a complex of opposite-wishes.

But Daydanda could not tell, from what her son had said, or what he showed, whether the parents were *burned*, within the child's meaning of the word. The son was not too certain, even that the heat had been responsible for death, directly. The room, when he first opened up the door, was filled with a thick grey cloud which dispersed too quickly to make sure if his guess was right; but he took it to be smoke...cold smoke. No one could breathe and live through a dozen heartbeats in that cloud, he said.

WHETHER THE cloud formed first, or the heat did its work beforehand, the two were surely dead when their children came back from the first swift trip into the forest that much was sure.

Whether they had themselves locked the door, and placed a taboo on opening it, or whether the daughter had obeyed the custom of her people in sealing it off, was also impossible to determine—now.

This much, however, was clear: that the children had had ample opportunity to learn the truth for themselves if they wished, or if it were proper for them to do so. There had been no difficulty opening the door, not even for her sons who were unused to such mechanisms. The daughter knew how to do it; the daughter would not do it. Finally: the daughter had been *purposefully* set free to develop without the protection of her Mother.

If Daydanda had been certain that the protection of a foster-Mother would also inhibit the growth of the Strange children, she might have hesitated longer. As it was, she asked her consort what he thought, and he of course replied: "It might be, my Lady, my dear, that these Strange people live only as parasites in the Houses of such as ourselves. See how their Wings are a semi-House, not settled in one location, but designed for transport. See how they chose a landing place almost equidistant from ourselves and our neighbors, as if to give the young ones a little better chance to find a Household that would accept them. It would seem to me, my dear, my Lady, that out course is clear."

Daydanda was pleased with his advice. And it was time for the Homecalling. The Lady sent out her summons, loud and clear and strong for all to hear: a warning to unfriendly neighbors; a promise and renewal to all her children, young and old.

DEE LAY on her mat in the chamber she still shared with Petey, and watched the T-Z, but she did not watch it well. Her mind was too full of other things.

The Mother wanted them to stay and…"join the Household." She wasn't sure just what that would mean. Doing chores, probably, and things like that. She didn't mind that part; it would be kind of nice to *belong* someplace…until the rescue party came.

That was the only thing.

She hoped the Mother understood that part but she wasn't sure. They couldn't just *stay* here, of course.

But it might be quite a while before anybody came after them, and meanwhile…she looked at Petey, sleeping with a smile on his small fat face, and on his round fat bottom a new kind of diaper, made by the bug-people the same way they made the sleeping mats, only smaller and thinner. That was so she wouldn't have to bother with cleaning the cloth ones any more.

Petey was certainly happier here, but she'd have to watch out, she thought. If the rescue party took too long to come, he'd be more like a bug than a human!

She went back to watching the T-Z set. She had to learn a lot of things, in case she was the only person who could teach Petey anything. Tomorrow, the very next day, she was going to start really teaching him to talk. He could say words all right, if he tried. And with the bugs just in and out of your head, the way they were, he'd never try if she didn't get him started right away.

She turned back the reel, and started the film from the beginning again, because she'd missed so much.

The Lady of the House was pleased.

THE END

If you've enjoyed this book, you will not want to miss these terrific titles...

ARMCHAIR SCI-FI & HORROR DOUBLE NOVELS, $12.95 each

D-71 **THE DEEP END** by Gregory Luce
TO WATCH BY NIGHT by Robert Moore Williams

D-72 **SWORDSMAN OF LOST TERRA** by Poul Anderson
PLANET OF GHOSTS by David V. Reed

D-73 **MOON OF BATTLE** by J. J. Allerton
THE MUTANT WEAPON by Murray Leinster

D-74 **OLD SPACEMEN NEVER DIE!** John Jakes
RETURN TO EARTH by Bryan Berry

D-75 **THE THING FROM UNDERNEATH** by Milton Lesser
OPERATION INTERSTELLAR by George O. Smith

D-76 **THE BURNING WORLD** by Algis Budrys
FOREVER IS TOO LONG by Chester S. Geier

D-77 **THE COSMIC JUNKMAN** by Rog Phillips
THE ULTIMATE WEAPON by John W. Campbell

D-78 **THE TIES OF EARTH** by James H. Schmitz
CUE FOR QUIET by Thomas L. Sherred

D-79 **SECRET OF THE MARTIANS** by Paul W. Fairman
THE VARIABLE MAN by Philip K. Dick

D-80 **THE GREEN GIRL** by Jack Williamson
THE ROBOT PERIL by Don Wilcox

ARMCHAIR SCIENCE FICTION CLASSICS, $12.95 each

C-25 **THE STAR KINGS**
b   y Edmond Hamilton

C-26 **NOT IN SOLITUDE**
by Kenneth Gantz

C-32 **PROMETHEUS II**
by S. J. Byrne

ARMCHAIR SCIENCE FICTION & HORROR GEMS SERIES, $12.95 each

G-7 **SCIENCE FICTION GEMS, Vol. Seven**
Jack Sharkey and others

G-8 **HORROR GEMS, Vol. Eight**
Seabury Quinn and others